MW01229161

All characters, events and places portrayed in this
book are Fictional and any similarity to actual
persons, living or dead, is entirely coincidental and
not intended by the author, (except maybe some for
fun)

Copyright 2020
James Allen Forrest

All rights reserved

THE ADVENTURES OF JOHN FARADAY BOOK 3

JAMES ALLEN FORREST

Table of Contents
Book 3

CHAPTER ONE

"All that Glitters"

Monday 08:00 January 2000

John was sitting at his desk, starring at the pen on his desk, he was bored. Nothing had happened in the universe for over a year that needed his help. Bob walked into the office: "What's up boss?"

John: "I'm bored, what can we do?"

Bob: "I don't know, everything seems to be running great."

John looked up at Bob: "I've got it, it is time for us to have some fun." Bob watched as the little head tilt and the gears started whirring in John's brain, he knew what was going to happen next, he decided to sit down and wait.

John took a piece of paper from his desk and started to write; Bob waited for him to finish. John wrote, then thought, then wrote some more. A few minutes later he pushed the paper over to Bob.

John: "What do you think?"

Bob: "You want me to call Dells Furgo and ask them to give me a list of Western states 1840-1880's gold robbery's where the gold was never recovered."

Bob: "Why, what are we going to do with that information?"

John: "We are going to have some fun—trust me."

Bob eyes rolling: "Well if that's the case Ok, I will get right on it."

John: "I saw that, I have something I want to research also."

Wednesday 08:00

John was sitting at his desk looking at his research when Bob walked into the office. John: "Well, how did you do?"

Bob: "I have a list of 25 gold robbery's that occurred where the gold was never recovered. Some of them were paid off by Dells Furgo, some were never insured. They all occurred in California, Arizona, Texas, and Nevada."

John excitedly: "Oh, that's great, I got a lot of data on my research also." Bob: "What did you research?"

John: "I am keeping that a secret till the end of the fun."

Bob: "Ok, what are "WE" going to do with the list I obtained?"

John: "We are going to try to recover the missing gold, using the "Big Dial" portable."

Bob-his eyes lighting up: "Wow—That *will be fun*, when do we start?"

John: "Tomorrow morning from my workshop, bring extra clothes."

Thursday 08:00

John was sitting at the table in the Florida room with Lora eating breakfast.

John: "Lora do we have any vacation scheduled for you and me yet?"

Lora: "No, we talked about it but never made a decision on the date."

John: "I have a few things cooked up for this week and if your schedule is clear, you could come too."

Lora: "I'm sorry honey, I have two yearly meetings scheduled this week that can't be rescheduled. I am available starting next Monday for a week though."

John: "We need to sit down and just schedule something after this week, we really do. It just seems that I am too busy or you are too busy and we haven't had any time for us, and now I am going to be gone for at least three days."

Lora: "I agree we will talk about a vacation next week and just plan it, ok?"

John: "Ok, for sure. The doorbell chimed. That would be Bob." John got up and answered the door. He opened the door to find Bob standing there with a suitcase in his hand.

John: "Come in sir, have you had breakfast yet?" Bob: "No, I was late getting up." John: "I think we can fix that." He and Bob went to the Florida room and sat down. Bob took a plate and filled it up with what was on the table and started to eat. John poured Bob a glass of orange juice.

Bob: "So, what is on the agenda for today, John?"

John: "We will start from your list and see what happens, oh I forgot to mention that Donna and Jack are going too, along with Sgt. Carter and his girlfriend Carla."

Bob: "How will all of us do this from the golf cart?" John: "You'll see." Bob finished his breakfast: "Ok, John, let's go see what you have cooked up." John got up and headed towards the workshop with his suitcase. John picked up the "doorway" backpack on the workshop table and opened the shop "doorway", as Bob started to go through the "doorway he stopped and looked at a probe sticking through the corner of the "doorway": "What's this John?"

John: "Oh, that's new, it is a cell phone transceiver, it allows you to use your cell phone inside the "VOID"." It automatically moves into the "VOID" when the "doorway" opens." Bob said: "That's great" and stepped into the "VOID". Bob followed closely behind John. Bob noticed immediately that a "Bullet" was parked next to the golf cart.

Bob: "How did you get this?"

John: "Look at the name above the door:" Bob looked above the door and saw "Faraday 1".

John: "After you left yesterday, I called Izzy and asked him if "Faraday 1" was available. He told me that it was scheduled to be scraped in two days. I offered to purchase the vehicle. The purchase was authorized by the Defense Department. I also asked Izzy if some of the equipment could be left installed since I might be using it for missions." Izzy said he would take care of it. I see he added the ramp and the light strip around the vehicle. I won't know what it is equipped with until I see inside." Suddenly the cabin door opened. Sgt Carter was standing there grinning. John looked inside the cabin, Donna and Jack were sitting up front at the right console and a girl John didn't know was sitting on the left console.

Sgt. Carter: "Well, are you guys just going to stand there or can we get this vacation on the road?" John went up the ramp and Bob followed him. They put their suitcases with the others stacked in one corner, and sat down in the Captain's chairs.

John: "Sgt did you, wait isn't your first name Timothy?" Sgt. Carter:" Yes" John looked at the girlfriend and asked: "What do you call him?" She started to answer when Sgt. Carter said: "uhh, you can just call me Tim. John smiled: "Ok, *Tim* why don't you introduce us to the lovely lady sitting up front?"

Tim: "This is my girlfriend, Carla. We wanted to go on vacation but we had no idea where to go or what to do, then you called and here we are."

John: "Jack why are you here?" Jack: "Believe it or not, it is for the same reason, we figured if you were going somewhere, it might be fun, thanks for calling us."

John: "Ok, we need to talk a little before we head out. Tim, have you checked out the vehicle yet?"

Tim: "Yes, General Leeson said it has all the features of "Faraday 3" except for the gun on top. He also had a GPS sensor installed on the under "doorway" probe that works from Donna's console. The "Bullet" was refitted with five full bedrooms, a very nice kitchen and the refrigerator and freezers are full of food."

John: "Carla may I ask what you do?" Carla: "I work part-time for a local communications company, I go to UNF in River City, my major is" Communications", my minor is "The Old West"." John chuckled: "The Old West you say still chuckling." John looked over at Bob who had his hand over his face and was shaking his head: "Bob go ahead and say it, go on—say it" Bob looked up at the ceiling: "It just never stops—never." John chuckled a little more then stopped: "Ok, Carla, the two people at the other end of the console are the "Fosters", Donna and Jack, they are newlyweds, Donna works for NASA and Jack works for me. The gentleman next to me is Bob Johnson, my security Chief, and I am John Faraday."
Carla: "Wow--The John Faraday of "Faraday's" Moon?"

Bob nodding: "Yes that Faraday." John smiled: "Ok, before we leave, I must inform Tim, Carla, Donna, and Jack that you will see things while on vacation that are highly classified. Repeating any of these things to anyone is a federal felony, one that will put you in a single cell for the rest of your lifetime. If any of you want to leave before you see anything you may leave now." John waited. Bob got up and turned towards the door. John: "Very funny Bob, but you are in neck deep already. Ok then, here is what we are going to do on vacation. First, we are going to investigate1840-1880's stolen gold out West that was never recovered. We will do this using a device I invented that allows me to see into the past. We will watch the robbery, we will follow the robber, and we will try to see why the gold was never recovered.
I know Tim has no questions; he just believes what I said is true."

Carla questions?" Carla: "I don't know what to ask."

Jack Questions? "No questions."
Donna before I ask if you have any questions, look at the console area in front of you. You will see a space to put a "doorway" unit, a power plug, and two copper connectors for that "doorway" to attach to. This is tied into your under "doorway" console so it will show on your screen. There is a switch on your console marked primary and secondary, primary is normal "doorway", secondary is the "Time "doorway"."

Donna looked at her console and saw all John was talking about: "No questions John."

CHAPTER TWO

"Go West Young Men-Go West"

John: "If there are no questions, John opened his "doorway bag" and pulled out the first location they were going to head to and handed it to Donna, input the directions please and tell everyone where we are going."
Donna looked at the paper and placed the town name into the "GPS" program. The console in front of her started to fill with information: "The town is in California and it is called "Sorrow"."

Carla: "I know that town, it is a ghost town."
John: "It is today, but not in 1842 when the robbery occurred." Donna set the coordinates, she nodded at Tim.

John: "Tim the coordinates are set, please take us to "Sorrow" California." Tim smiling looked at Carla: "Yes Sir."
Five minutes later Donna said: "We are here."

John: "Donna show our position on the main screen." Donna flipped a switch and the area below them appeared on the big screen; everyone watched the screen.

John: "Go closer and see if we can find "Sorrow." Donna moved the camera closer to the ground. An old ghost town appeared.

John: "See if you can find something with the town name on it, try the bank." Donna moved around; several buildings had the town name "Sorrow" she continued to look for the bank. A big brick building came into view, on the front it said "Bank of Sorrow". John: "Wonderful, pull back to 100 feet above the town and hold." John took out the" doorway" from the bag and took it over to Donna's position. He put the unit into the cubby hole that was made for it and plugged it in, then hooked the box to the two copper nipples that were sticking up out of the console. John turned the switch on the console marked "doorway" on. "Is everyone ready?" John turned the unit on: "Donna there is a small display that should be lit up in front of you, what is the date?"

Donna: "It says todays month and year and time." John: "Select the switch I talked about to "secondary". Donna selected the "secondary" position". John: "What is the date now?" Donna: "It is the same date." John: "Good, that is correct, he turned the big knob to "2", Donna what is the date now?" Donna: "It is still the same date." Good, that is correct, John turned the big knob to 4, what is the date now?"

Donna: "The date is todays date in 1950." John looked up at the big screen, there was not much of a change. He looked back down at the "box", and noticed the small knob was not set correctly. He set the small knob and moved the big knob again. Donna: "What is the date now?" Donna the date is: "today 1841. "John looked up at the big screen. There was the town with people moving around.

Tim: "That's incredible." John: "Donna, do you think you can put the date on the big screen." Donna looked around on the console, she flipped a switch and the date appeared at the bottom of the screen. John: "That's great Donna, thank you."

John: "Does anyone have any questions now?"
Tim: "What happens now?" John: "We wait for the robbery to occur, then we follow the robber until he does something with the gold he steals, after that maybe we can discover what happened to the loot." John moved the big knob one notch the date changed to 1842. He pushed the "hold" button, then held it down and moved the big knob to the middle and released the button.

John: "Now we can use the big knob to move 500 hours forward or backward, Donna, what time did the robbery take place?" Donna looked at the paper: "It says the robbery occurred at 3:55 pm just before the bank closed." John: "Ok, that is two hours from now, John moved the big knob one tick, now it is one hour from now. How about some food I'm hungry?"

Donna: "That's a great, idea, come on Carla let's see what's in the kitchen. The two of them disappeared into the back. The guys followed to help. They opened the fridge and found a bunch of food, ate and watched the main street for forty-five minutes on the big screen on the kitchen wall. They cleaned up the kitchen and went back to the main cabin. They all had their eyes glued to the big screen. The clock clicked off to 3:50pm. A seedy looking character rode up on his horse, got off and walked into the bank with his saddle bags. Everyone assumed he was the robber. Six minutes later he walked quickly from the bank got on his horse and headed east from town.

John: "Ok, Tim, we can follow him by using light controls, just keep him in sight. Tim easily kept the robber in sight. They could see no one chasing him yet. He must have gone 3 or 4 miles into the desert when he suddenly stopped and galloped off the road into the brush. He stopped at a large rock. He had previously dug a 3-foot hole next to the rock, he got off his horse and tossed the saddlebags with the gold into the hole, quickly covered it up, then climbed up on top of the large rock and checked to see if anyone was around. He did not see anyone.

John: "Donna, use infrared and check the area for a mile around us." Donna checked: "There is no one but the posse coming up hard behind him about a mile back."
The robber got back on the road and slowly rode away from the posse. A mile down the road he became aware of the posse, he attempted to outrun them. Shooting erupted and the robber fell from his horse. They watched as the

posse surrounded him. The robber made another attempt to fire his gun but two shots from the posse finished him off.

The posse checked his horse for the stolen gold but found none. They tied the robber's body onto his horse, and attempted to back track the road back to town by looking for any tracks. The posse looked for over an hour then gave up. and went back to town.

John: "Ok, go back to the rock and zero in." Tim moved the "Bullet" back to the rock and backed off about 20 feet. John pulled a chair up to the "doorway" and moved the big dial one click at a time for 500 hours. No one approached the rock. John" Ok, let's go back to present date. John made the adjustments and the counter moved back to the present date. They all looked at the big screen. Not much had changed, the dirt road was still there.

John: "Donna what happened to the bank?"
Donna looked at the paper: "The bank was bought by a Los Angeles bank in 1885 and the town closed up in 1899."
John: "Is the LA bank still in business?"
Donna: "Yes, it's a well-known bank with its headquarters in Sacramento."
John: "Well, who's for digging next to the rock?" All hands went up. John got up and retrieved a folding military style shovel from the locker and held it up for view. Who wants the thrill of digging up stolen gold from the ground?" Donna looking at Jack: "Do you have two shovels?" John: "Why yes I do." John pulled a second shovel from the locker and took both to Donna and Jack.

John: "Donna, on your panel there is a "doorway display" switch, one side is marked "Small the other side is marked "Large", switch to "Large" please." Donna placed the "doorway" switch to "Large", when she did a 7 ft. high by 4 ft. wide doorway opened on the back wall of the cabin and a small probe 3/16 in. thick and 1/4 in. long poked through the "doorway" from a small box on the upper corner of the "doorway".

Jack: "That's cool, what is the small box at the corner of the "doorway"?" John: "That is a probe through the "doorway" that gives us sound and cell phone use when the "doorway" is open. "Now through the "doorway" you could see the big rock 20 feet away. John looked at Donna and Jack: "Sunglasses, put em on if you got em, and remember it is probably a hundred degrees out there and if the saddle bags are still there, they will probably be rotten, be careful how you bring them out of the hole. Donna smiled at Jack: "Come on, and they started out the "doorway" towards the big rock". The rest of the crew watched as they started to carefully dig the hole. They were down about 2 and a half feet when Jack hit something. Donna stopped digging. Jack bent down and carefully removed more dirt with his hands, then put the shovel back into the hole and lifted out the saddle bags. Donna took them from the shovel and placed them gently on the ground. They back filed the hole. Jack gave Donna his shovel and carefully picked up the saddle bags, then he and Donna walked back through the "doorway" into the cabin.

John: "Bring them into the kitchen and put them on the counter under some paper towels." Carla ran ahead and put down the paper towels. Jack laid the saddlebags on the paper towels. They all stood there for a minute or two just looking at the saddlebags. John: "Ok Jack, you two open them up and let's see what is inside." Jack moved back to let Donna open the bags. Donna held up the bags at the middle, both bags stood up on their bottoms.

Donna: "They are not rotten, the leather just feels a little aged.", she opened the left bag and looked inside, then put her hand inside feeling what was there." She started to pull out 5 oz. marked ingots until the bag was empty, then she opened the other bag and pulled out more 5 oz. ingots until it was empty. They counted the ingots, there were 50 ingots 250 oz's. of gold. Everyone starred at the shiny gold ingots.

John: "Let's see, gold was going for about $280 an oz. today so that makes them worth about (John was doing the math in his head) $70,000, someone else check my numbers." Donna: "I did, it is $70,000. She marked it on the paper."

John: "So, are we having vacation fun yet?" Everyone yelled: "Yes we are."

John: "Carla, how about you?"
Carla: "I am still digesting that we just went back in time 150 years and dug up stolen gold." Tim looked at Carla: "I told you we were going to have fun didn't I." Carla nodded yes.

John: "Ok, it is almost 5 pm. Let's go somewhere and have dinner then come back and feel the gold, John got up and got a small cardboard box from the storage locker and put the gold bars into it, marked it with the info put the paper in the box and closed it up, then placed the box back into the locker."

John: "What do you say, Carla "The Old West minor" where would you like to go to dinner?" or if you don't know I will make a couple of suggestions." Carla:" What are your suggestions?" John: "Old Tucson, the movie set or Tombstone. They both have nice restaurants. Carla: "I would love to go to Tombstone Arizona."
John: "Donna: "You heard the lady, so set a course please, Tim, Tombstone Arizona please. And off they went. 5 minutes later they were above Tombstone.

John: "We need to find a good out of the way place to park, John looked around the edge of town then pointed to a large pile of wood. Tim, pull up to the rear of that pile of wood facing away from town and face it with the doorway. Tim did so, Now slowly push through the wood until we come out the other side, Tim slowly moved the "doorway" through the wood. Suddenly the wood disappeared and the country side stood in front of them. Perfect Tim. Shut down the engines" Tim did.

Donna: "What just happened?"

John explained: "The "doorway" doesn't know there is a pile of wood there, remember when we boarded the Sarin ship in space, the "doorway" didn't know there was a metal wall in front of it, it just went through it. It is crazy, but if you stop and think about it becomes clear." When we go to dinner the "doorway" will be left open, anyone or anything could accidentally go through the open "doorway", so we leave the invisible "doorway" open in the most likely place no one could stumble through it."

Bob: "What if the "doorway" closes after we leave?"

John smiling: "That is an excellent question Bob, we would be stuck in Tombstone Arizona for a while— except for this, John got up and removed a backpack from the storage locker and placed the strap on his shoulder, inside is another portable "doorway". Well, pardners, let's go get some grub shall we, I will go out first and check the area, then motion for you to follow." John walked up to the "doorway" and looked left and right, then stepped out onto the dirt lot. He looked around and held up two fingers and motioned them to come out. Tim and Carla came out and stood next to John, who looked around again and motioned for all to come out, Donna and Jack and Bob came through the "doorway".

John: "Shall we find the restaurant?" Donna and Jack held hands along with Tim and Carla and headed to the street. Bob and John followed. John looked at Bob: "Remember where we parked." It was 11 pm., they all had a wonderful time, the food was great and they had walked the town to see the sights.

John: "It has been a fun and long day, I think now would be a good time to head back to the "Bullet" and get

some sleep, for tomorrow is going to be another fun day."
All agreed.

John: "Bob where did we park?" Bob pointed to a spot
at the edge of town: "We are over there". John looked at
Tim and Donna who were smiling trying hard not to
laugh. John: "Bob, just how many beers did you have
with dinner?" Bob slurring his words: "I don't know."

Donna put her arm through Bob's arm: Come on
Cowboy let a navigator show you where we parked." She
turned Bob around and they all went to the other end of
town and back into the "Bullet". After they all had
entered the "Bullet" Carla said: "Oh look, a bunny
rabbit." A rabbit had evidently gone through the open
"doorway" into the "Bullet". John: "Ok, form a half
circle, bend over with your hands out and scoot the bunny
back out the "doorway". They did and the rabbit went out
the "doorway".

John: "Donna turn off the "doorway" please. Donna
did so. Tim let's move the "Bullet" away from the
woodpile out to the edge of the desert please." Tim
moved to the console started the engines looked at the big
display and moved the "Bullet", then shut down the
systems.

Everyone went to the back and went to bed.

CHAPTER THREE

"Vacation, Day 2"

06:30

John was up, and in the kitchen making breakfast. The bacon was frying and he was working on cracking 10 eggs into a bowl when Donna came out of the bedroom and joined John. Donna: "Here, let me help and took over the egg job." Jack appeared and joined them: "What can I do?"

John, "There is some nice frozen blueberry waffles in the freezer and maple syrup in the fridge, some might like them for breakfast. Jack put the maple syrup on the table. About that time Bob, Tim and Carla joined them in the kitchen. Jack asked who wanted blueberry waffles and proceeded to put them in the four-hole toaster. Tim and Carla set the table. Donna finished the eggs just as Jack finished the waffles. They put the fresh food on the table. Bob had put coffee in the coffee maker and it was ready, he got frozen orange juice from the fridge and made a pitcher full and put it on the table. John mentioned there was bread if anyone wanted toast. Breakfast went quickly. Donna and Carla started doing the dishes and Bob helped.

They all sat at the table and talked about how much fun the day before had been.

John: "Well today, we will try to do two finds, the first is a big one, a stage coach robbery by two men in Arizona, the take was four gold bars in a strong box. If you are ready, let's get cracking pardners." John got up and went forward, picked up his folder and sat down. Tim and Carla went to the left console, Donna and Jack to the right console. Bob sat down next to John. John opened his folder, thumbed through some paperwork, pulled out a sheet and handed it to Donna who looked at the paper. John: "Donna, where are we going today?"

Donna: "We are going to a town in Arizona called "Murphy" located about 60 miles west of Tucson."
John: "Carla do you know of "Murphy". Carla: "Yes, it is a small town in the middle of several dozen gold mines."

John: "Very good, it is a waypoint for gold to be delivered to Tucson by Dells Furgo. I'm guessing it is smelted into bars and turned over to the stage office for delivery to Tucson."

Donna set a course for "Murphy", and Tim take us out of here." Tim started the engines and headed for "Murphy", 5 minutes later they were there.
John: "Donna, tell us about the robbery please."
Donna looked at the paper: "Well, the robbery took place in 1875 around noon 2 days ago from our time 5 miles outside of town."

John moved his chair up to the console next to Donna and turned on the "doorway", and started to adjust the dials as he watched the big screen. All watched the screen as the time went backwards and stopped at the year 1875 two days before the robbery.

John: "Place us just outside the city alongside the road, but still able to see the stage depot. We will wait for the stage to leave and follow it." Tim did so. John moved the dial on the "doorway" to 11 am. The stage was sitting outside the depot. They watched and waited. Three men came out of the depot, two men were carrying out a strongbox from the depot. One got up on top of the stage and the other two handed the box up to him. It looked heavy, the man still on top of the stage strapped down the box and then sat down in the driver seat. One man on the ground got up into the other seat on top. He picked up a shotgun from the floor. The driver took up the reins and the stage started to leave the depot. The depot agent waved goodbye to them.

John: "Ok, Tim things are *afoot*, let's move down the road some and see if we can find our bad guys." Tim slowly moved the "Bullet" down the road, but still was not out of range of the stage. Everybody watched the big screen and looked for the bad guys. Suddenly Carla yelled: "There they are behind that big rock" They all looked at the two men on horseback, guns drawn waiting for the stage to come by. Just before the stage got to the rock the two men lurched from behind the rock and held their guns on the two men on the stage. One of the robbers said: "Throw down your guns, and the box, and get down." The two men on the stage tossed their guns down to the ground, then the strong box and got off to the ground. One robber looked at the two drivers: "One of you unhook the horses from the stage." The stage driver unhooked the horses and one robber got off his horse and walked over to the strong box and shot off the lock, he pulled out two gold bars and put them in the mounted robbers' saddlebags. He pulled out two more gold bars and put them into his saddlebags. He reached down and picked up the guns the stage riders threw down to the ground and put them into his saddlebags. He kept the shotgun and got back on his horse. One robber looked at the two men on the ground: "Start walking", they started walking back towards the stage depot. The other robber grabbed the stage horse team reins and the robbers started off east towards Tucson with the team. Tim followed them as they went down the dirt road. They must have gone 2 miles with the team. The robbers stopped. One robber turned the team back west towards the stage station yelled and swatted the lead horse on the rump. The horses started to run west. The robbers took off again east for their camp 5 miles away. The robbers took a dirt road to the left and rode another 2 miles to their camp. The camp was up against a high rock bluff with a 15x20-foot outcrop of rock that acted as a canopy 15 feet from the ground. Let's start digging a hole for the gold right here under the rock canopy. We will go on to Tucson and come back in a month and then head to Mexico. The other robber agreed. They quickly dug the hole in the soft sand and tossed all four gold bars wrapped in a shirt into the hole then filled it in. One robber made a fire pit with rocks over the buried gold, gathered some firewood and started a fire inside. The other robber said: "That was smart and looked at his partner who was holding the shotgun on him."

Hey: "What's with the shotgun?" The answer to his question was the shotgun pellets going into his chest." The other robber laughing: "It makes it easier to split the take." He tied his dead partner to his horse, led the horse to the edge of the outcrop and pointed the horse north, yelled and slapped the horse on the rump with the barrel of the shotgun, the horse took off and disappeared still going north. He rode back to their camp, cleaned up the camp area, and erased footprints. The small fire had already gone out.

Donna: "They were really violent back then."

John: "Normally the robbers would shoot the stage drivers, --no witnesses." The now lone robber slowly headed back to the main road, and turned east towards Tucson and slowly rode along, he was in no hurry. He had gone about a mile when he heard noises behind him. He turned and saw two riders coming at him fast. As they got closer, he realized they were the two stage drivers now with rifles and riding the team horses. He pulled his hand gun and fired at them then realized they were too far away for his hand gun. The two riders stopped, both took aim with their rifles and fired. The robber saw the rifle gun smoke and then two 40 caliber bullets hit him in the chest. He fell off his horse to the ground. The two stage drivers rode up to the robbers' body and got off their horses. One checked the robber: "He's dead. He will never know the rifles were inside the stage on the floor, or that we would catch the team horses when they headed back to the station depot." They checked the robbers saddle bags for the gold and found none. They tied the robber on his horse and went back to the station depot.

John: "Let's wait and see how many people are sent out to find the gold, he moved up the date by one day?" They all watched the overhang; John would move the time up by one hour. He did this every few minutes. It was now two days after the robbery. Five men came into the clearing where the gold was buried, two of them were the stage drivers. They tried digging a few places within the clearing, but no one tried digging in the fire pit. The group continued to watch as people kept coming back every few days to the clearing to search. No one again went near the fire pit. On the fifth day no one showed up to search at all.

John: "Well, should we go to our time see if it is still there?" All hands went up. John set the "doorway" to present time. John: "Tim, back off to 100 feet above the site please." Tim did so. As they looked down, they could see the changes that occurred over the years, the dirt road was now blacktop. The road up to the overhang was graded and graveled. There were a few houses in the area but none close to the overhang. John: "Ok Tim, let's take a look at the overhang." Tim slowly moved back to ground level and stopped 30 feet from the middle of the overhang. There were 4 picnic tables spread around the clearing, and three trash bins. Donna: "Look the fire pit is still there, it has been used a lot over the years but it is still there."

John: "Any ideas on how to check on the gold bars?" Bob spoke up: "How about a picnic?" John looked over at Bob: "Why Bob that is a great idea, everyone agreed."

John: "Bob, it is your plan, take it away." Bob thought a minute: "We will move one table, and put it 10 feet away from the firepit and 4 feet to the left, we will move the rocks of the firepit 4 feet to the left also. We will face the "doorway" straight at the firepit 4 feet from the right side. We will have a picnic, when it gets a little dark, we will dig in the old firepit location 4 feet from the "doorway", how's that? "

John: "Jack, what do you think of that plan?" Jack: "I say we look for a picnic basket to fill with food, I'm hungry." Donna was already heading towards the kitchen, the others followed, they started looking in the cabinets. The second higher cabinet they checked had a picnic basket in it. John couldn't believe it. The women started to take stuff out of the fridge to use to make sandwiches. They even found a bowl of potato and macaroni salad. They had pickles and cold cuts, chips and dips.

Just as the basket was packed Tim opened another door in the kitchen: "Hey there is another large fridge in here, Tim opened the fridge door, "It's full of drinks, water, soft drinks, and beer." Everyone grabbed a drink; Bob grabbed a beer and the basket. Tim moved the "Bullet" into position next to the rock wall, Donna opened the large "doorway". John grabbed the "doorway" backpack, slung it onto his shoulder, and walked up to the open "doorway" and looked around: "Ok Bob, it's your show."
Bob picked up the basket, went through the "doorway" and put the basket on the sand in front of the firepit. He then walked over to a picnic table and asked Jack to help him move it. They placed it about 4 feet out from the old firepit. Donna and Carla started to move the firepit rocks 4 feet left of the current location, John put the backpack

"doorway" on the picnic table and went back into the cabin to get the shovels. He came back and laid them up against the rock wall where the old firepit used to be. Tim picked up a shovel and carefully moved the burnt wood and charcoal to the new firepit marking the old firepit with an "X", and leaving the shovel leaning against the rock wall.

Bob: "Everyone did great, let's eat." And they did. As it started to get dark Bob said: "I get one shovel Tim you have the other. Everyone else watched the road." Bob and Tim picked up the shovels leaning near the "X" and started to dig. Tim: "I hit something hard I'm going to use my hands." Bob stopped digging. Tim reached down and pulled out a gold bar and placed it on the ground: "That thing is heavy." Bob was now moving sand with his hands, found a gold bar and laid it next to the first one. Now Bob and Tim started moving more sand with their hands, they both pulled up another gold bar.

John: "Go ahead and check, but I think that is all the bars." Bob used the shovel again to look. They found no more bars, so they filled in the hole. Bob, Jack, Tim, and John picked up the gold bars any carried them into the cabin and set them on the floor, the girls picked up the basket, tossed the trash in the containers and returned to the "Bullet". Bob went out again to check the site, removed footprints as much as he could and checked the old location of the firepit, then returned to the "Bullet".

Everything looks good out there. Donna: "I have a vehicle that just turned onto our road and is heading this way."

John: "Tim, move us back and up a couple of hundred feet." Tim did so. They watched the vehicle drive into the clearing; it was a sheriff's deputy. He got out of his car and walked around the site with his flashlight. He then proceeded back to his car and left. Carla let out a sigh of relief. John: "Are we still having fun?" a resounding "*Yes we are* echoed in the cabin."

John: "Bob, bring one of the bars into the kitchen and we all can get a close look at it"

Bob picked up one of the gold bars, went to the kitchen and placed the bar on the counter. John: "Well, let's see. It has 400 oz. stamped on the bar and a serial number. I'll bet numbers are on all the bars, those will come in handy when I talk to Dells Furgo. There are 4 bars, each at 400 Oz's. times $280 is." Donna cut in: "That's $448,000.

John looked at all the group: "That's about 120 pounds of gold. It boggles the mind; I had hoped to do two sites today but it didn't work out. Donna what time is it?" Donna: "It is a little after 9 pm." John: "Well, I don't know about you guys, but I am bushed and I hope to do two more sites tomorrow." Bob: "Me two, I am going to hit the sack."

Donna squirming in the chair looking at Jack: "Jack and I don't mind going to bed early, Jack smiled and shook his head yes."

Tim: "No, it's a good idea, we can hit it hard in the morning." John: "Ok then, Bob, dig out a cardboard box and let's put the 4 gold bars in the locker, and mark the box with the info we just had and hit the sack." John said goodnight to the others: "Tim if you would, shut down the "Bullet"." The rest left for the back. Bob found a box for the gold bars, he put them, and the paper into the box and then into the locker, Tim shut down the "Bullet" and they all hit the sack.

CHAPTER FOUR

"Vacation, Day 3"

06:30

John was up and started making breakfast again. He was quickly joined by the others. They made and ate breakfast then gathered in the main cabin. John picked up his folder and sat down at the console next to Donna, he thumbed through the papers and handed Donna one.

John: "Donna where are we going today?"

Donna: "We are going to "Bullet" Arizona, that seems appropriate, it seems the "Bullet" Savings and Loan had a small robbery in 1851, 100 Oz's. of gold nuggets. Robber unknown. The robbery occurred at 9am just after the bank opened."

John: "Donna input coordinates, Tim get ready for speed." Donna nodded at Tim, Tim started to "Bullet" Az., a few minutes later they were there. "Bullet" was 25 miles north of Tucson nestled at the foot of the mountains 2 miles from the pass through the mountains. Tim parked 200 feet above the town. Everyone looked at the big screen. It was a small town, not more than 12 buildings, 2 outhouses behind the General store. There were 4 people on the street.

Carla: "Wow, this place in the middle of nowhere is desolate."

John: "Donna, what time is it?" Donna: "It is 7:45 local and the morning of the robbery." John turned on the "doorway" and started to adjust the big dial, they all watched as the time on the screen moved back to 08:45 the morning of the robbery year 1851. Tim placed them looking down at a brick building with "Bullet Savings and Loan" above the door. There were now two people on the street. At 08:55 a man walked up to the front door of the "Savings and Loan", looked around then proceeded to open the front door. As he opened the front door a scruffy looking rider came into town and watched him open the door and go into the building. He parked his horse 50 feet from the Savings and Loan, he waited. An "OPEN" sign went up in the window of the Savings and Loan The robber got off his horse and went into the bank. Two minutes the robber ran out of the Savings and Loan with a large heavy bag in his hand, he stuffed the bag into his saddle bag and quickly headed out of town towards the mountain pass. As he started away from the bank the same person that opened the bank came running out with a pistol in his hand, he managed to get off two shots before the robber disappeared down the road, he started yelling that the Savings and Loan had been robbed, he also noticed a storm was brewing near the mountains. Thirty minutes later the robber stopped near an old house with a barn. He could see that it was empty. He rode his horse up to the barn. He carefully got off his horse, his left arm was bleeding badly from the bullet hole in his shoulder from the gun the bank manager had shot at him with. He opened the barn and went inside. He found some rags and bound the wound. He decided he would hide the bag of gold here, head for the next town across the pass, see the doctor there and come back later, to pick up his loot. He noticed some loose boards on the floor near the front of the barn. He pried up three boards and dug out enough dirt to bury the bag of gold. He put the bag in the hole, covered it up with about 6 inches of dirt, and replaced the three boards. He looked at his work and nodded. He took his horse out of the barn and closed the door again. The storm was getting bad, it had started to rain, he headed towards the pass.

John: "Ok, let's keep track of him to see why he never returned." Tim slowly followed him up the mountain pass. The storm was really intense now, heavy rain, lightning, and wind. Just before reaching the pass summit a large bolt of lightning struck the robber and his horse. Both fell to the ground.
Donna and Carla said: "Oh my God at the same time."

John: "Wow-I guess Karma strikes hard sometimes." They watched a few more minutes to see if the horse or the robber got up, neither did.
John: "Ok Tim, let's go back to the barn and wait." Tim parked the "Bullet" 100 feet up and 40 yards from the barn. One hour later a group of five men rode onto the old homestead following the blood trail, it was still raining hard and had been for at least 45 minutes. The blood trail ended 30 yards from the house and the barn. The men headed to the house to search, and then to the barn. They came up with nothing.

John: "We must assume the blood trail got wiped out by the hard rain."
 The group of men left and headed up toward the pass. The "Bullet" waited. About an hour later the group of men came back from the pass carrying the body of the robber on their way to town.

John: "Alright let's see what this place looks like now." John moved back to current day. Everyone looked at where the barn was. The house was gone, what was left after the barn had obviously burned was on the ground.
John: "Donna, what kind of company do we have around us?"

Donna: "I see two ranch homes, 3 miles away."
John: "Does anyone remember where the loot was buried?"

Bob: "I can see the spot in front of the barn, just behind where the barn doors fell outward."
John: "Donna open the large "doorway" please, Tim put us 20 feet in front of where the barn door was." Tim positioned the "Bullet". Donna opened the large wall "doorway". John got up and pulled a shovel from the locker and handed it to Bob: "Remember that bag has probably rotted away, take a box the size of the bag with you to use in case it has rotted." Bob jumped up with the shovel, looked in the locker for a box and bolted for the barn.

Jack: "Gee, you think Bob was a little excited." Everyone laughed. Bob reached the barn door and started digging. He pried up the wood planks that were behind the barn door. After removing the planks, he started to dig, he didn't have to dig far. Suddenly Bob brought up what was left of the bag of gold buried in the hole. He carefully put the remains into the box, he then cleaned out what was left of the gold nuggets and put them into the box. He felt around with his hands and pulled out a few more nuggets. When he couldn't find any more nuggets, he filled in the hole and came back to the cabin, and took the box to the kitchen. Everyone followed him and looked in the box, gold nuggets were obvious and shiny. Bob put a stopper in the sink, emptied the bag into the sink and then the rest of the box. He placed paper towels on the counter, turned on the faucet, and started to wash off the dirty nuggets, he handed the wet nuggets to Donna who was standing behind him looking around his shoulder. Donna wiped them dry and put them on the paper towels. It only took a few minutes to finish. They all looked at the pile of different sized gold nuggets glittering on the counter.

Jack: "You know I remember seeing a food scale." He started to look in the cabinets. In the second cabinet he opened the door and pulled out a food scale and placed it next to the pile of gold nuggets.

John: "Bob, you found em, you weigh em." Bob zeroed the digital scale and started to slowly pile the nuggets in the middle of the scale. The scale only went to 30 oz. so he had to do the scale several more times. They added the count and the weight came out to 102 Oz's. John: "Let's see 102 times 280 is." Donna cuts him off again and says: "$28,560." John: "How do you do that?" Donna holds up a small plastic device smiling: "Calculator." Everybody laughs.

John: "Ok Bob, put the gold nuggets in the box, write the numbers down." Donna handed the piece of paper to Bob to put in the box. Bob wiped out the box with a damp paper towel then put the nuggets into the box. They all went back into the cabin. John: "Donna, what time is it?" Donna: "11:15 am." John: "Let's have lunch and do another find, what do you say?" The group didn't say a word they just headed into the kitchen to make lunch. 12:15 pm

Everyone had re-assembled in the cabin again. John thumbed through his paperwork: "Alright this one should work; he gave the paper to Donna." Donna took it and read the paper.

John: "Donna, where are we going?"

Donna: "We are going to "Racoon" Nevada. It was a bank; it looks like gold bars maybe three were taken in the year 1855 at 2 pm. "

John: "Donna set up the coordinates, Tim get ready to roll. Donna: "Ok, go to it Tim." Tim pushed the throttle forward. A few minutes later they were there.

John: "Donna, show us "Racoon" Nevada please." Everyone looked at the big screen. The town was only four buildings and an outhouse. John: "Donna, where was the gold stolen from?" Donna: "The paper says there was a "Racoon" Bank."

John: "Tim, get a little closer, look at each building."
They all looked at the buildings one at a time.

Jack: "There it is "Racoon Saloon and Bank"." John
was holding his sides and laughing. John stopped
laughing and started to set up the "doorway" the group
watched as he moved the time back to the year 1855 1:17
pm, same day as the robbery. We have about 43 minutes
to go."
John: "Carla how much school do you have left?"

Carla: "I graduate next year." John: "Were you able to
use any of the state money for school." Carla: "No, I took
out a $12,000 student loan for all four years total."
John: "Tim what about you, are you staying in the
Marines?" Tim: "Yes, I also graduate next year and plan
to go to OTS and become an officer."

John: "Well, that is wonderful, you will make a good
one. I hope you will call on me or Bob if you need
assistance." Tim: "Thank you Sir." John took out his
notebook and wrote in it for a couple of minutes then put
it away.
1:55 pm

John: "Ok, let's keep a sharp lookout, it is almost
time." Everyone was watching the front of the Saloon.
Suddenly a side door opened and a man with a bag came
into the alley. He walked quickly to the outhouse opened
the door and dropped the contents of the bag into one of
the two holes. He closed the door and started to run
behind the two end buildings.

John laughing: "Did he just toss the gold bars into the
crapper?" He stopped and picked up 2 bricks and put
them in the bag and continued to run. John: "Donna get a
closeup of that man." Donna brought up the image of the
man on the big screen. They all looked at the man as he
continued to run. Bob: "That guy is at least 90 years old."
Suddenly the man tossed the bag with the two bricks
away into the tall grass and kept running. Now three men

came out the side door of the Saloon, and went to the rear of the building. One man pointed to the running man: "There he is he shouted." They all took off after him. The old man was a good 50 yards ahead of the other three men. Now more men came out of the Saloon and started to chase after all the men. Suddenly the old man fell down. A bunch of the other men gathered near the tall grass where the old man had thrown the bag with the two bricks. The first three men reached the old man on the ground. They bent down. They yelled back: "He's dead, one of the three men was a doctor. He examined the old man: "He died from a heart attack probably related to the running and his age." One of the three men chasing the old man said: "Where is my bag with the gold bars?" More men showed up and started to hunt for the bag of gold bars. They started to search along the rear of the building. The search went on for a good 15 minutes. Most of the men were standing right next to the tall grass where the bag was laying. Three men were actually standing in the tall grass between the bag of bricks and the bunch of men watching the search. One of the men in the bunch turned and started to walk towards the three men in the tall grass, as he did, he kicked the bag of bricks. He bent down and picked up the bag and yelled: "I found it; I found the bag." He walked out of the tall grass toward the bunch of men. Everyone searching ran to the man holding up the bag. One of the original three men took the bag and looked inside. He pulled out one of the bricks. He looked at the man that gave him the bag: "Where was the bag?" The man answered: "It was in front of the three men standing in the tall grass." The man with the bag called the three men out of the tall grass: "Where are the gold bars that were in the bag?" One of the three men said: "I don't know we were just standing there watching the search." The man holding the bag drew his gun and shot dead the man he asked the question of. The other two men held up their hands. The man with the bag said: "Search them and take these two to jail and start searching the tall grass." Some men led off the other two men and others started searching the tall grass. The search went on for 30 minutes as the group watched.

John: "Well, I have seen enough, how about we just move forward, Tim keep us pointed at the outhouse please." Tim did. The group all agreed. John moved the "doorway" to present time. The town was now deserted. The only building that was left was the Saloon, at least the outhouse was still there laying on its back.
Donna: "Is there anyone around close?" Donna: "No, I see nothing."

John: "Do I see a hand to do some digging?" Everyone looked at each other and laughed.
John: "Ok, I will go, after all these years it will all be soil and dirt." John got up and grabbed a shovel from the locker, Tim, move us to within 15 feet of the front of the downed outhouse please", Tim did so. John walked through the open "doorway" towards where the outhouse used to be. The group gathered around. John started to dig. Only dirt and soil came up. John had gotten down about 3 feet when he hit something solid. He dug it out with the shovel. It was a gold bar, he kept digging and found another gold bar, John continued to dig and found a third gold bar. John dug a little longer but failed to find anything else. He filled in the hole and asked someone to help him take the gold bars into the kitchen and put them into the sink. Jack and Bob picked up the two bars and everyone went into the kitchen. John: "Donna, please close up the doorway?" Donna did and followed them into the kitchen. John turned on the faucet and used soap and warm water to clean the gold bars. He sat them on the counter on some paper towels. John looked at the bars, they all had 400 oz. stamped on them. John: "Donna how much are they worth?"

Donna: "They are worth $336,000; she made a note on the paper." John: "Bob, a box please to put the gold bars in." Bob went and got a box. John put the gold bars into the box along with the piece of paper.

John: "Another nice find. Donna what time is it?" Donna: "It is 3pm."
John: "If you all want, we can do one more find today, that would make up for the one we are behind, show me some hands if you want to continue." All hands went up. John thumbed through the folder, and he pulled out a piece of paper and handed it to Donna.

John: "Donna, where are we going?"
Donna: "We are going to "Sweetsprings" Texas. Year 1857 the robbery was at 8 am: from the "Sweetsprings" bank. It says 2 bags of $50 gold coins, but it has no value. Maybe it was not insured." Donna put in the coordinates and nodded at Tim. A few minutes later they arrived. Everyone looked over the town. It was in the middle of nowhere, and miles from any other towns, it had a main street two blocks long. After a close look at the stores there was no "Sweetsprings Bank" to be found.

John: "Ok, it might not be there anymore. No big deal." He started to move the clock back to year 1857: "I think I can get to within 15 minutes of the robbery." They all watched as the clock moved to year 1857 and 7:45 am. John" Ok, we have 15 minutes to locate the "Sweetsprings Bank". Tim started to move down the street looking for the "Sweetsprings Bank". Carla: "There it is, the last building on the street. Sure enough, the sign said "Sweetsprings Bank". Tim set up to watch the bank. About 7:50 two men on horseback tied up their horses across the street from the freight office and waited. There was one person on the street. At 8 am: an "open" sign went onto the inside glass of the front door. The two men started towards the front door. They entered the office, 30 seconds later a shot rang out. The two men ran from the office each carrying a large bag of something that looked heavy. They ran across the street and jumped on their horses. Immediately four men came out to the street from one of the stores and one from the Bank. The clerk from the bank let go with as many shots as possible, so did the other four men. The two robbers held tight to the heavy bags as they were hit by bullets and raced east out of town. At the end of town, they turned and hid behind the last building. The other men mounted their horses and were hot on their trail. The posse did not see the hiding wounded robbers and continued on down the road and out of site. The robbers then turned south and continued into the country side. Tim followed them. They must have ridden for an hour and stopped near a small lake with no one around. They got off their horses and went down to the water's edge to get a cold drink.

One said: "Jake what are we going to do? We are both shot up. Who knows how much longer we can last?" The other said: "There is a small town about 3 miles from here, that has a doctor. Let's bury the bags and head there we can come back later."

Jake: "Ok, Slim, but we don't have the strength to bury anything." They found a wooden box next to the lake big enough to hold the large two bags. The put the bags into the box and walked about three feet into the lake. They put down the box upside down on the bottom and pressed it into the mud as far as they could. They went back to their horses and started for the small town 3 miles away.

Tim kept following them. After about 2 miles Slim fell off his horse. Jake stopped and knelt down to Slim and listened to his chest, he was dead. He got back on his horse and again headed to the small town which was just over the rise in the road. At the top of the rise in view of the town Jake fell off his horse. The group waited for 10 minutes. The posse appeared coming fast, they had Slims horse with him tied to it. They stopped to check Jakes body; he was dead also. They tied Jakes body to his horse and headed back to town. Tim went back to the lake and faced the "Bullet" towards the water.

John started to turn the big dial back to present time. As he changed the display, they all watched to see what the area would look like when John was finished. Jack: "What happened to the lake?" The lake had vanished.

John: "Donna, is it possible to get a recent weather report for this area?" Donna: "I will try—I got something yes, there has been a two-year drought in the area." John: "The lake probably vanished because the spring that was feeding it stopped due to the drought, but the edge of the lake is easily visible, who would like to dig for gold?" Tim and Carla raised their hands. Tim got up and took two shovels from the locker.

John: "You might want to consider sunglasses and a hat, and you are looking for remnants of the wooden box, rotted bags and gold coins." Carla ran back to the rear compartment; she came back with two Cowboy hats smiling: "We got these in Tombstone." John looked over at Donna and Jack: "Did you guys get some hats also?" Donna and Jack both nodded yes. John laughed.

John: "Donna, what is the temperature out there?" Donna: "I already looked; it is 99 degrees. John: "Ok kids, go to it." Tim and Carla walked through the open "doorway" and to the edge of the lake. Tim pointed to something on what used to be lake bottom. He looked back at the "doorway": "We see an indention that might be the old wooden box." They started to dig. As they did the outline of a wooden box took shape. They continued to dig around the box until they got to the bottom of the box. They reached the bottom of the box with a foot all the way around the box being dug out. Tim used the shovel to pry up one side of the box and then moved around and pried up the other side of the box. Then they both put their fingers under opposite sides of the box and gently pulled up the box until it came loose of the dirt. Sitting on top of the dirt were two bags of something. Tim and Carla carefully lifted the bags and placed them one on each shovel.

Carla: "The bag is really heavy." They picked up the shovels and brought them back through the "doorway" and into the kitchen. Donna tore off some paper towels and put them on the counter. Tim and Carla put the shovels on the paper towels. Tim placed the stopper into the bottom of the sink, then put one bag into the sink, as he did it came apart and spilled gold coins into the bottom of the sink. He turned on the water and started to rinse off the coins. Carla put more paper towels on the counter and dried off the coins with a dish towel as Tim handed them to her. She stacked them in columns on the paper towels. When she ran out of space with the first bunch of paper towels, Carla tore off another bunch and continued stacking the coins. It took a third bunch of paper towels to contain all the coins. Tim removed the sink stopper, cleaned out the sink with a few paper towels, and tossed them in the garbage. They all were mesmerized by all the glittering stacks of coins. John took one coin from a stack and looked closely at the coin: "It is definitely a $50 gold coin." He moved over to the food scale. He placed the coin on the scale. It weighed two Oz's. John counted the coins, there were two hundred, there must have been a hundred in each bag. John looked at Donna who was smiling. Donna: "They are worth "$112,000."

John: "Actually they are worth more than that, at auction they might be worth twice or more because they were from 1857. Donna what time is it please?"

Donna: "It is 5pm. And all is well." John looked over at Donna who was smiling.

John chuckled: "How about we go back to "Old Tucson", have dinner, see all the sights, and shows, come back here, and talk about what we have done and I will tell all of you about what we are going to do tomorrow, our last vacation day."

Donna whining: "Oh, tomorrow is our last day?"

John: "Yes, it is but it will be the best day you will ever have on vacation. So, go wash off the dust and change clothes if you want, Donna and Jack, drag out your hats and we are off to "Old Tucson the Movie set" Tim, Carla, Donna, and Jack headed into the back room. John looked at Bob: "What's the matter—no Cowboy hat, we'll just have to get you one?" Bob: "I don't know it just seems kind of boring."

John: "Do you like trains, they have an old steam engine to ride at "Old Tucson"?"

Bob: "Well why didn't you say so, I love old trains." John and Bob went in the back to clean up.

5:30pm.

John and Bob were in the main cabin waiting for the two couples. Finally, they all came into the cabin. Tim and Carla sat down at the left console and Donna and Jack at the right console.

John: "Ok, Donna put in the coordinates for "Old Tucson please, Tim, take us to the Movie set." Donna nodded at Tim. They were there in a few minutes.

Donna: "John do you have any idea where to park?" John: "Take a look at the main street, start at the train station and go to the other end of the street." Tim took the tour of main street.

John: "Look there is a small shed at the rear of the old courthouse, go through the shed and put the "doorway" in the rear wall." Tim parked the "Bullet" and turned off all systems except the "doorway". John put the "doorway" backpack on his shoulder and they all piled out. John led them slowly to the main street. The walked down main street until they found a place to eat, then went in.

7 pm.

John was sitting on the bench outside the restaurant. Tim came out and sat down beside him.

Tim: "John, thank you, Carla and I have had a great time on vacation. I was planning to ask Carla to marry me on vacation."

John: "Well that's wonderful, I know a perfect place."

Tim: "Where 's that?"

John: "The old courthouse steps down the street, Bob has his camera, you guys have your Cowboy hats, it would make a perfect picture for your family and kids. You could talk about the picture for years."

Tim: "I love it, let's do it."

John: "Ok, you take Carla out a little ahead of us when we leave. We will follow and Bob will have his camera ready, and afterwards, we will all take a nice train ride." Tim agreed. Bob, Carla, Donna, and Jack came out of the restaurant. Tim grabbed Carla's hand: "Let's take another walk down the street." They started to walk hand in hand towards the end of the street and the Old Courthouse.

John turned to the group and whispered: "Slow down let them get a little ahead, Bob, get your camera ready." The group let them get about 11 feet ahead. As they got to the end of town Tim slowly walked over to the steps of the "Old Courthouse and stepped up two steps to the entrance before the doors, with Carla. He let her get a foot or so ahead and dropped her hand. As Carla turned around to see Tim on one knee Donna saw what was happening and elbowed Bob to start taking pictures. Tim was holding a box with an engagement ring out to Carla.

Tim: "Carla, I love you, will you marry me?"

Carla starting to tear up: "Yes, of course I will. I was hoping you would ask me on vacation." Tim put the ring on Carla's finger.

Carla was in full tears and hugging Tim, Donna was in tears and hugging Jack, Bob was fortunately still taking pictures. John was a little misty. A stranger walked by and John grabbed him and ask if he would take a group picture for them. The stranger took Bob's camera and took several.

John: "Well, that was super, now Bob wants to take a train ride if that's ok?" The group walked back to the train station at the other end of town. Carla and Donna sat together and clucked. John, Bob, Tim, and Jack sat together. Bob made them all ride the train four times. After the train ride John bought Bob a Cowboy hat picked out by Donna. After that they all went back to the "Bullet"

9pm.

The group were all sitting in the cabin. Carla was showing off her engagement ring, the men were congratulating Tim, and then they talked about the gold finds and how much fun they had doing it.

10:30pm.

John: "I promised I would tell you what we are going to do tomorrow, well, we are going on another hunt but not like before. We will not go looking for stolen gold. We will kind of be looking for gold but this is something that has been lost for a hundred years, and it's famous. It is located in Arizona. Would anyone like to guess what it is?" John waited and looked at Carla.

Carla raised her hand: "Is it in the Superstition mountains east of Phoenix?"

John: "Yes, it is.

Carla was jumping up and down (Tim was getting a kick out of Carla): "Is it the "Lost Dutchman Gold Mine"

John: "Yes, it is—good guess, and after that I am hitting the sack, see you all in the morning." John left the cabin and went to bed.

CHAPTER FIVE

"Vacation, Day 4-Last day"

O6:30

John wandered into the kitchen. Donna, Jack, Tim, and Carla had already started breakfast. John asked what he could do. Tim: "You could make coffee." John: "Actually I can't make coffee; I don't drink it so I don't know how to make it. He looked at the table" I will make a pitcher of OJ." John went to the freezer, got the orange juice and proceeded to use the blender. John had just put the OJ on the table when Bob wandered in. John: "Good morning, Bob, we didn't wake you, did we?" Donna and Jack started to chuckle. Bob just got a cup and poured himself a coffee and sat down at the table. They all ate, cleaned up and went into the main cabin. Everyone sat down at their post. John picked up his folder and sat in the chair, Bob sat next to John.

John: "I suppose you are all excited to start todays hunt, and so am I, however I want to talk a minute.
First---We are not going to mine the mine even if we find it.
Second---We will not tell anyone where the mine was if we do find it.
Third---We need to very careful, lots of people have died and have been killed trying to find the mine.
As I see it, we have two ways to do this:

Way one:
We follow Jacob Waltz to the mine. This may be the
slowest way to find the mine. He was a bartender in a
saloon at "Tortilla Flat "Arizona and had a small ranch
not too far from there. Both are outside my mine search
area. The problem here is we don't know when he will go
to the mine.
    Way two:
 I have researched the clues that were left by Jacob Waltz,
they are contradictory, vague and many. They tell you
what you can see from the mine site, but without
reference points mean nothing. However, there is one clue
that stands out to me and I will tell you what that is later.
So, I think for fun we might see if we can follow Waltz
from the Saloon first, we might get lucky. So, hands up
for Way one: please. Tim, Carla, Jack, and Donna all
raised their hands. Ok. "Way One" it is. Donna, I have all
the information here in my papers I will just give you
locations. First, we are going to 1864 "Tortilla Flat"
Arizona. That's the Saloon where Jacob Waltz worked as
a bar tender. John held up a printed picture of Waltz and
gave it to Donna."
Donna input the coordinates and scanned the picture to
the big screen, then nodded at Tim, a few minutes later
they arrived. The town had 20 buildings at least.
    John: "There may be only one Saloon, the name of the
Saloon is unknown, so let's see if we can find it. They
started to check each building. Visibility was good there
was still just enough daylight left. Tim slowly moved
down the center of the street looking at the building
fronts. Bob spoke up: "There is a Saloon. There was no
name just "Saloon" on the sign. John: "Keep looking
there might be another." Tim moved to the end of the
street turned and went down the other side. There were no
more Saloons and Tim moved back to the first Saloon, it
was located in the middle of town with an alley on both

sides and two outhouses out back. John moved his chair up to the console next to Donna, he turned on the "doorway" and started to adjust the big dial forward to nighttime, he stopped at

11pm. Jacob time

John: "Tim we need to watch the bar and locate Jacob Waltz. We don't know when he arrives, so it might take some time. Move the "doorway" into the rear of the Saloon, 8 feet off the ground and Donna use the small image." Tim put the "Bullet" in the back corner of the room to see most of the bar." Tim did some skillful maneuvering and did just that. All of the bar was in view.

John: "I will now move the clock ahead 1 day until we see Mr. Waltz." John moved the clock forward one day at a time. They had been watching now for over two hours, and gone ahead eight months. Donna and Jack had taken turns moving the dial ahead 1 day at a time.

Suddenly Jack said: "Isn't that Waltz coming in the side door?" They all looked closely at the man.
John: "He sure looks like the picture. Let's watch and see what happens". The man sat down at a table and ordered a beer and started to drink. The man asked for another beer. The bartender brought the beer and sat it on the table: "Jacob are you working tomorrow?"

Jacob: "No, I am going to Tucson for two or three weeks, I am leaving tonight after this beer, I will see you in a few weeks." Jacob finished his beer got up and left through the same side door he came in.

John: "Ok, maybe we just got lucky, keep him in sight." Jacob went towards the rear of the Saloon, he kept looking behind him. As he reached the open ground, he stepped up his pace and disappeared into the darkness. At the edge of the wilderness he stopped, turned and hunched down watching behind him. John: "I feel good about this, he keeps checking for someone following him. Donna is anyone following him?" Donna turned on her night vision: "Yes, two men with one mule full of supplies, but it looks like they have lost him, they are wandering around trying to find him." Jacob now headed south east at a fast pace. Tim continued to follow him to a large rock. He again hunched and watched and looked into the darkness.

John: "Donna, is he being followed now?"
Donna: "No, they gave up and went back to the town. Also, there are two mules behind the rock Jacob is standing next to and one it is full of supplies." They all watched as Jacob picked up the two mules and continued south east toward the Superstition mountains. Everyone was excited.

1:30 am. Jacob time
They had been watching for and following Jacob for almost 3 hours. He was approaching the edge of the Superstition mountains, he changed direction and headed straight south. One hour later Jacob turned and headed straight east into the mountains.

2:30 am. Jacob time. 12:30 pm cabin time
John: "What time is it here in the cabin?" Donna, it is lunch time. John: "Why don't Carla, Jack, Donna and Bob go to lunch and Tim and I will keep tabs on Jacob while you eat?" Bob got up and headed to the kitchen saying:" I don't need to be asked twice to go to lunch." The rest followed Bob. Tim and John continued to watch Jacob. He stopped as he got slightly into the mountains.

John: "I was expecting this, he is going to make camp until morning. Nobody would go into those gullies and canyons in the dark even if you knew where you were going." Tim and John watched as Jacob set up camp. He had picked a small u-shaped gully that had large rocks in the front, he lit a very small fire, knowing that no one would see the fire. John figured he had used this gully before. The lunch group came back from the kitchen and brought John and Tim something to eat. John thanked them for the food and gave them a status. And they talked a long while.

John: "Donna, what time is dawn Jacob time?"

Donna: "Let's see, dawn is about 6:45am his time, about 4 hours from now. "

John: "Ok, we can try and get 4 hours sleep now, that would catch us up with Jacob's time and we wouldn't feel so sleepy later. We are always going to be about 6 hours different until we are finished. Tomorrow he should be at the mine, and will be for weeks, at which time we can adjust our time back to normal to match his. I know this is crazy but we must stay on Jacob time until we can catch up. So, Donna, set an alarm for 6am: Jacob time and we can try to sleep. Those of you that want a bed to sleep in go ahead, someone will come and get you." The women left the cabin. John, Bob and Tim dozed off. John could hear the alarm going off, he opened his eyes. Bob and Tim woke up slowly. John looked at the big screen: "Oh, crap Jacob is gone, all his gear and the mules were gone." Tim walked over to Donna's console and turned on the infrared view and looked at the big screen.

Tim: "There he is about a half a mile into that canyon." Tim went back to his console and caught up to Jacob. John went to Donna's console and turned off infrared vision. He looked at the big screen and all was ok. About that time Donna and Carla came back to the cabin.

Donna: "Did everything go ok?" John looked at Tim: "Yes all is fine." Tim just smiled.

They watched Jacob for the next two hours. He ducked in and out of ravines and canyons steadily heading in one direction, --East, his movement though was slow overall because of the terrain. John was able to gain an hour because of the slow travel. Now their clock and Jacobs were only off 1 hour. It was now noon Jacob time, he stopped. They watched him tie up the mules and find a place in the shade to rest. He laid back on the cooler rock and fell asleep. John moved up the time 30 minutes, Jacob was still asleep, John moved the time up another 30 minutes, their clocks were now the same. Jacob was eating something he must have taken from the pack mule. He continued eating and drinking water.

It was now 1:30 pm.
Jacob finished eating, looked around at the surrounding area, nodded his head and started out again. One hour later he stopped again and tied up the mules He spent a few minutes looking up and wandering around the small area he was stopped in. He walked back to the mules and removed four large empty canvas bags, then walked to a dead tree 20 feet away next to the rock face. He looked behind the tree, there were four ropes hanging down the rock, almost invisible the same color as the rock. He carefully attached each bag to one rope.

Donna: "What is he doing?"
John: "The mine is up above him. After he fills the bags with gold, he lowers them back to the bottom because he can't carry the heavy bags back down by himself."
After Jacob finished with the bags. He went to the end of the canyon and started to climb up using a very small ledge that slowly went up 50 feet to the top of the canyon. At the top was a cave closed up by a rock wall.

John: "That's good, the clues say he built that wall to close off an old attempt to dig down into the mine. If the clues are right the mine is below him. Jacob walked by the cave on a slightly downward slant and suddenly disappeared. The group was trying to figure out where he had gone. John: "Tim put us directly across from the closed-up cave wall." Tim did so.

Jack: "Look, the ropes with the bags are being pulled up." They watched as the bags were pulled up and then disappeared into a two by two-foot hole in the rock.

John: "Tim, take us a few feet higher. Tim moved the "Bullet" up three feet. Now everything became clear. There was ledge on the rockface about 3 feet wide and 12 feet long and six feet tall a foot from the rockface, four feet at the edge of the ledge. The wall on the edge of the ledge slanted inward towards the rockface, and stopped about 8 inches from the rockface. It was a natural tunnel completely hidden from the ground. From the ground the rockface looked solid. Jacob entered the tunnel by using the 2-foot-wide hole at the right end.
John: "Tim, move the "Bullet" nearer to the left end of the tunnel. The left end had a similar hole that was about 3 feet long and two feet wide.

John: "Look at the left end of the tunnel, A hole about 3 feet wide slanted slightly downward going into the rock face. There is the "Lost Dutchmen Mine." Jacob reached the left end with the bags and crawled inside.

The group all watched the hole. They could hear a pick being used inside the hole. About two hours later Jacob pushed out a full canvas bag from the hole, he then emerged and pulled the canvas bag back to the right-hand 2-foot-wide hole. Tim moved back to the right side of the tunnel. Jacob was tying the bag to one of the ropes. When he finished, he pushed the bag over the side of the ledge and started to lower it to the ground, the bag stopped half way down the 50-foot drop. Jacob leaned over the edge of the hole to see what was wrong. He could not see what had happened. Jacob climbed out of the hole onto the wide footpath and tried to pull the rope towards him. When he did Jacob lost his balance and went over the ledge. He grabbed the edge of the 2-foot-hole as he went over and hung on with both hands. He tried to climb back up to the hole but the rock was too smooth for his shoes.

John: "This is nuts, Donna open the large "doorway", Tim get us closer to the edge of the footpath so I can jump to it." Tim moved the "Bullet", When the "doorway" was close enough John stepped onto the rock wall footpath, he leaned over the edge of the footpath and said to Jacob: "Take my hand I will pull you up." Jacob grabbed John's hand and John pulled him up onto the tunnel footpath which started at the 2-foot entrance to the tunnel.

Jacob: "You saved my life, thank you. I owe you for that. What are you doing here?"

John: "Observing."

Jacob: "Observing me?"

John: "Yes, look Jacob, I 'm not sure how to handle this situation yet. I need to think a few minutes, in the meantime please don't ask me any more questions, all right?"

Jacob: "You seem to know who I am so I will wait for you to think." John: "Thank you, Jacob" Jacob waited. John: "Jacob, do you feel that you owe me for saving your life? And if you do, what do you owe me?"

Jacob: "I would owe you anything within reason."

John: "I want you to believe me when I say that we don't care about your gold mine or the gold in it."

Jacob: "You said we, are there others observing also?"

John: "Yes, please don't ask more questions, I cannot give you answers, and I can't explain why. It is for your own good that I say nothing."

Jacob: "Alright I agree no more questions."

John: "Could we balance the debt with a favor from you?"

Jacob: "Anything within reason."

John: "Let me help you fill the other three canvas bags, I would love to see inside the mine, we should be able to fill the bags in about an hour."

Jacob: "Well, I don't know how you intend to fill all those bags in an hour, but if you can I would like to see it. You have a deal: "Jacob held out his hand. John took his hand and shook it.

John: "Jacob I have to ask you to face the rock wall please." Jacob turned and faced the rock wall. John looked towards the "doorway"; Bob I need the 18V hammer drill with the flat rock bit. They are in the tool locker."
A minute later Bob stuck his hand through the "doorway" and handed John what he had asked for.

John: "Jacob you can turn around now. Jacob saw the drill in John's hand. Now we can go into the mine, I assume you have coal lamps inside?" Jacob nodded, they both dropped into the 2-foot hole and walked to the mine and crawled inside, John looked through the entrance and could see the coal lamps had lit up the inside of the entrance. It was much larger inside, as big as a cave. He crawled through the entrance. Jacob was sitting a few feet away. John looked at the cave wall in front of him. The quartz vein was 18 inches wide, slightly downward to the end of the cave 20 feet away. The vein was slightly pink in color and more so near the end.

John: "Jacob thank you for letting me see this, it is amazing. Do you have any idea how far back into the rock wall the vein goes?" Jacob: "No, I have only been here twice before and have barely mined the vein. You see it just as I found it."

John: "Well, let's get busy, he adjusted the drill setting to the picture of the "hammer", put the drill up against the vein of quartz and pressed the trigger." The drill ate through the quartz like it was butter. John chopped out large nuggets in no time flat. Jacob was smiling as the nuggets started to rain down on the floor.

John looking at Jacob: "What do you think, is this quick enough for you. Jacob: "That thing is unbelievable and started to scoop the nuggets into the second bag. The bag was filled quickly and the other two bags filled before the hour was up. John continued to hew out sections of quartz and filled the floor with it. John looked at all the nuggets on the floor: "That should make it a little easier on you the next time you come back here."

Jacob: "Thank you, you know you never told me your name."
John: "I know, remember the less you know the better off you are and your debt is paid, you will never see me again. But you can remember me, John moved over to the rock wall on the other side of the cave, he carved the initials JW" into the wall and then and as an afterthought added a dash and JAF.

Jacob: "How about you carve out a piece of quartz to keep as a souvenir?" John thought about it for a minute and said: "Thank you Jacob." John went back to the quartz wall and carved out a three-inch square of pink quartz., he looked at Jacob and tossed the square a couple of times into the air smiling. Jacob laughed.

John: "Come on I will help you get the bags down to the canyon floor below." John and Jacob pulled the three heavy bags to the other one laying at the end of the tunnel. Jacob tied them up and they lowered them down to the canyon floor together.

John: "Remember, nothing happened here today." John put out his hand again to Jacob and shook his hand. Goodbye my friend Jacob Waltz. If you would face away from me one more time, and count to ten. Jacob turned and started to count, John pushed the drill towards the "doorway", Bob took it from him, John put the golden quartz cube in his right hand and put his left hand towards the "doorway" Bob pulled John through the "doorway" back into the "Bullet"

Jacob reached 10 and turned, seeing John was gone: "Goodbye Observer and smiled." John: "Tim, pull away and go to the bottom of the canyon please." Tim did so. The group watched as Jacob made his way to the canyon bottom, packed the mules and started to leave, they watched as he disappeared at the end of the canyon.

John looked at Donna: "Donna, time to go home please, wait a minute, did you all have a good time the last four days?"

Jack: "I think I can speak for Donna and myself, we had a wonderful time, we couldn't have planned a more fun vacation."

Tim: "I agree we also had a great time, John watched as Carla nodded and played with the new ring on her finger."

Bob: "I had a good time too, I was bored a little but I got over that and enjoyed myself, maybe it was the train rides." Everyone laughed.

John: "How would all of you like to see inside the mine before we go?" All hands raised. John: "Ok. I will take two of you at a time for a few minutes to see the mine. Tim and Carla are first. Tim, take us back up to the ledge. Tim maneuvered the "Bullet back up to the ledge, this time he put the "doorway" right on the pathway facing the mine. John got a flashlight out of the storage locker, he looked at Tim and Carla: "Are you ready?" They nodded. John led them to the ledge and the hole to drop through. John went first into the drop hole, then he helped Tim, and Tim helped Carla through the hole. John led them to the mine entrance:" Now the inside is much larger, like a large cave:" John went in first, Carla next, and Tim followed. Inside the mine was now lit up really bright. John pointed out the vein across the wall. He gave Tim the flashlight so he and Carla could get up close to see the vein of quartz.

Carla: "Wow, this is beautiful, you can see the gold specks in the pink quartz.

John: "I believe that if you were to follow the vein downward into the rock, you would actually find some smaller veins of solid gold that had melted out of the quartz." Tim took his turn looking at the quartz vein.

Tim: "Thanks John for this opportunity, this is really amazing, I have never seen anything like this before." They finished and made their way out of the mine and back to the "Bullet" cabin. It was now Jack and Donnas turn. John led them to the ledge as before, and into the mine. They checked out the gold vein with the flashlight as Tim and Carla did. When Jack and Donna had finished looking, they all went back to the "Bullet" cabin.

John: "Ok Bob, are you ready?"
Bob: "I'm good, I have seen mines before, and I saw the chunk of quartz that Jacob gave you for a souvenir."

John: "Ok, then there is something that has been bothering me, Jacob Waltz told me in the cave this was his second trip to the mine. Carla, you have a good knowledge of the "Old West", in your opinion what would have happened if Jacob Waltz had fallen and died on the canyon floor?" Carla thought for a few seconds: "The legend would not have continued or even started, he would have come up missing and forgotten."
John: "And he would not have died in 1891 many years later sick in the back room of a friend who was taking care of him."

Donna excitedly: "John, are you saying we were there to save Jacob Waltz from dying that day?"
John: "It sure is something to think about isn't it, to think that fate or the universe stepped in to make sure what was supposed to happen, did happen. Suddenly the group was silent and thinking.

John leaned over to Bob and whispered: "Maybe in 1947 also. "
Bob whispered back: "Kind of gives you the willys don't it?" John chuckled: "Ok, let's go home."

Donna entered the coordinates for home and nodded at Tim.

John: "Well, I suppose you all want to know about the mine and what happens next?" John started to tell them more about the mine and what will happen to all the found gold.

John: "I want you all to come to my house for breakfast 30 days from today and get the rest of the details. They stopped at the "Faraday's" moon entrance to drop off Donna and Jack, John: "I will see you all later." then went on to the workshop.

John: "Carla, have you ever taken a ride in the "VOID" in a golf cart, because now is your chance?" Carla: "No, sounds like fun though.

John: "Bob, you can go into the house, I will be back in a minute. Tim load your bags into the golf cart and back the "Bullet" up next to the golf cart, that's its new home."

Bob went through the workshop and into the house. John got into the golf cart, Tim and Carla were in the back seat and their bags in the cart bed.

Tim: "So John, why are you taking us home?"

John: "I bought the "Faraday 1" from the government, I told them I might take it on missions and Izzy equipped it for such. That is why it will be parked from now on next to the golf cart. So, where can I drop you kids?" Tim told John where to go. Later John returned and parked the golf cart next to "Faraday 1". He went through the workshop and into the house. Bob was sitting at the Florida room table with Lora. John gave Lora a kiss and a hug and sat down.

John: "Well, that was quite a trip, four days of fun, fun, fun. Right Bob?"

Lora: "Bob was telling me about the trip. It sounds to me like you guys had a lot of fun. I'm sorry I missed it"

John pulled the square pink quartz piece of vein out from behind his back and handed it to Lora.

Lora: "Oh, wow, this is so beautiful, look at the gold specks in the pink quartz. What are you going to do with it, John?"

John: "I plan to mount it in a silver frame and put it on my desk, anyway the trip was great, I even bought the "Faraday 1" from Uncle Sam."
Bob: "I remember you mentioning that. How did you swing that?" John: "Izzy mentioned they were about to scrap her. So, I asked if I could buy her and use it in possible missions if needed. When I said that he authorized the upgrades we saw and would send me a bill."

Bob: "How much did they sell "Faraday 1" to you for?"
John: "The charged me $1000."
Bob "Are you kidding me, $1000 bucks and all that stuff they did to it?"

John: "Well, they were going to scrap her, I couldn't have that, besides I didn't ask Izzy to do that other stuff, that was his idea." I guess they thought if it was used on a mission, we might need the *stuff.*" Bob: "Oh, that reminds me, they installed a mini-gun mount on top of "Faraday 1", in the front center of the "Bullet", they removed it and put the gun in one of the lockers, along with a bunch of ammo. I verified that by looking at the weapons console, there was a power button marked as "Mini-Gun." There also is a celling door in the front center that opens to access the gun, to mount the gun, and change the ammo belt inside the cabin."

Lora: "Does this mean we have our own hotel room when we go on vacation?" John;" Why, yes it does and according to Bob its loaded for bear."
Lora:" Way to go Mr. Faraday, Good purchase."
Bob: "I see your point; it was really nice for those four days."

John: "That reminds me Bob, I want you to call that settlement attorney, what's his name, ummm Dewy something, I can't think of his last name. I want him to handle dealing with whoever about the gold return and the reward for finding it. He owes me a big favor for helping him out of trouble back a ways. Have him come see me Monday morning. Bob: "I know who you are talking about, I can't think of his last name either, I will call him in the morning.

John: "Oh, one other thing, find out who holds the student loan on Carla. Getting that student load paid off would be a nice wedding present." Bob smiled got up and left.
Lora: "What wedding present for who?"
Tim (Sgt. Carter) asked his girlfriend to marry him while we were on vacation. Bob has all the pictures. And I forgot to tell him to get many copies made. I'll tell him tomorrow." John was eyeing the empty couch.

Lora honey: "How long before supper?" Lora smiled: "About an hour or so. Why don't you wait on the couch?" John complied.

CHAPTER SIX

"Attorney what's his name"

Monday morning 08:00

John was sitting at his desk going over the gold numbers before he saw the attorney today. He looked at the silver stand holding the pink quartz cube on his desk. John loved it, it sure was neat. In the sunlight it lit up the office like a disco night club. Jenny came to the door: "John a Mr. Cheetum is here to see you." John: "Thank you Jenny, send him in. John moved around to the table in the office and sat down, he motioned for Dewy to sit down. John: "How have you been Dewy?"

Mr. Cheetum: "I have been good; I see you are doing quite well."

John: "I do ok, listen Dewy I need a favor done that will make us even, are you interested?"

Dewy: "Why yes, I would be, what do you have in mind?"

John handed Dewy the paperwork on the recovered gold: "This gold was found from robbery's committed in the 1880's out west and never recovered. I would like you to contact or locate the alleged owners of the original gold and negotiate a recovery settlement. If no owner can be located you would follow state procedure for found property."

Dewy: "Where is the gold now?"

John: "It is in the bank account of a corporation called "Gold Finders Are Us." It's in a Faraday Bank vault here on my moon. The gold will be sold at whatever the daily price of gold is on the contract date. The finder's fee will be deducted and the balance will be sent to the found owner on the paperwork."
Dewy: "What is your expected finder's fee?"
John: "Not less than 10 percent, I don't see that as a problem since they are receiving much more than the original gold was valued. Do you?"
Dewy: "That is a good point, maybe a slightly higher finder's fee is possible, negotiating a better finder's fee might be part of the fun."
John: "That is the right attitude."
Dewy: "Now what about my fee?"
John: "All of this is phone calls; I was thinking that a "Great Job Dewy" and a hearty "We are even now" would be appreciated and maybe a slight "I owe you one Dewy".
Dewy nodded: "I see what you mean Mr. Faraday."
John: "Please call me with any problems."
Dewy: "Is there a time limit on this?"
John looked Dewy straight in the eyes: "Nooooo, take the whole week if you want and come back next Monday."
John: "Hey Dewy, I heard a good lawyer joke last week."
Dewy looked at John and waited for the joke. John: "What do call 100 lawyers at the bottom of a lake?"
Dewy: "I give up"
John chuckling: "A good start." Dewy: "Oh, a really good one, I'll pass it on." Dewy took the paperwork and left the office. John walked to the office door as he watched Dewy leave: "Jenny, have the office fumigated please (Jenny knew who Dewy Cheetum was) and laughed." John went back to his desk and stared at his new shining paperweight. Jenny came to the door: "John there is a Mr. Terry to see you." John: "Send him in Jenny" John got up to meet Mr. Terry at the door. Mr.

Terry was the head of the five member people's council on "Faraday's" moon. They handled any problems from the local resident domes. John held out his hand as Mr. Terry came to the door.

John: "Mr. Terry nice to see you again, it's been too long. Please sit down at the table, can I get you a refreshment?"

Mr. Terry sat down: "No refreshment thanks Mr. Faraday."

John: "Oh, please call me John." Mr. Terry: "Ok, John, I am here to ask you to addend a complaint meeting with the council in an hour. The is really the first one we have had since the council was established more than a year ago. I am sorry to say it looks like it is going to be a bad one. I would like you as an observer if you wouldn't mind."

John thinking this might be interesting: "I would be delighted to attend; I will bring Bob Johnson if I may. I have been a little lax on not attending the last few meetings because your group was doing fine. So, I will see you in about an hour at the meeting."

Mr. Terry got up and extended his hand: "Thank you Mr. Faraday." John got up: "John, call me John." As Mr. Terry left the office. Bob, bounded into the office and noticed John muttering to himself.

John looked at Bob: "Why can't people just call me John?" Bob: "They respect you that's why—just go with it, anything going on?"

John: "Yes, we are attending a peoples meeting in less than hour as observers." Bob: "Oh, good that sounds like fun, oh, WOW look at that quartz cube. That is a crazy setting its in, when did you have that done?"

John: "I went to see a friend in the jewelry business. He made the setting for me, its silver. He kept asking me if I wanted to sell it to him." John chuckled. They sat and talked; John told Bob about the meeting with Dewy

Cheetum. Bob: "Ya, he is quite a prize. If you threw something wet on him it would just slide off." John laughed: "Oh, you do know Dewy?"

John: "Well, it's time to go to the meeting, and after I will buy you lunch." John and Bob left the office and went downstairs to the peoples meeting. They walked in and sat down in the audience section which was darkened so the three people in front of the council could not see into the audience. John and Bob were the only ones there.

There were five council chairs filled with council members sitting at a table in front of John and Bob about thirty feet away. There were three chairs about six feet apart in front of the council chairs, there were three people sitting in those three chairs facing the council. John could not see who they were.

Mr. Terry stood up from the middle council chair: "This monthly meeting of the people's council will please come to order; he pounded a gavel on a round piece of wood on the table in front him. Mr. Gravis you are the complainer, please stand and tell us your complaint." Mr. Gravis stood turned and pointed to the second man: "This man and his fellow foreigners run a horrible eating restaurant, the food is terrible and the meat served is questionable, and could very easily be local animal pets that have gone missing. It is the same for the grocery store also run by foreigners. Poor food and dirty all the time. It has to stop they all must be made to leave, he then sat down."

John: "I see where this is going, call Jack and ask him to come down here please."

Mr. Terry: "The defendants here are Mr. Ying from the restaurant and Mr. Sing from the grocery store. (John started to chuckle slightly. He knew both of these men and they were both fine and honorable men.) Mr. Ying please tell us your side."

Mr. Ying: "The man is crazy. My food is inspected daily by me and weekly by a local inspector, you must have the reports, just look at them." Mr. Ying sat down. As he did Jack walked in and sat down next to John.

Mr. Terry: "Mr. Sing, please tell us your side." Mr. Sing told the same story and ask the council to look at the reports. Jack leaned over to John: "What's Gravis doing here?"

John: "You know Mr. Gravis?"
Jack: "Yes, he works on a construction crew, been here about a month."
John: "Tell me about him."

Jack: "He is a good worker, but a troublemaker, he is also the biggest racist I have ever seen." John looked over at Bob and smiled. Bob: "Oh boy, here we go."

Mr. Terry: "The council after hearing all the testimony and after investigating the records has come to a decision. All the records indicate that the complaints have no merit. The attitude of the complainer is evident. It is the decision of this council that the complainer be immediately barred and ejected permanently from "Faraday's" moon, that is the final decision. Mr. Gravis, you may of course go to arbitration, that is your choice."
Mr. Gravis: "Yes that I will, I demand arbitration, someone here on the moon must have some sense."

Mr. Terry: "Mr. Faraday are you in the audience?"
John: "Yes, Mr. Terry can someone please turn up the audience lights. Mr. Terry flipped a switch at the council table, and the audience lights came on."

John: "Mr. Gravis, an arbitration requires a minimum of three arbiters. By chance there are three already here, myself, Agent Johnson, and Jack Foster. If you would give us a few minutes please. John turned to Jack and Bob: "Personally I would love to grab this idiot by the scruff of the neck and toss him out the first "doorway" to Earth. I assume you agree with me about this butthead?"

They both nodded. John: "Mr. Terry: Arbitration is over and we concur with the council, please call two security officers and escort this man off of "Faraday's" moon."

Mr. Terry pressed a button and the two security officers standing outside the council chambers came in and walked to the council table.
John: "Excuse me a minute boys." John walked up to the council chamber table: John: "Officers may I speak to Mr. Gravis for a minute before you escort him to his apartment?" The officers nodded yes. John grabbed Gravis by the arm and pulled him a few feet from the table.

John held up his index finger to Gravis: "You see this finger, Gravis; it contains a fingerprint that is recorded when any of my "doorways" are accessed. If you ever attempt to access any "doorway" to my moon I guaranty you may never be found again. And tell your friends that may be here, that we will be watching them because of you and we will tell them that also, now get off my moon and don't ever come back, John looked at the security officers, thank you Officers and walked back to Bob and Jack."
Jack: "What did you say to him?"
John: "I just said he was a despicable person and to get off my moon and never come back, that's all."
Bob: "Ya, I'll bet"
Mr. Terry came over to John: "I would say the laws you setup work well." John: "The council did what it is designed to do, and you did it very well." They were joined by Mr. Ying and Mr. Sing; John said it's nice to see you both again I'm sorry about what happened today. Mr. Ying: "Mr. Faraday you have nothing to apologize for, these things happen sometimes." John, Bob, and Jack left the council chamber.

Bob: "Hey, what about that lunch you were going to buy?"

John: "I forgot, let's go to Ying's place for lunch, you too Jack." Jack smiling: "I can't today Donna is expecting me for lunch on the houseboat, sorry." Jack smiling waved as he headed for the houseboat.

John looked at Bob who was smiling: "Bob stop thinking that, oh what the hell it's kind of fun, come on let's go to lunch." John and Bob went to lunch at Mr. Yings restaurant. They had just sat down when Mr. Ying came over to take their order. Mr. Ying: "Whatever you want is on the house today—just order and he handed them a menu. He came back in two minutes and took their order. The food was great as usual. John thanked Mr. Ying and they went back to the office. They both admired Johns pink quartz paper weight for a while then the day ended.

Tuesday 08:00

John was studying some of the construction reports. He thought to himself: "We have built up almost 50 percent of this moon. Everything so far has gone great. It can't get any better." He tossed the report onto the desk. He was still bored. John got up and walked out to Jenny's desk. I am going over to Jack's office. I will be back in a little while. At that he left his office and went to Jack's office. Jacks' secretary Debbie was behind her desk: "Hello Mr. Faraday what can I do for you?" John: "I just came down to see Jack."

Debbie: "Oh, I'm sorry, he is out at a construction site somewhere, he said he wouldn't be back until tomorrow. Do you want me to tell him you stopped by?"

John: "No, it wasn't important, just visiting." John went back to his office and stopped in front of Jenny thinking, "Jenny asked if he needed anything: "John came out of his stupor and looked at Jenny. John: "Oh, no, I was just thinking, it has been boring lately around here. I know what will help, a "PINBALL machine, Jenny I'm going to River City, see you tomorrow." John turned and

left for home. He walked into the Florida room. As he did
Lora came around the corner from the kitchen.
Lora: "You are home early, what's up?"

John: "I got bored at work and decided I need a
"PINBALL" machine at work to help me think."
Lora laughed: "Let me guess, you got to thinking about
that old machine you used to play when you were a kid,
the one with the "Derby Winner" horses on the glass
scoreboard, right?"

John: "Yes, that's the one, I guess that is kind of
pathetic, isn't it?"
Lora: "Absolutely not, you had fun playing that machine
so, let's go buy it, I will go with you."
John looked at Lora: "You know, that's why I love you
and gave her a big kiss."

Lora: "Oooo, maybe we should hurry and buy it and
come back home *early*."
John: "Sounds like a deal, John grabbed Lora's hand and
headed to the car."
They went downtown to see "Vinnie" a friend of John's
that was in the "PINBALL" machine business John had
been there before. Vinnie saw John and Lora before they
got into the store, he met them as they came through the
door. Lora gave Vinnie a hug.
Vinnie: "So what's up, you got that itch again, you still
looking for that machine you played as a kid?"

John: "I know I won't ever find that machine, but I
want a "PINBALL" machine in my office."
Vinnie: "So go look around, you can start over to the left.
As John started to the left Vinnie grabbed Lora by the
hand and put his index finger to his lips.
Lora: "What?"

Vinnie: "Now you go over to the right the third
machine from the wall in back on your right."
Lora followed Vinnie's instructions. As she got to the
third machine she stopped in front of the machine and

looked at it. It was called "Kentucky Derby" and had three pictures of horses on the back glass and their names under the pictures, one of the names was "Citation". Lora hollered: "John, John come here quick."

John came running at Lora's request. He looked at the machine: "Oh my god, this is the machine I have always looked for." He looked back at Lora and Vinnie who was standing there with a huge grin on his face. John: "Ok, what's going on?"

Vinnie chuckling: "I got this machine in the store three days ago, I realized it was the one you have always been looking for. I had my machine guy look it over. The inside has been modernized but the machine is perfect, just like the one you used to play. I was going to call you tomorrow."

Lora: "Vinnie, let me buy this machine for John's birthday next month." Vinnie: "Ok, come into the office and we can do the paperwork. John why don't you plug it in and play it while we do the paperwork. There is a rocker switch underneath the front to play without using a quarter."

John: "How much is the machine? Vinnie: "Do you care?" John shook his head no. Lora and Vinnie went to his office. Vinnie: "Ok, here is the paperwork, it has a lifetime warranty."

Lora: "Well, how much do I owe you Vinnie there is no amount on the paperwork." Vinnie: "Lora you can fill in any amount you want I, suggest $1000, there is no charge. John has been a true friend to me and has been there for me when I needed a friend. This machine is a partial payment to a friend." Lora was all teared up now. She looked at Vinnie and gave him a hug and wiped her eyes. They went back and watched John play the machine: "You were right Vinnie; it is exactly the same machine, is the tilt turned on."

Vinnie: "No the tilt is off, to turn it on you have to open the front, and pull up the top, it works like your car hood, there is a bar inside you lock into the top to hold it up. The tilt switch is clearly marked. If you will tell me where to ship it, we can get it there tomorrow, unless you want it later."

"Very funny, get it later, very funny." John gave Vinnie his office address on "Faraday's" moon.
The both thanked Vinnie and went back to the house. John said: Lora I am so excited to be getting that machine."

Lora smiling: "How excited are you?" John looked at Lora: "Let me show you how excited I am."

CHAPTER SEVEN

"PINBALL"

Wednesday 08:00

John was again sitting at his desk; he was dreaming about his "PINBALL" machine arriving. He got up and went to Jenny's desk. Jenny I am expecting my new "PINBALL" machine today. Would you call security and ask them to make sure the delivery guys find the building, ok?"

Jenny laughing: "Yes boss, I can do that if I get to play it. I am a pinball wizard." John smiling: "Ya, ok with me." John went back into his office and stared at his pink Quartz.

Wednesday 10:00

John was about half asleep. Jenny came to the door and said Mr. Cheetum was here. John motioned to Jenny to send him in. Dewy came in and sat down at the table. John joined him at the table. John: "What's up Dewy?"

Dewy: "I have finished with the first four robberies. All four were able to supply documents backing up their claims.

The total Oz's of gold was 3000 oz. worth $852,000.

I got a 15 percent recovery fee of $127,800

You owe $724,200. Gold went up $4 an oz. yesterday. The $50 gold coins can stay on deposit here. An ad will run in the closest newspaper to "Sweetsprings" for one week. If there is no claim the gold is "finders' keepers" I told the newspaper to notify your security Chief Bob Johnson of any news. Here is the payoff paperwork. The bank here should be able to handle the payments and the deposit to "Gold Finders Are Us"."

John: "Dewy, all this is great, you really did a great job, were there any comments from the Payees? "
Dewy: "John, these guys were chomping at the bit to get the recovered gold value. They came up with the paperwork literally in hours after I called them. I believe they might have gone as high as twenty percent recovery fee to get the money. Anyway, the numbers are frozen now. Good luck on those $50 gold coins. I believe the auction price on each coin could be 3 or 4 times the actual value of the gold."

John: "I appreciate the job you did; our debt is clean and if I would need something like this in the future would you be available?"
Dewy: "Thank you John, call me anytime." John got up with Dewy. John held out his hand. Dewy took John's hand and said: "That gesture to me was worth more than any payment. Dewy turned and left the office. Bob walked in to the office: "I saw Dewy leave; how did that go?" John: "Bob would you believe we got 15 percent finders fees.

Bob: "No, that's great, what were the total recovery fees."

John: "It was $127,800, and the $50 gold coins are on hold for the ad running in the newspaper."
Bob: "What in the world are you going to do with all that money?"

John: "I don't have a clue, if you come up with any ideas let me know."
John: "Listen I am waiting on a delivery, would you mind taking this paperwork on the gold bank payments down to Ed Long at the bank, I talked to him yesterday on the

phone and he said he would be happy to do it for us, and then come back up here."

Bob: "Sure I will be right back." Bob took the paperwork and left.

John sat back down at his desk. He was fixated on the pink quartz when Donna walked in to the office.

John standing up behind his desk: "Donna this is a nice surprise. What brings you here?"

Donna looked at the pink quartz paper weight: "Wow that is some display it is beautiful especially in that silver setting, she moved to the side of John's desk: "I was waiting for the right time to talk to you but I decided it was more important to just come here. I wanted to thank you for pointing me at Jack, I know you did it on purpose. I talked to Lora about Jack before we got together and she told me what you had done. I never knew my father, he died when I was two, my mom died two years ago. All my relatives moved away or died before I was four. My mom never spoke of them. I never realized what happiness was until Jack came into my life, she was biting her lip to hold back the tears." John stepped forward and gave Donna a hug.

John: "When, I told you before that I considered you all as family, I meant that." John bent down, opened a desk drawer and offered Donna a tissue. You and Jack were alone, now you're not. Life is about being around people that care about you. You have that again."

Donna smiled at John: "I am thankful for that too." Donna wiped her eyes again.

John: "Jack mentioned you two were spending a lot of time together on the houseboat."

Donna: "Yes, we both love the houseboat. We still use Jack's place here also. Oh, I forgot to tell you, my new office now is here in this building, NASA said because of the time I spend in the "VOID" I should be here."

John: "Well that's great, we can see you more often."
As he finished talking Bob and Jenny came into his
office."

Jenny: "John, you have a delivery waiting in front of
my desk."
John: "Perfect timing, you three stay here I will be right
back." John ran out the door and came back with two men
pushing a large flat dolly with his "PINBALL" machine
on the top of it.

John: "Just put it over here behind the office door,
there is plenty of room and a power plug." The two men
carefully moved the machine into place, removed all the
wrapping, one man took off the face in front of the
machine and opened the top, in the bottom was an arm
that went up and fit into a slot to hold it open about two
and a half feet. He removed a cardboard box from the
inside, opened the box and placed two metal balls in a slot
next to the spring plunger that shoots the ball out to play.
He showed John the two extra balls and placed the box
back inside where it was before, he motioned for John to
come over to the machine, John moved over to the
machine, the man showed John where the "tilt" switch
was, it was in the "off" position. The man put the lid
down, put the front face back on and plugged the machine
in. All the lights came on.

The man: "Ok, sir just press the red button and have a
nice day."
John: "John thanked the men and they left." As they
disappeared from the office everyone gathered around and
admired the "PINBALL" machine.

John: "I have been hunting for this machine for years,
I played on this machine many hours as a kid."
Bob: "Well, go ahead and push the red button. "
John: "Jenny is the resident expert here; Jenny, give it a
go." John motioned towards Jenny to come to the
machine. Jenny stood in front of the machine and pressed

the red button. All the displays for scoring zeroed out, all the lights came on. Jenny shot out a ball. The sounds made John feel like a kid again. John, Jenny, Bob, and Donna played the "PINBALL" machine the rest of the afternoon.

Thursday 08:00
John was at his desk admiring the pink quartz paperweight again.

Bob came in and sat down and then they both admired the pink quartz paperweight.

John: "Bob, when does the newspaper ad on the $50 gold pieces end?"
Bob: "If there is no reply, they belong to you next Wednesday morning."

John: "No, not me they belong to the "Gold Finders Are Us" account."
Bob, "Oh ya, that's right. How about a mid-morning snack? I am kinda hungry."

John: "Ok, I could use a donut." They asked Jenny if she wanted anything, she declined, and they went downstairs to the donut shop, and then back to the office. Bob was drinking his coffee and eating some kind of breakfast sandwich, John was drinking orange juice and eating a glazed donut." Bob was thinking about playing the pinball machine, he looked over at John. John had his eyes closed and was concentrating on something. Bob was thinking that was not a good sign.

John opened his eyes and looked at Bob: "Bob, call Izzy and ask him to come and get "Faraday 1" ready for action, and deliver it back with the squad at the workshop at 08:00 tomorrow. Get Jack and Donna up here ASAP." Bob jumped up and looked at John: "What are you planning?"
John smiling: "I'm planning to finish my juice and donut." Bob ran from the office. Jenny came in: What's going on?"

John: "It looks like a problem has arisen on "CEBO".
We are going to be gone several days I assume."
Jenny said: "Great, I can play with the "PINBALL
machine" while you are gone."

John smiling: "What if I lock the office door?" Jenny
smiled and pulled out a key from her pocket and wiggled
it at John, and went to her desk. John: "I guess she has me
there."
John called Lora and told her there was a problem on
CEBO and they would be gone a couple of days.
Lora said: "Ok, you boys be careful."

CHAPTER EIGHT

"Extinction Event"

John waited for Bob to return and Jack and Donna to arrive. Bob came back and sat down, and started to finish his food. John waited until he was finished.

John: "Bob, what have you done so far?"

Bob: "I called Jack and Donna and they will be here any minute."

As he finished Jack and Donna walked into his office.

Jack: "What's up John?"

John: "I just got a message from Kayla, there seems to be something very wrong at "CEBO". She will meet us at the "doorway" station ASAP, we can be there in 1 hour or less, John stopped talking and held up his index finger and closed his eyes for a minute.), No, check that, Kayla and Toma will meet us. If Bob is done feeding his face, we can go down to the parking lot and get into my golf cart and take it to the to the workshop and get into "Faraday 1" and take a trip to "CEBO"."

Bob: "I'm finished."

John: "Do you kids need to get anything to eat or anything else before we go?"

Jack: "Donna why don't we pick up a sub sandwich and a couple of drinks downstairs on our way out."

John: "Bob there is a small cooler in my closet, why not fill it up with some cold waters and bring it with us. Be sure to put in some orange juice for Kayla and Toma."

Bob: "Ok, sounds good." They all headed downstairs. They arrived at John's workshop and "Faraday 1" about 10 minutes later. John opened the door and they all got in. John sat in the driver's seat, Donna at the navigator's position and Jack, and Bob picked chairs to sit in. John turned on the power and all the consoles came up. The big screen was waiting for information.

Donna: "Ok, "CEBO" coordinates are loaded hit it." John pushed the "Auto Cruise" button, the big screen filled with a picture of where they were and where they were going. John closed his eyes and told Kayla they were on the way.

Donna: "How does that work with you and Kayla?"

John: "We have a very strong link between us. Kayla or I just concentrate on what we want to say to each other and we can hear each other in our minds." Donna nodded and thought about what John said. Then she smiled, looked at Jack, and closed her eyes. Jack noticed what she was doing and smiled: "I know what you are thinking woman." John just smiled.

Thirty minutes later they got to "CEBO", Kayla and Toma were waiting. John opened the door and they climbed in.

John: "Donna there is a bunch of comm badges in that small storage hole in the console, would you grab a few and hand them out please?" Donna did so.

John: "So, what is going on?"

Kayla: "Toma you tell them what it is."

Toma: "Two days ago, our scientists discovered a large asteroid on a possible collision course with "CEBO". It wasn't close enough to get any more information so we asked for your help to come and check it out."

Donna: "Give me the coordinates and we will all take a look." Toma gave Donna the coordinates, she nodded to

John, and John again pushed the "Auto Cruise" Button. The big screen filled with information.

Donna: "It's about 1.3 million miles away and at its current speed it will reach "CEBO" in 30 days, if we wait a few minutes more we can get a lot more information."
Donna: "John in five minutes put us in front of the object." John watched as the object got closer and closer.

John took "Faraday 1" out of "Auto Cruise" and placed her directly in front of the object."
Donna: "Ok, let's see what this big boy has to tell us. Donna entered some commands and waited for the big screen to supply the answers. They all watched the big screen. The big screen filled with data.

Donna: "This is a big one, it is round, 10 miles wide, doing 44,000 mph, no atmosphere, and it is a solid iron and nickel asteroid. John back off a little and go left of the rock, I want to get more stars to see to configure its trajectory. John did so. Donna watched the big screen. The updates completed. Donna: "Oh my God, it will hit "CEBO" dead center in 30 days at a 50-degree angle. John this is an extinction event."

Kayla: "What is an extinction event?" Donna: "Kayla in 30 days this monster will destroy all life on "CEBO"."
Toma:" That was the preliminary finding by our scientists." Donna did some more checking and looked at her console screen: "John this asteroid is bigger than the one that hit Earth 65 million years ago and is going to hit at the same angle that wiped out 90 percent of all life on the planet. If this one hits "CEBO" there will be no life left." Donna entered some more commands.

John: "Back off a good distance from the center of the asteroid." John did so. Donna entered some more commands into her console. She waited for the results and watched her console. She looked at the results.

Donna:" John these readings are damn strange. The readings would make you believe that this monster is making course corrections as it moves towards "CEBO"."

John: "Donna can you backtrack the asteroid and see where it came from?" Donna: "Sure that's easy." Donna entered some commands and the display showed where the asteroid originated."
John: "Toma do you recognize that solar system?"
Toma: "Yes, I am familiar with it. Toma looked at the system again then at Kayla."

Kayla: "John, we need to return to "CEBO" as fast as you can."
John: "Ok, right after I look at the rear of this asteroid." John moved the "Faraday 1" around to the rear of the asteroid and got closer. They all looked at the strange looking things at the rear. Donna take a picture of that and print it." Donna did."

John: "Donna set a course for "CEBO" please. Donna nodded at John. John pushed the throttle to maximum and sat back in his seat and didn't say a word all the way back.
They arrived at "CEBO" quickly. John parked the "Bullet" close to the "doorway" structure and opened the door.

Kayla: "Stay here I will be back shortly." They waited. Twenty minutes later Kayla returned with her father Kaylon. Kaylon sat down in a chair. John closed the "Bullet door." John noticed he was wearing a comm badge.

Kaylon looked at John: "Four years ago we were contacted by the Soschi They wanted to join the planetary Council. We treated them like any other planet applying for membership. It was all done without ever meeting them. Negotiations took months. They had space craft but did not like leaving their planet, they also had not discovered the "VOID". During the talks we discovered their planet was an ocean world. They were not what you would call a humanoid species. The only land on their planet was an island built by them 20 miles square, crisscrossed by canals and used strictly for industrialization. They built their machines on the island. Then near the end of the negations we got a request from the Soschi. The message simply asked to "taste" one of us. We assumed we had mistranslated the message. While attempting to figure out what the message meant, another message was sent, this time the message was translated the same as the first with an extra paragraph. The extra paragraph read "and the body can be freshly dead". We immediately ended negations with them and declined their admittance. We received several threats from them over the next few months, then they stopped, and we never heard from them again. We sent two scout ships and a probe into their solar system 1 year ago to check on them. The two ships never returned. The probe transmitted data for 2 weeks before going dead. The data received from the probe might have indicated their oceans were dying, but the data was incomplete."

John: "Before anything happens, we are going back to the asteroid and do an intensive scan of the asteroid. Would you consider coming along with us now?"
Kaylon: "I would consider it an honor; I was hoping you would ask."

John: "Donna set the course please." She did and nodded at John. John pressed the "Auto Cruise" button. In a few minutes they were back in front of the asteroid.
John: "Bob would you show Kaylon the picture please?"
Bob got up and went to the printer in back. He came back with the print and handed it to Kaylon.
John: "Donna I want close up pictures of the entire asteroid, is it easier to do pictures if I give you control of the "Bullet"?"

Donna: "Yes, that would be fine, that way I can move and position the camera at the same time." John transferred control to Donna and she started to take pictures. An hour later Donna was done and the pictures were printing.

John: "Let's go to the table in the next room and discuss our problem." Donna just for grins close the under floor "doorway", and turn on the cellphone transceiver. Donna did so. They all went into the back room and sat at the kitchen table. John put the pictures on the table and everyone looked at them. There are drinks in the cooler on the counter and probably in the fridge through that door next to the counter.

John holding one of the close ups of the rear of the asteroid: "Toma do you know what the tubes are on the rear of the asteroid?"

Toma: "Yes, they are fusion pulse rockets. Kaylon agreed, they work from hydrogen collected from space or a large tank somewhere or both they are very efficient. They used 50 of them spread out 500 feet apart in two circles one inside the other to drive the asteroid. Course corrections can be made by turning on or off selected rockets. The number of rockets used is 20 percent needed to drive the asteroid forward. The rest are extra rockets in case some are lost."

John: "Do we know from the pictures how the rockets are controlled?"

Toma: "They can be controlled by a control box or manually or both. One of the pictures has what could be a control box. Toma picked out the picture and handed it to Kaylan. Kaylan looked at it and nodded then gave the picture to John."

John: "What would happen if we destroyed the rockets or the control box."

Toma: "Destroying the control box would stop the asteroid from correcting its course but at this point it wouldn't matter, it is too close to the planet. As for the rockets, they are buried in the asteroid except for the cone that sticks out about two feet on a tube. Destroying the rockets is possible I suppose by slicing off the tube at ground level. The problem is that the asteroid is now close enough to still hit the planet even if we damage the rockets." John listened and watched Jack start drawing on the back of one of the pictures. He was whispering to Donna while doing it.

John: "So Toma your suggestion is to slice off the rocket end tubes and hope the asteroid moves past the planet."

Jack looking at John: "No, there is another way if I may."

John: "Please go on Jack."

Jack: "Toma, what is the thrust of one of the fusion pulse rockets?"

Toma: "That's easy each rocket of this type has around 22,000 pounds of thrust."

Jack: "How many rockets does it take to correct the course of the asteroid?"

Toma looking at Kaylon: "I would say no more than 6 rockets."

Jack: "So any six rockets of 22,000 pounds of thrust or smaller as long as they equal 132,000 pounds of thrust would work, is that right?"

Toma: "Yes that is right."

Jack: "Can you supply enough of the rocket type on the asteroid to use?"

Toma:" Yes, but it would take weeks to get here and then it would be too late."

Jack: "John here is my plan; we get the equivalent number of rockets needed from Izzy. They can be put on a trailer attachable carrier that has a portable crane, the trailer can be hooked to the "Faraday 1", I can have a stand built to my specifications to hold the rockets on the asteroid, I just need to talk to Izzy's engineer. We attach an electronic controller using the Starlight sensor for the rockets to select which direction they point, all on one side or half pointing one direction and the other the other direction, all we have to do is input one location and press a button. We leave the fusion pulse rockets alone. After we position the new rockets to the front of the asteroid, we destroy the controller box. Now we use our own rockets to turn the asteroid and send it back to the Soschi home planet."

John: "Kaylon, Toma, what do you think?"
Kaylon: "Is this the type of crazy plan that you always come up with that gets the job done?"
John laughing: "Yes sir, it is, I only hire the best crazy people."

Kaylon looked at Toma: "Well, what do you think Toma?"
Toma looked at the diagram Jack made and remembered what Jack said: "I don't see how it can fail."

Kaylon: "I have to stay to see this work, John I am an observer, do what you must." John: "Let's go to the cabin. They all got up and left the kitchen for the main cabin. Donna: "Set a course for my workshop." Donna did. John pressed the "Auto Cruise" button.

John: "Jack and Bob get on the horn with Izzie, go to the kitchen and work out the details. Tell him we are on our way to the workshop, oh, we don't need the squad just Sgt. Carter to drive." Bob and Jack left the main cabin for the kitchen table. Thirty minutes later they arrived at John's workshop, John parked the "Faraday 1". Bob and Jack came back to the main cabin.
Bob: "Everything is set, Izzy has 6 25,000-pound thrust rockets being attached to the stands Jack set up with Izzy's engineer. The "Faraday 3", stands, rockets, and the Starlight controller box will be here in four hours."

John: "Well, why don't we go into the house and have some orange juice and tell lies for four hours. Everyone laughed and left the vehicle. They all were sitting in the Florida room when Lora came home. She stopped in the doorway: "Well, are we having a nice party?" She gave Kaylon a hug, and Kayla, and Toma, You people have nothing better to do than hang out with my husband and drink all my orange juice? They all nodded yes. I see the pitcher is empty do I need to make some more juice? They all nodded yes again. Lora chuckled, took the pitcher and went into the kitchen." A few minutes she came back with the full pitcher of juice and placed it on the table.

Lora looking at John: "Do I need to ask what is going on?" John shook his head no.

Lora: "Then I will go into the house and find something to do." Lora turned and left, Donna followed, Kayla followed Donna. The others looked at John: "It's ok, they are just going off to cluck." John mimicked talking with his hand. They all nodded. Bob got a phone call looked at the phone and answered it.

Bob: "Alright that's good see you then. That was Izzy, he is going to be 30 minutes early. Everything is ready, he is testing the control unit to make sure it works. He will be here in (Bob looked at his watch) 30 minutes. They all sat down and went over the plan with Jack again. Donna and Kayla returned. A few minutes later John said: "Izzy will be here any minute, let's go to the workshop." They all followed John to his workshop. John opened the "doorway" to the "VOID": "We can wait in here. We will see Izzy when he arrives. Toma looking at a big plastic flashlight sitting on the workbench: "What is this, John?" John picked up the big flashlight with the rubber band around it. This used to be a 6v hand light. I removed the bulb, and moved the reflector to the rear of the case. John picked up a 2 in. long floating piece of stainless steel, I installed a rolled-up piece of material the military scientists made. It is like the orange cones I toss into the void for light, but it is much brighter. John took the 2 in. bar of metal and put it into a slot he had made in the rear of the flashlight. Suddenly a very bright light projected out through the front of the flashlight. John shined the light around the room, see no batteries. It also works in the" VOID" John took out the metal piece and shoved the light through the "doorway", it lit up a wide area, John pulled the light back through the "doorway". It also works this way, he put the metal piece under the rubber band to hold it steady, when he did the light came on again. The metal doesn't need to be in the light, just close to the material inside the light to work. "

Toma: "I understand why it works in the "VOID", why does it work here, out of the "VOID".

John handed Toma the metal piece to look at. The black substance on the stainless steel 2 in. bar is "VOID" floor. That why the light works here, out of the "VOID".

Toma: "Explain *stainless steel*. I know what steel is, but what is *stainless steel*? Kaylon was intently listening to the conversion.

John: "Stainless steel is ordinary steel with other stuff added to it when it is made. It becomes stainless steel after the process, it will no longer rust. Let me show you, John walked over to his wood bin, he picked up a piece of steel and a piece of stainless steel. Look at these pieces of steel. One is rusty because of access to water or moisture the other piece is not. There is also one other difference, again John walked to the open "doorway", he tossed both pieces of metal into the void. One fell to the floor the other floated above the floor, the floating one is stainless steel. Toma stepped through the "doorway" picked up the two pieces of steel and dropped them again. One fell to the floor the other floated. He picked up the two pieces and brought them back and handed them to John. John tossed them back into the wood pile.

John: "Stainless floats on the "VOID" floor. That is why the "Bullet", (John pointed to the "Bullet") floats in the "VOID". Toma, I assume you use steel in your buildings, right? Toma nodded, what do you do when it starts to rust?"

Toma: "We paint it, then scrape off the rust and paint it again."
John: "Then I assume you don't have stainless steel?"
Toma: "No, we have never had stainless steel."

John smiling: "Well, we will have to fix that won't we?"
Toma: "Yes I would like that and I want to understand about the stainless steel, it won't rust, it floats in the "VOID" and if you add the "VOID" floor to it, it also floats out of the "VOID" John: "You got it., see that was easy, I wish transparent aluminum was as easy."
Toma: "We have transparent aluminum."

John smiling: "Well then, we will trade the formula for stainless steel for the formula for transparent aluminum."
John looked at Kaylon.
Kaylon: "Seems like a good trade to me." As they finished talking the "Faraday 3" Bullet pulled up outside the workshop.

John: "Here is our ride." They all followed John out to the "Faraday 3". There was a long trailer behind the "Bullet". Six inches off the ground and with a crane on one side. On the trailer were two stands that had been built to Jack's specifications. Each stand had three rockets fastened to the stands. One stand could rotate and had a motor attached to it and what looked like a battery pack with solar cells to charge them. The rocket stands were both fastened down. The "Bullet" door opened and Izzy stood in the doorway. The ramp went down.

Izzy: "Those of you that are out to blow stuff up please come on board." John and Bob laughed. They all went aboard, the squad was sitting behind Sgt. Carter who was sitting in the driver position, Donna moved to the navigator position, John, Bob, Jack, and Izzy sat in the middle. Kaylon, Kayla, and Toma sat behind John.

Izzy: "John, it's all yours." John got up and stood by the door: "Izzy are you coming along?" Izzy: "I wouldn't miss this for anything, besides someone needs to keep tabs on my rockets." John closed the cabin door.

John: "If we need to make a stop at "CEBO" speak up now." No takers. Donna set course for the asteroid and bring us to the front of the rock, but with the sun behind us please. Donna looked at John thinking a second: "Yes sir." She set course and nodded at Sgt. Carter.

John: "Sgt. Carter *full* speed ahead." Sgt. Carter pushed the throttle fully forward. Gentlemen sit back in your chairs it will be quite a ride. John smiling walked over to the squad: "You guys just couldn't miss the action, huh?" They all nodded. They all watched the big monitor. Twenty minutes later they were sitting in front of the asteroid.

John: "Ok Jack, It's your show."
Donna: "John we have something strange here."
John: "Jack it's not your show yet, sorry." What is the strange Donna?"

Donna: "I noticed this when we were here before. Off in the distance behind the asteroid I have seen something reflecting light, a glint, or flash from the sun. There has to be something there to produce the flash, but there is nothing on radar and it is following the asteroid, it is the same distance from the asteroid as when we were here before."

John: "Sgt. Carter head straight at whatever it is half power, Donna bring the camera up and take pictures as we go by. They flew right by the object and stopped and turned around to face the rear of the object. Anybody here know what that was, it looked like a small scout ship?"

Kaylon: "I think it was a Soschi scout ship."

John: "Donna do you think they know we are here?"
Donna watched as the ship slowly turned around and
faced them: "I would think that answers your question."
John: "Sgt. Carter move directly above them and target
the laser, they moved forward toward the scout ship, as
they passed the ship, Donna took more pictures, Sgt.
Carter fired the laser, the scout ship exploded in a fireball.

John: "Donna get the pictures printed please. Sgt.
Carter being us back to the front of the asteroid. Sgt.
Carter and Donna stay alert, there could be more ships.
Kaylon, Toma, Kayla, Izzy, Bob and Jack let's go to the
table in the kitchen. John led the way to the kitchen. They
sat down at the table.

John: "Is there a chance that the scout ship was
controlling the asteroid?"
Kaylon: "I don't think so, they might have been there to
solve a problem, but if the asteroid went off course or was
discovered, they could say they were simply monitoring
it, and were going to warn us." I do think they would have
notified their home world when we were destroyed."

John: "I tend to agree with Kaylon. Kaylon how
much does the council know about what is happening?
They were informed about the asteroid and its path. They
had already decided what was going to be done if the
asteroid could not be stopped."
John: "And what was that if I may ask?"

Kaylon: "The planet killer was loaded aboard a ship
orbiting one of the outer moons. If "CEBO" was
destroyed, they were to deliver the bomb to destroy the
planet of the Soschi."
John: "Well, that takes care of any doubts I had about
sending the asteroid back to Soschi. Ok, Jack once more
the show is yours." One of the squad brought the pictures
Donna took. The all looked at what was showing on the
other side of the scout craft windshield. The Soschi were
ocean creatures, the ship was filled with water They had a

large head, two large eyes, a large mouth with many sharp
teeth, A body about 2 feet long and four tentacles coming
out of the bottom of the body. Their resemblance to an
Earth octopus was startling.

John: "Ok, Jack what is your plan, please?"
Jack: "The first thing we do is destroy what we think is
the control box for course correction rockets.
The second thing we do is install the rocket racks on the
front of the asteroid and weld them to the iron-nickel rock
with short bursts of our laser I had them build four flat
wide feet on the bottom of each rack. After the racks are
installed, all facing the correct direction, the rocket stands
controller box will be hooked up to the Starlight system
aboard the "Bullet", the system communicates to the
rocket stands using wireless, there is a small door at the
end of Donna's console with a u-shaped open hole at one
end, open the small door plug in the controller box, close
the door and the system is live. (the cord supplies power
and signal) Press button marked" Arm Starlight System
the system will ask for coordinates. Donna will enter the
coordinates for the target, once input the system will show
those coordinates on the box and ask them to be verified.
Press enter to verify, after verification the "Fire" button
will turn green. If the "Fire" button is not pressed within
30 seconds the system will automatically reset and turn
off.

Once "Fire" is pressed the system will be automatic. It
will fire the rockets to turn the asteroid around, once the
asteroid is turned to match the entered course the other set
of rockets will rotate opposite the first set, and fire to stop
the turn, after that either side of rockets will fire to keep
the asteroid on course back to the target.

Jack: "So, Sgt. Carter let's go practice your welding on
the control box. Maneuver the "Bullet" over the suspected
Fusion controller box and fire short bursts until it melts."
Sgt Carter moved the "Bullet", turned on the laser, put the

crosshair on the target control box and using short bursts melted the control box.

Everybody watched and checked the fusion rockets to make sure they were still operating, they were,

John: "Donna watch for course deviations, "they waited.

Donna: "Small course deviations occurring, she waited, and no correction, in fact the deviation is slightly to the right."

John: "Ok, so far so good."

Jack: "Let's open a large "doorway" and get the rocket stands onto the asteroid. Sgt. get us right up close to the front of the asteroid." Sgt. Carter perfectly parked the "Bullet" to ground level. And shut down the engines. The Marines got busy unstrapping the rocket stands with Izzy.

John and Sgt Carter opened a large "doorway" right next to the trailer with the rocket stands. After the doorway was open, the Marines used the crane to unload the first rocket stand. The crane easily moved the non-rotating rocket stand through the "doorway" and it was placed on the surface of the asteroid. Then they moved the rotating rocket stand onto the surface offset from the first by six feet forward towards "CEBO" so the rocket blast would not hit the first rocket stand. Jack checked the measurements. They needed to plug in a 10-foot cable from the rotating rocket stand to the non-rotating stand. Izzy had a special half suit for the cable hookup. It was made to fit over the head as a helmet and over both arms down to the waist where it is tied off. It allowed whoever had it on to work a short time in real space, that was because the half suit was pressurized from the "VOID" as was the air to the suit. One of the Marines that was trained on the suit put it on and stood next to Jack near the open "doorway".

Jack looked at the Marine: "We will push one end of the "doorway" in to within 6 inches of the cable. You will grab the hanging cable, then pull it back into the "VOID" and walk it over to the other stand, plug it in and twist it until it locks. "The Marine nodded; Jack pushed the right side of the "doorway" close to the rotating rocket stand. The Marine put his arm into space and grabbed the cable and pulled it into the "VOID", he then stepped left, put his arm again into space, plugged in the cable on the first rocket stand and twisted it until it locked. He pulled his hand back into the "VOID".

Jack "Are you alright?" The Marine nodded yes. Jack and John closed the "doorway" and put it away into the bag, and everyone outside went back into the main cabin. Izzy had the rocket controller up front and was sitting in the chair next to Donna.

Jack: "All is done, the cable is hooked up, Izzy hook up the rocket controller please." Izzy opened the small door next to Donna and plugged in the rocket controller, then closed the door, and sat the controller down next to Donna, then he went back and sat down in the middle seats.

Jack: "Ok, Sgt. Carter lets weld the rocket stands feet to the asteroid." Sgt. Carter maneuvered the "Bullet" to the first rocket stand, as everyone watched he started to weld the inside feet first. The welding was working really well. The first stand was finished in fifteen minutes and Sgt. Carter moved to the rotating stand, he finished the rotating stand then he and Jack checked all the welds. They were perfect.

Jack: "John, all has been installed and checked.

John: "Kaylon with your permission we will continue."

Kaylon slowly nodded.

John: "Power up the rocket Starlight System controller and enter the target coordinates please. Donna pressed the "Arm Starlight System" button, the system asked to enter coordinates. Donna entered the Soschi coordinates.

Donna: "I have a green "Fire" button.

John: "Kaylon I believe as the Head of the Council of Planets you should press the "Fire" button."

Kaylon: "You are right John. Kaylon got up and moved next to Donna, he looked down at the green "Fire" button he muttered "God forgive us." And pressed the green button."

All watched the screen, at the front of the asteroid all six rockets fired. Donna watched for a course deviation for the asteroid.

Donna: "It's working, the asteroid is turning, they watched as the asteroid made a wide right turn and kept turning, about five minutes later the rockets shut down. The rotating rocket stand turned to the right locked into place and started firing again. About 5 minutes later the rotating rocket stand shut down.

Donna: "Watch the speed of the asteroid slow to zero and then start to pick up speed. They watched the asteroid get slower and slower and reach zero speed, then the speed started to increase.

John: "Donna how long will it take the asteroid to reach 44,000 mph again and then how long to the Soschi?" Donna loaded some data into her computer: "It will take about two hours to reach optimum speed and in 62 days it will be close enough to their planet that it will be unstoppable.

John: "Thank you Donna, please set a course for "CEBO"." Donna did and nodded to Sgt. Carter. They were there in a few minutes. It was a somber time in the cabin on the way to "CEBO". Kaylon, Kayla, and Toma got off the "Bullet", hugs were exchanged, John told Toma to come visit him at the workshop and bring the transparent aluminum formula to trade for the stainless-steel formula. He said he would. John said just tell Kayla you are coming and if you can't get a ride tell her to tell me to come and get you. John closed the cabin door.

John: "Donna, let's go home", Donna input the coordinates and nodded at Sgt. Carter. They were home in 30 minutes.

John opened the cabin door. John said goodbye to Izzy and the Marines, he told all of them and Izzy they had done another fine job. Bob, Jack, Donna waved goodbye and got off the "Bullet", they all watched as the "Bullet" "Faraday 3" disappeared into the distance.

Donna: "John, I want to thank you for not making me have to push the green button."

John smiled: "That was the least the "Omer" could have done after Jack saved their bacon." By the way Jack, nice job again, and the weekend starts now.

Jack: "Thanks boss." Then he looked at Donna: "Why don't we get takeout and go out on to the lake and have a nice weekend Mrs. Foster?"

Donna: *Oooo*, I love to hear "Mrs. Foster"."

John: "If you kids get into the golf cart, I will take you to "Faraday's" moon." Jack and Donna held hands and got into the back of the golf cart.

Bob whispered: "What do you bet they don't get to takeout."

John smiling: "No bet, come along or are you going to take off?"

Bob: "I will take off from here, thanks, see you Monday maybe" Bob headed to the workshop "doorway".

John got into the golf art and delivered Jack and Donna to "Faraday's" moon, then went home for the weekend.

CHAPTER NINE

"The Gold"

Wednesday 08:00

John was sitting at his desk waiting for Bob to arrive: "Hey, how about a little "PINBALL"?" He got up, walked over to the new machine and turned it on. Rather than plugging and unplugging it all the time he had a rocker power switch installed on the front of the machine. The ball loaded and John shot out the ball, he was wildly happy when Bob sauntered in. He stopped and sat down at the table.

Bob: "I have some great news. The newspaper article on the $50 gold coins turned up no claimers. The coins are now the property of "Gold Finders Are Us."

John: "That's good news. Let's get everyone together for lunch and then come back and discuss what to do with the money."

Bob: "Ok, I will call Tim, and Jack and we all will meet here at 11:30."

John: "Sounds like a plan, see you later." Bob left. John went back to the "PINBALL machine and played till 11:30.

Bob, Jack, Donna, Tim, and Carla all showed up at the same time. John took them downstairs to the restaurant and they had a nice lunch. After lunch they all went back to John's office and at sat down at the table.

John: "Wow, that was a nice lunch, wasn't it?
"Everyone nodded, before we start, I would like to hear
what is happening with Tim and Carla."
Tim nodded at Carla: "We sent out the wedding
invitations last week, and are waiting for reply's, the
wedding is two weeks from next Sunday. "
Donna: "We got your invitation; we are attending and I
will send it back today."
Bob: "I got it too and we will be attending and my wife
will send it out today."
John: "We didn't get one."
     Carla: "We didn't send you one, Tim and Carla waited
a few seconds and burst out laughing, because we brought
it with us, she held up the invitation and handed it to
John."
John pouting eyes down and closed: "He looked up at
Tim and Carla with one closed eye (the pirate eye),
everyone laughed. And we will attend and Lora will send
it back today. John continued. well, we are here to discuss
what will happen to the money recovered from our
vacation together a week or so ago.
     I am happy to report we got more of a recovery fee
than the expected 10 percent. We got 15 percent. All the
funds are deposited in a corporate account under the
name" Gold Finders Are Us (GFAU)." Everyone
chuckled. The amount of fees recovered is $127,800. And
there is more good news, the $50 gold coins also belong
to "Gold Finders Are Us", no one claimed the coins. Now
we have no way to determine the value of what they are
worth unless they are auctioned off. So, let's hear some
thoughts on what to do with the $127,800." John waited,
no one spoke up.
     Bob: "John most of us have not had to deal with this
amount of money. I know you must have an opinion on
what to do from your own experience. Why not tell us

what you think and then we can decide or make other comments."

John: "Is that what you all want me to do?" They all agreed.

John: "On the coins, my thought was to put 10 coins in each of our names in trust and left in the account. Each of you will be appointed as directors of "Gold Finders Are Us." One year later another 10 will be distributed. None of us can withdraw our coins for 5 years after the last distribution. After next year's distribution the lot of coins left can be left alone or will be auctioned off at the director's discretion. There will be a yearly meeting here in January in this office, the day to be determined by the CEO of the corporation. Doing this meeting meets all the legal requirements for the corporation. The attorney for the corporation will handle all the legal stuff. I use the same attorney. John yelled out to Jenny. Jenny came to the door. Jenny, will you get your note pad and come sit with us please. Jenny left and returned with her note pad and sat down. Jenny you are to take official notes for the "Gold Finders Are Us "corporation. Jenny acknowledged. I call the first meeting of "Gold Finders Are Us" corporation to order.

My first act as temporary CEO is to elect myself, Bob, Tim, Carla, Donna, and Jack as the directors of this corporation and they will be paid a salary of $1 after each meeting. All hands show for consent. John raised his hand, the others followed. The first vote is complete and was unanimous, the before named individuals are elected as directors.

The second act will be to add an official secretary (Jenny) to the corporation with a salary of $5,000 a year to be paid after each corporate yearly meeting in January, plus today. All directors vote now. John raised his hand, all the others did also. The second vote is complete and is unanimous.

The third act will be to name a Permanent CEO to be elected for 1 year in January or until the next official corporate meeting and a new CEO to be elected each and every January for a salary of $1 a year. I submit the name of Tim Carter for the first CEO to take effect immediately after this meeting. All directors vote now, and Tim you can vote for yourself, John raised his hand. All others raised their hand. The vote is unanimous the new CEO is Tim Carter effective at the end of this meeting. The meeting will now go on hold for discussion.

Alright we need to talk about the $127,800. I suggest we grant each of us $10,000, and leave the rest for whatever. And there is something else I have been meaning to do and just never got around to it, The Faraday corporation will donate 2 million dollars into a separate account inside this corporation to be called "Vets Fund" to be administrated by the directors to award no interest loans to veterans of $ 10,000 for first home purchase. Later we can determine other rules as to what happens to the loans under some different circumstances before we hand out any money. The fund we can setup now and we can discuss the rules at the next called meeting or wait until January for the second official corporate meeting occurs. Do any oppose the new fund? John waited. Jack raised his hand: "Can we donate another million to the fund?" Who could turn that down, Ok, I think that takes care of the money?

I now reopen the meeting. We have a suggestion to grant each director $10,000 from the recovered fees fund. All in favor raise your hand. All raised their hand. The vote is unanimous. We have a suggestion to create a new fund called "Vets Fund" as part of the "Gold Finders Are Us." Corporation and a donation of 2 million dollars from the "Faraday Corporation" and a donation of 1 million dollars from the "Foster Corporation", to be placed in fore mentioned fund, a show of hands is requested, all hands were raised. The vote was unanimous. As a side note John Faraday will not be accepting the $10,000 recovery fee payment (John looked over at Donna and Jack and they nodded no also) and Jack and Donna Foster will not accept the recovery fee. If there is no more business today, I ask for a vote to end this meeting. John waited. This meeting of the "Gold Finders Are Us corporation is concluded. Next official meeting will be in January next year and presided over by the new CEO Tim Carter. Jenny, please type up those minutes, order a new cabinet for your office for the "Gold Finders Are Us" corporation and place them in a folder in the new cabinet."

John: "Well, how was that? Everyone was pleased how it all came out. Ok. Bob, I guess I will see you later? Bob got up, waved at everyone and left. The other four were still sitting at the table. Is there something else?"

Donna: "Have you two made any plans for a honeymoon?"
Carla: "We started to talk about it, but not yet. Why?"
Donna: "We would like to offer you two the houseboat for a week if you would like something like that. It is wonderful out on the waterways and the lakes, quiet and private. We really enjoy it."

Donna: "Well, you guys talk it over and we can talk later, and you can see it docked below on your way out." Jack and Donna got up Donna gave John a hug they left. Tim and Carla thanked John again.

John: "Listen you two, you and the others here today are as close as any family can be. And all of us are extremely lucky that it turned out that way. Carla, the 20k you guys will get will pay off your student loans next year when you finish college. Tim you will come out of OCS as a young lieutenant. I hope I don't lose you as a valuable member on our missions. Anyway, you two are about to start your own adventure, Now get out of here."

Tim: "My company commander indicated that me and my squad was always to be assigned with you on missions. I don't know what will happen after OCS."

John: "Tim your company commander showed up here one day. Jenny told me there was someone who wanted to see me, in walks this Marine Bird Colonel and asked to talk to me about you. He told me he was your Squadron Commander.

His name was ummm—Pennington, I think. Tim nodded yes. He asked about our missions, I simply told him that you and your squads' performance was the deciding factor on every mission whether they turned out bloody or not.

I have a feeling he was a little skeptical of the things General Leeson was telling him about the squad and you. Anyway, he thanked me for my honesty and left. That was around two missions back not counting the most recent. He did not say if the conversation was confidential or not, it doesn't matter you know me, I would have told you given the chance anyway. That's the end of the story."

Tim: "Thank you again for everything."

John: "Your welcome. And I am looking forward to the wedding and by the way Carla, Jack's houseboat is really nice you definitely want Donna to show it to you before you make a decision." Tim and Carla left the office. John went back and finished his PINBALL" game and went home.

CHAPTER TEN

"The Big Undo"

18 Days until Soschi dies
08:00 Wednesday

John was sitting behind his desk admiring his pink quartz paper weight. Bob came stumbling into the office and sat down in front of John. Bob watched John ogle the paperweight.

Bob: "You know what you should do with that paperweight?"

John: "No, what?"

Bob: "You should take it and find out what the gold would be worth by the ton if mined. Then find out what the pink square itself is worth, then put that information on the pink square in gold writing. Now that would be cool."

John: "Bob, you want to know what I think about your idea, (Bob started to say no), I think that it is a great idea. What a conversation piece it would be. The killer would be value per ton mined. Then you could tell the story about where it came from, yes let's do it today." We will go to the jeweler down stairs and have it done." Bob: "Really?" John: "Of course not, it was a dumb idea."

We don't want to tell people where this came from, how would we explain it?"

Bob: "Oh Ya, I guess you are right."

A month later:

John: "Hey, was Tim and Carla's wedding a blowout or what. The best part was his best man drunk, dancing on the water fountain and then falling in."

Bob: "No, the best part was the other three Marine buddies who jumped into the fountain to haul out the best man before he could drown. He just kind of laid face down in the fountain for a while before they jumped in to pull him out."

John: "That was some wedding alright. Donna told me Tim and Carla did decide to use the houseboat, and they had a great time. Tim said he couldn't wait to do some fishing. After they came back, I asked Tim if he caught any fish, he smiled and said no, but I did get to use my pole." Bob laughed, and John was laughing and holding his sides. They calmed down and Jenny came to the door and said: "John you have a visitor."

John: "Send them in. John looked toward the door to see Kaylon come through the door, John noticed he was wearing a comm badge. Kaylon held out a comm badge to John and Bob, they put the comm badge on their sleeve, what a surprise, have a seat."

Kaylon: "John we have big trouble, the Soschi sent us a message an hour ago, they apologized for the asteroid, they have disbanded their military and destroyed all 30 of their ships but one. They have decided not to leave their planet for at least 100 years. They don't seem to know the asteroid is coming at them, we must disarm the asteroid before it hits their planet. Do you have any idea what we should do?"

John: "Well, a trip to the asteroid is necessary no matter what we do. How much time is left until the asteroid hits their planet?"

Kaylon: "18 days. About the same amount of time "CEBO" had until the asteroid was diverted."

John: "So you want the team to go back to the asteroid and see if it can be stopped?" Kaylon: "Yes"

Bob, call Izzy, see if "Faraday 3" is available, call Sgt. Carter to drive it if it is, call Jack and Donna, hopefully everything we used is still on "Faraday 3", I'm talking about the rocket stand controller, ask Izzy if it is on the "Bullet". Kaylon is Toma available to go? Kaylon nodded yes. Izzy can go if he wants to, there is no need to put Kayla in danger. I think that does it. Kaylon while we wait for some answers, how about a glass of orange juice and a game of "PINBALL?"

Kaylon: "Orange juice yes, what is "PINBALL?" John led Kaylon over to the "PINBALL" machine and showed him the basics. While he was playing, he went and asked Jenny if they had any orange juice. Fortunately, they had some in the small fridge. She came back with a glass for Kaylon. Jenny asked if Kaylon was from "CEBO" like Kayla, John told her that Kaylon was Kayla's Father the Head of the Planetary Council on "CEBO".

Jenny looked at John: "And you have him playing "PINBALL" in your office, the universe must be laughing its ass off. John nodded his head, chuckled, took the glass of juice, smiled, and went to his office.
Bob returned an hour later. Kaylon sat down to listen.

Bob: "Ok, "Faraday 3" will be available tomorrow morning ready to go at 08:00. Izzy said he would go to watch. Sgt.Carter is driving no squad required. The rocket stand controller is still on the "Bullet" and still hooked up. Jack and Donna will be at the workshop. I think that is everybody.
John: "Kaylon do you need a ride back to "CEBO"?"

Kaylon: "No I brought the golf cart you gave Kayla. I parked it in the special spot she told me about in the "VOID"."

John: "Ok, I will walk you downstairs to the cart, tomorrow I will meet you and Toma in the "VOID" near your "doorway" structure around 08:30." John and Kaylon went to the parking lot. John waved as Kaylon left on the old golf cart. John went back upstairs and talked to Bob a while. He played a couple games of "PINBALL" and went home.

06:30 Thursday 17 days till Soschi dies

Bob, John, and Lora were sitting in the Florida room finishing breakfast.

Bob: "John what do you think has to be done to fix this problem?"

John: "Way too soon for a plan, there are some things that don't add up but they won't be clear until we do a look see. If your done eating let's go to the workshop."

Bob: "I'm done, Lora thanks for the grub. As usual it was great."

Lora: "Thank you Bob, you two be careful today, I agree with John, something just doesn't feel right about this whole thing." John and Bob got up and headed to the workshop.

John opened a big box that was sitting on the work bench. Bob watched as the top opened? "What's in those small boxes?"

John: "If you give me a minute, I will show you." John took out one of the small boxes and opened one end. He reached inside the box and pulled out a green plastic cylinder with a handle on top. On one end it had a clear screw on cover and on the other end there was a parallel square slot open on the rear end.

Bob: "This looks like the flashlight you showed me before."

John: "Very attentive Bob, that is exactly what it is. This is the final version I had made, simple and easy to use. John picked up an orange color plastic 1/8 x1x2 in. bar inside a metal box on the workbench. There were 10 or 15 of them in the box. He placed the bar on the workbench and it floated. He picked up the orange bar and placed it into the slot on the flashlight, it clicked in and locked. A very bright beam lit up the whole workshop. John placed the flashlight on its butt and it floated above the workbench." He handed the light to Bob to inspect. Bob grabbed the handle and checked out the slot where the orange bar was inserted. He pulled out the bar and the light went out. Bob unscrewed the front and looked inside the light. He could see the reflector near the back of the tube. He put the orange bar back into the slot, the flashlight again lit up the workshop.

John: "I discovered if I wrap the bar in tin foil and put it next to the light it will not work, so you could store the light and the bars without making the light work. The light still works in the "VOID" of course without the bar." John opened the "doorway" to the "VOID", he took out another small box, opened it and pulled out another flashlight, a red one, he picked up another bar from the metal box and placed it into the rear slot, the light came on. John removed the orange bar, placed it on the workbench and went through the "doorway" The light lit up the area in front of the "doorway". John walked back into the workshop.

John chuckling: "So, they work in and out of the "VOID", they come in different colors, they don't need battery's, they have no bulb to burn out and they will be out in time for Christmas."
Bob: "What about the battery companies?"

John: "Very good Bob, a subsidiary of the Faraday Corp. called the "Johnson Lite" Corp will sell the lights to the battery companies for $3.50 each, plus $2 for the orange bar which the Johnson Corp also makes. Each box comes with a plastic orange bar in a tin foiled carry case and a light, 20 to a big box. I believe that the stainless bar can be cut down to 1/16 of an inch, maybe even stainless foil would work and save manufacture cost and you don't have to change the size of the plastic bar since it is hollow. There is a lot of testing to do before it is released to the public. Of course, the CEO of "Johnson Lite Corp" would be in charge of that."

Bob: "I don't know what to say."
John trying to keep a straight face: "Oh, have you met the new CEO Larry Johnson?"

Bob: "What?" John smiling:" Gotcha." And started to laugh. Bob just shook his head. Anyway, let's take six of these and six bars and put them in the "Bullet" which should be here any minute. John took six bars and wrapped them in tin foil. He handed Bob six lights and they walked into the "VOID", the "Bullet was there, the ramp was down and Sgt. Carter was smiling as they walked up. John: "What, did you swallow a bug or something?"

Sgt. Carter: "No, I am just glad to see you both."
About that time Donna and Jack showed up, said hello and got into the "Bullet" cabin."
John: "Well, I guess we had better get in or we will miss the trip." Bob and John got aboard, John shut the door and sat down. Bob started to put away the lights, John asked for one and kept an orange bar, gave the rest to Bob, and he put all the stuff away and sat down.

John looked at Donna and Sgt. Carter, pointed his finger and said: "Onward Great Steed?" They all laughed. They rolled into "CEBO" about 30 minutes later, Kaylon, Toma, and Kayla were standing next to the "doorway" station. John opened the door and the ramp went down, he stood in the doorway. Kaylon came up the ramp shook John's hand and sat down, Toma did the same, Kayla boarded and looked at John directly: "I had nothing to do this afternoon, she smiled. I didn't think you would mind. "John directly: "You know you are always welcome, but only if I get a hug."

She nodded and gave John a hug, then sat down next to Kaylon. Bob handed out comm badges.

John: "If everyone is ready, Donna input coordinates for the asteroid, Donna did and nodded at Sgt. Carter. And they were on their way. John nodded off, everyone else watched the big screen as the two dots came closer and closer. About 30 minutes before the trip to the asteroid was over John got up, stretched and picked up the new light that was laying on the floor at his feet. He brought it over and sat down next to Toma. He held it up and showed it to Toma. Toma had seen the prototype before.

John: "I just had this made, it works like the prototype you saw before." Toma took the light from John and inspected it. Kayla watched also. When Toma had finished John gave him the orange bar. Toma looked at the bar and then at the light and put the bar into the slot. Fortunately, he had the light pointed at the back wall. The light was very bright. Toma pulled out the orange bar and the light went off.: "That is very handy, I suppose it works in the "VOID" without the orange bar?"
Kayla: "That light has no power source?"
John: "No, none other than the orange bar. "

Kayla: "What gave you that idea?" Well, you know I have been using the orange cones from the beginning, when I first saw the new "Bullet", Izzy had installed the new cone material light around the bottom of the "Bullet", the scientists had improved the material used in the cones to make a brighter light. I applied that material to the inside of the light and placed a reflector in the rear of the light. The orange bar is a hollow piece of plastic with a piece of stainless steel with "VOID" floor material grown on it inside the orange plastic bar." When the orange bar is inserted in the slot it makes the light work."
If you are interested in this device you can talk to Bob, he is the head of the Johnson Lite Corporation. I'm sure we

can work out some kind of deal." Toma looked at Kaylon and Kaylon nodded.

Donna: "Ok, we are pulling up to the asteroid."

They all looked at the big screen. The asteroid was apparent, it looked like it was heading into the system sun.

Bob: "Where is the planet; I don't see the planet?"

Donna: "Bob, look at the display I put on the big screen. It was a picture of the solar system with the sun in the center, the planet circling from left to right and the asteroid heading straight into the sun. The planet is orbiting the sun from the left, the asteroid is going straight ahead. As the planet moves around its orbit it comes closer into the asteroids path until they intersect,"

Bob: "Oh, I get it now, thank you for that description, Donna."

John: "Let's get a close-up view of the rear of the asteroid."

Sgt. Carter maneuvered the "Bullet" up behind the asteroid.

John: "Are all the fusion rockets still working Toma?"

Toma: "It looks like they are."

John: "Donna is the asteroid still on course for the planet?"

Donna: "Dead on course, in fact it has gained a two-day lead to its target. So, we are at 15 days until it hits."

John: "Ok, let's take a look at the rocket stands up front of the asteroid." Sgt.Carter moved the "Bullet" to the front of the asteroid. The rocket stands look as we had left them one stand pointing left and the other pointing right.

John: "I can't believe they don't know that asteroid is headed at them, they would have sent a ship to check it out."

Bob: "Why didn't they destroy the rocket stands themselves or attempt to stop the fusion rockets."

John: "Donna, would you like to handle that one."

Donne looked at Bob: "The only way to stop the asteroid from hitting the planet is to turn it like we did. They have no way to control either the rocket stands or the fusion rockets, remember we destroyed their controller box to move the asteroid left or right, and we have the controller for the rocket stands. And destroying either would tell us they know about the asteroid." Bob nodded.

John: "Let's go get some answers, Donna set a course for the planet, let's go look around. Donna set the course and nodded to Sgt.Carter. In almost no time there were above the planet.

John: "Donna, a full scan using everything we have please." They all watched the big screen.
John: "Sgt. Take us over their industrial island please."
Sgt. Carter moved the "Bullet" over the island. Parked in the middle was a ship they said they had."
John: "Donna how high are we above the planet?"
Donna: "We are 1000 miles above the planet."
John: "Sgt. Take us to 500 miles, and Donna start an infrared scan please."
Sgt. Carter moved the "Bullet" to 500 miles above the planet."
Donna, scan around the industrial island 25 or thirty miles from shore, go all around the complex. Donna scanned around the island. They all watched the big screen.
John: "There on the screen, what does that look like to you Kaylon?"

Kaylon: "Why it looks like 14 ships under water."
John: "Yes, it is and I'm guessing they know we just saw them."
Donna: "John, I have some kind of a launch indicated from the surface; it is coming from the industrial island."

John: "Is it coming right at us, and when will it hit us?"

Donna: "It is right at us, and we have two minutes."
John: "Put it on the screen please."
They all watched the missile coming up from the surface.
John: "Donna close the under floor "doorway", Sgt. move us 50 miles left or right of the missile please." Donna closed the under floor "doorway" Sgt. Carter moved them out of the way."

John: "Ok, Donna re-open the "under floor "Doorway" with no radar." Donna re-opened the under floor "doorway" The missile immediately came into view, they watched it as it continued on without changing course.
Donna: "What made you think it might be the radar?"

John: "It was obvious they saw us. It was not likely the probe was seen, so they had to be tracking the source of the radar signal. Let's see if that can be proved. Put us back over the underwater ships and Donna turn the radar back on. Sgt Carter warm up your laser weapon and we will take a shot at the next missile if they launch one."
Everyone watched the big screen.

Donna: "I have another launch; you were right John."
John: "Sgt. Carter please. They watched the big screen as Sgt. Carter used his roller ball crosshair to target the missile, a blue light illuminated the warhead of the missile and then 4 seconds later an explosion occurred.
John: "Kaylon, do you agree this was a Soschi ruse from the beginning?"

Kaylon: "Yes, you are right. It was a setup."
John: "Donna how deep were the 14 Soschi ships in the water?"
Donna: "They were no more than 50 feet deep."
John looked over at Sgt.Carter.
Sgt. Carter anticipating John's question: "Fifty feet is not a problem?"

John: "Sgt Carter put us back over the 15 Soschi ships at 4 miles above them, target and destroy them, please use 5 second dwell time."

Sgt. Carter: "Yes sir, he moved the "Bullet" over the ships, targeted the ships, then pressed the "Fire" button." They watched as multiple blue beams went to each ship, the one on land at the industrial complex blew up first, then the other 14 exploded underwater, all within 2 or 3 seconds."

John: "Donna, how many buildings do you think are on the industrial island? Donna started a count from the picture, it looks like less than 100 buildings."
John: "Sgt. target all the buildings on the complex please except the one with a tower that looks like a transmitter, and continue firing until they are destroyed. "

Sgt. Carter: "Yes sir, targeting all buildings on the island, except one, firing will commence twenty buildings at a time until all are destroyed. Sgt. Carter pressed the "Fire" button."

They all watched as the laser fired on 20 buildings at a time until they exploded or were left burning, then fired on the next 20. In less than 10 minutes the industrial complex was completely destroyed and burning except for one building. John: "Good shooting Sgt."
John: "Kaylon, the ships on the ground we destroyed I was not worried about, it's the other 15 I am worried about. Where are they?"

Kaylon: "How do you intend to find them?"
John: "I must think like and become the Soschi commander. I must put all the facts together and make a reasonable guess."
Bob was watching John; he knew anytime John would make that decision. He continued to watch, then he saw it, the head tilt, the stare forward. He just waited for it to happen. It took less than 10 seconds.

John: "Donna set a course for "CEBO", Sgt. Carter *Full* power to "CEBO" we need to catch them before they get there."

Donna set the course and nodded to Sgt. Carter who pushed the throttle to full power.
Kaylon: "John what made you think they went to "CEBO"?"

John: "This isn't about power or war, this last mission for the Soschi commander is for revenge, revenge against the Council for rejection, revenge for turning their weapon against them, he knew he had no chance to stop the asteroid. But now he has to hurt those who had hurt him. He doesn't care if they all die because all of his planet will die with him. Now he just wants to kill as many of you as possible."

Donna: "We are half way to "CEBO"."
Toma: "Half way to "CEBO", How fast does this craft go?"
John: "Keep watch we are coming up on them quickly. Donna use the radar but when we see them turn it off. Sgt. power up weapons if they are not up now."
Everyone watched the big screen.
Donna: "15 minutes from "CEBO"."
Another 5 minutes passed.

Donna: "John I have 15 ships on my screen, turning off radar." 8 minutes to "CEBO"."
Sgt. Carter: "I have targeted all ships, 5 in. laser 5 sec dwell time 4 minutes to targets."
John watching the big screen: "That's right get closer slightly above them."
Sgt. Carter: "1 minute to targets. Slowing down."
Everyone was glued to the big screen, suddenly 15 blue shafts of light sprang towards the 15 ships., in 5 seconds all 15 ships exploded. John sat back into his chair: "Sgt. full stop please.

Kaylon: "I want you to think about something, what if this whole affair was the Soschi military? What if the civilian population had nothing to do with the attacks?

At this point their industrial island is gone, their access to space is gone, all of their military higher officers are gone. They will not be back in space for 200 plus years. I will be back in a few minutes." John went to the back to get a drink. Bob and Kayla followed John. In the back John got a drink from the cooler and sat down at the table.

Bob and Kayla sat on the other side of the table. Kayla looked at John: "You are giving Father a chance to stop the asteroid, aren't you?" John smiled, looked at Kayla and nodded.

John took a couple of swigs from his drink: "Your Father is a smart and gentle man, John took another couple of swigs from the drink: "Ok, that should be enough time." John left the drink on the table, got up, and went back to the main cabin and sat down. Bob sat down in his seat, and Kayla sat next to John.

Kaylon: "John, I have been thinking, maybe it would be the right thing to try and contact the Soschi, maybe if the general population was not involved, we should try and stop the asteroid, what do you think?" John looked at Kayla and smiled: "Sir, that would be a diplomatic decision for the Council, even though I would agree, that would not be my decision." I am here at your request."

Kaylon: "Well, I think we need to at least attempt to contact the Soschi."

John: "Donna do we have that capability on the "Bullet"?"

Donna: "Yes sir, with the right frequency, and it would automatically run through the language translator."

John: "Donna how much time do we have to change the course of the asteroid?" Donna smiling: "Two days, sir."

John: "Donna set a course to the asteroid please, Sgt. *Full* speed ahead one more time please." Donna nodded at Sgt. Carter and he pushed the throttle full forward.

John: "Donna, work with Kaylon, he probably knows the frequency."

Toma: "I know what the frequency is, Toma got up and walked over to Donna and gave her the frequency." Kaylon then went over and sat down next to Donna. Jack came over and sat next to Bob. Thirty minutes later they were back to the asteroid. Kaylon attempted to contact the Soschi. Donna had put headphones on Kaylon. They tried the contact several times. After 10 or 12 tries another voice started to talk to Kaylon. They conversed for 30 minutes then ended the conversation. Kaylon thanked Donna, took off the headphones gave them back to Donna and sat down behind John.

Kaylon: "You were right John, the people knew nothing of the plot, after we destroyed the underwater ships some of the lower rank military confessed to the whole thing. They were also unaware of the asteroid coming at them. They now realize it will be several centuries before they recover. It is only the technology they lost, everything else has not been affected. Because of the pollution of the island destruction, they are moving further out to sea. They thanked us and said if we could not stop the asteroid they understood. They asked us to not contact them again."

John: "Ok, let's use the rocket stand controller and get this big rock out of the way. Donna turned on the rocket stand controller.

John: "Let's talk about this for a minute. What is the best way to do this?"

Jack: "We will do it the same way we did it before. Donna will input a coordinate and the asteroid will be turned to that coordinate. "

John: "What coordinate would that be Jack?"

Jack: "Good question."

John: "Look we just need to send the asteroid somewhere that is not at the planet, how about we send it above the planet towards the sun, then after it passes the planet, we then send it into the sun. Jack, can you control each rocket firing."

Jack: "Yes it can be done."

John: "What if we fire one left rocket pulsing the rocket to get the asteroid to spin a little. Then when the right rocket stand is facing down to the bottom of the planet, we fire all the rockets on the right stand to bring the nose up to go over the top of the planet."

Donna: "That should work if we can get it to spin a little. Jack and I can work on that."

They waited for Jack and Donna to work that out."

Jack: "Alright we are ready to try to spin the asteroid. We tied the rocket controller into the navigation system. We made it automatic. Donna press the button. "Donna did, the left rear rocket engine started and did four quick pulses. They waited, as they watched, the asteroid started to slowly spin to the right. Just before the right rocket stand got to the bottom the three rockets fired for about 20 seconds. The asteroid started to go up slightly. After a few minutes the left rocket stand fired again to stop the spin. The asteroid stopped spinning and continued to climb. One hour later Donna said: "The asteroid is now over the top of the planet we will let it go awhile longer just to be sure, but at this point it will not hit the planet any longer. They waited another hour to give the asteroid more room. Then Jack and Donna reversed the rocket stand technique, stopped the spin again and then Donna reprogramed the asteroid to head into the sun with the rocket stands guiding it. "

Kaylon looked at John: "Your people are quite something."

John: "Thank you, I know, they all know their jobs very well. Donna disconnect the rocket stand controller, and set a course to "CEBO" please, standard speed Sgt. Carter." They started back to "CEBO".

Kaylon: "John would you and Toma join me in the back room please?"

Kaylon, John and Toma got up and went to the back room, they sat down at the table.

Kaylon: "Did you serve in your military as an officer or a commander?"

John laughing: No, I was a ground mechanic on a very special aircraft. I served in California at Beale AFB."

Toma: "I know that base from a couple of scout ship missions. Did you work on the aircraft you called the "SR-71 Blackbird"?"

John: "Yes, but how would you know that?"

Toma: "We used to watch it fly on its missions, that was quite an aircraft, if I remember it flew about 2400 miles per hour, we never figured out why it never melted, your aluminum melts at those temperatures. "

John laughed: "That was because it was not made out of aluminum. It was made from titanium, to withstand that heat."

Toma: "Oh, I am not familiar with that metal." John nodded.

John: "Kaylon, Why the interest in my military service?"

Kaylon: "John, you seem to have a natural ability to command. We have few commanders like that, and all of them were highly trained for years to get there. If you could pass on advice for my commanders, what would it be. What is it about your natural ability to command?"

John thought for a few seconds: "A **good** commander listens to advice from questions asked by him to his people. A **great** commander takes that advice and acts on it." It's one thing to have a good plan, it can be devastating to have a bad one.

Kaylon: "That seems to an excellent description of command. Thank you, John, I will pass that on."
Donna:" We have arrived at "CEBO" John."

John: "Thank you Donna." John got up and opened the door and stepped into the "VOID". Kaylon, Toma, and Kayla followed and stood at the base of the ramp. Kaylon shook John's hand as did Toma and Kayla gave John a hug. John watched as they walked away from the "Bullet", he got back into the "Bullet", closed the door and said: "Home please Sgt. Carter and sat down." Thirty minutes later the" Bullet" pulled up to John's workshop. John opened the door. John: "Wait a minute before you leave, I want to give you guys something. He walked over to the lockers and took out one of the new flashlights. He handed it to Sgt. Carter. Tell me what you think Sgt.?" Donna and Jack were watching. John was holding an orange bar in his hand.

Sgt. Carter looked over the light: "What does it do, it looks like a flashlight with missing pieces?" John: "Here put this in the slot." He handed Sgt. Carter the orange bar. Sgt. Carter inserted the bar into the slot and it locked. The light brightly shone on the wall. Sgt. Carter looked again at the light and removed the orange bar: "Is this a new kind of battery?"

John: "No, battery, this light has no battery, no bulb, and works inside and outside the "VOID". and is very bright, and it floats, on water, and the console. Put the bar back in and place it on the console. Sgt. Carter laid the light on the console, it jumped to an upright position and floated above the console. Sgt. what use would a Marine have for that light?"

Sgt. Carter: "Are you kidding, the fact it has no batteries or bulb means it is a light, and never fails." John went to the locker again he gave Sgt. Carter another light and orange bar and tossed a light to Donna and Jack, he also gave them each an orange bar: "Jack, what kind of use would you have on a boat for this?"

Jack: "An unlimited use, it could even be used as an emergency light that never goes out and you don't need electric lights which drain your batteries on the boat. John: "Sgt., one of those lights is for your personal use and give the other one to Izzy." Oh, by the way, Bob has just become the CEO of Johnson Lite Corp, the new company formed to make and distribute those new lights."

Donna: "These are great there are so many uses for them."

John nodding: "Yes, I think there might be a couple of more in the locker. Why don't you take another one and you too Sgt. Carter, two for you?"

Donna went to the locker and got the last two and handed one to Sgt. Carter, John handed them each another orange bar: "Donna let me show you all one more thing, give me one of your lights, Donna handed John one she had taken from the box and an orange bar. The orange bar also works this way, John held the bar underneath the light and it worked. The bar just has to be close to turn on the light. And if you don't want the light to work with the bar lying next to it, just wrap the bar in tin foil, or move the bar away a few inches, that keeps it from working." Bob, I never tried one thing, Donna put the orange bar in the slot on your light, Jack, give me the other orange bar, Jack did. John took the light from Donna and pointed it at the wall, then he put the second orange bar under the light, when he did the light became twice as bright. Bob, we just learned that you need to put another slot or slots on the light, experiment with multiple bars. An obvious selling point don't you think?"

Bob: "That's for sure." John: "Ok, see you all later and walked down the ramp." Bob, Donna, and Jack followed him down. John: "Oh, Bob, before Sgt. Carter leaves get a couple more of those lights and orange bars and give them to Sgt. Carter to put in the "Bullet" locker please." Bob quickly walked into the workshop pulled out two small boxes of lights and two orange bars wrapped in tin foil and came back to the "Bullet" and handed them to Sgt. Carter.

John: "You guys can go ahead and take off; I want to talk to Sgt. Carter a second, Bob why don't you take Jack and Donna to "Faraday's" moon and then come back here?" Bob" "Ok, I will be right back."

John: "Tim I can see the real value for those lights for you and your squad, if they agree, you let me know and I will supply you with the first new batch. The others are just proto types but they still work, and a rubber band around the light will work just fine to hold an orange bar to the bottom of the light."

Tim: "Thanks John, I'll let you know at our next Corporate meeting or sooner."

John nodded and went into the workshop. Bob was just returning from dropping off Jack and Donna.

John: "It looks like it's possible to add multiple slots on the light, just redesign them. What a way to increase orange bar sales, brighter light, add more orange bars.

John: "I would say Mr. CEO you have a lot of work to do to get these things off the ground." Bob: "Sounds like a plan to me, Boss." They both went into the house.

One week passes.

08:00 Monday Johns office:

John is playing "PINBALL". Bob comes in and sits down at the table. John stops playing and sits down with Bob.

John: "What's on your mind Bob?"

Bob: "I have a drawing for the new light and I wanted you to look at it and tell me what you think." Bob pushed a drawing of the light over to John.

John: "Well, tell me what you have done and I will follow it on the drawing."

Bob: "Look at the slots first, there is one on top of the handle facing to the rear of the light, there are two on the bottom of the light also facing the rear, and two on the rear of the light facing to the right of the light."

John: "The number of slots is abundant, maybe the two at the rear are not necessary, that's more than enough for general use. I see you changed the round barrel of the light and made it square like a normal flashlight, that seems to work better than my original design. I like it. Have you tried changing the size or makeup of the stainless steel inside the orange bar yet?"
Bob: "No, that is my next project."

John: "Well, this is your lucky day, I got bored last night and I made an orange bar with stainless foil and one 1/16 of an inch. John got up and went to his, desk, he opened the top drawer and took out two lights and a few bars wrapped in tin foil. These are the result. I made a bar with the 1/16 width, and one with the Stainless foil. They are marked as such. Would you like to test the bars?"

Bob: "Absolutely ". John handed Bob the two lights and the three bars. Bob looked at the bars, one was marked foil, one was marked 1/8, and the last was marked 1/16.
Bob put the original1/8 in. bar in one light and shined it on the wall: "John got up and turned out the office lights. Then Bob put the 1/16 in. bar in the second light and shined it on the wall. I don't' see a difference."
John looked at the wall: "Neither do I."
Bob removed the 1/16 in. marked bar and inserted the bar marked foil; the light shined on the wall: "I don't see a difference on this one either. We just made a lot more money on the orange bars."

John: "I would say you have done well so, far. Keep at it."
Bob: "I just thought of other stuff that needs to be done. We can open the "Johnson Lite Corp" business on the

first floor of this building, that makes it secure, easy to protect, and easy to control the making of the orange bars and gathering the floor material. It makes shipping easier, and I can hire people that already live here to make the orange bars."

John: "Very good Bob, who knows we may make a business man out of you yet."

Bob: "Thanks John, I will get right on the orange bars and the new light ASAP."
John: "To use a phrase I have heard before "Sounds like a Plan":" Bob laughed, got up, took the three orange bars, his drawing and left."
John watched Bob leave the office and nodded, then went back to his "PINBALL" game.

08:00 Tuesday Johns office:

John was sitting behind his desk. He had his feet on the desk, and he was thinking about a rousing day of "PINBALL". Bob came roaring into the office.
Bob: "Izzy called me he loves the light and wants to order thousands I sent him a picture of the new design and he loves that too. "
John: "Well, that's great but you don't even have a business location yet to start selling them."

Bob: "Let's go down to the first floor and check out availability, come on." John: "Ok, you can buy me a donut." They headed downstairs to the lease office."
John and Bob went inside. The girl behind the desk recognized them: "Mr. Faraday and Mr. Johnson how can I help you?" John explained why they were there.
Sharon (from her nametag):" Earl is due back in a minute, he went to get us some donuts. Would you like to wait?"

Bob: "Why don't we go get our donuts and come right back?" John: "I like that idea, Sharon we will return to see Earl." Bob and John left and went to the donut shop.
There was only one other person in the donut shop,

John: "Excuse me Sir, would you be Earl?" The man turned around: "Mr. Faraday, yes, I am Earl, how did you know." John explained.

Earl: "Look, you get your donuts; I will take these back to Sharon and I will come back here and we can sit at a table and talk about what you need. "
John: "Ok, that suites us." Earl sped off to deliver his donuts.

John: "Well don't just stand there buy us some donuts, and I want an orange juice." John and Bob ordered their donuts and sat down at one of the tables. Earl shortly came back and sat down with them. They discussed what Bob needed and finished the donuts.

Earl: "I believe I have available exactly what you need, why don't we go look at it?" Earl led them to the office space. On the way John made a call to Jack. At the office space Earl was showing them the interior of the open office space. It seemed very nicely centrally located inside the dome. Jack came in and joined John and Bob.

John: "I invited Jack for his engineering knowledge. Bob was not sure how to lay out the walls. Jack found a blank piece of paper on one of the rear counters and called Bob over to the counter. Jack: "What do you want to do here?"

Bob: "Well, we will have a store area up in front, a production area in the rear for the orange bars, a small office for me near the restroom facilities, and a storage area for supplies." Jack started to draw on the piece of paper. When he finished, he showed John and Bob what the store would look like from above.

Jack: "The easy one is your office next to the restroom facilities. Jack pointed to it on the paper, the next one is the store up front; this has a movable wall with shelves if you need to expand, the next is your storage area on the opposite end from your office, it also has a movable wall for expansion, and finally in the middle of the back, a large area for your production of the orange bars that can easily be doubled or tripled when needed as you start the business."

Bob: "Wow, that is perfect, John agreed, Earl was impressed."

John to Earl: "Jack is my Chief engineer on "Faraday's" moon." Earl: "That makes perfect sense, if you want, we can go back to my office and talk lease and we could go over the paperwork Mr. Johnson."

Bob: "Ok, I would like that, Bob looking at the drawing."

John: "Thank you Earl, I know you will take good care of Agent Johnson."

Earl asked: "Agent Johnson?" John: "Yes Earl, Agent Johnson is the Security Chief for "Faraday's" moon. He is starting his own business as a trade partner with Faraday Corp. Bob you go with Earl, Jack and I will go back upstairs, I will see you later for the details. Bob nodded and walked off with Earl."

Jack: "That was interesting to watch as you made Earl understand who Bob was."

John: "Earl has been here since the beginning, he is a hard business man, not a crook, just a little slippery. Now he will be doing his best for Bob, and that was my only goal." Jack smiling: "Mission accomplished Mr. Faraday."

John and Jack went back to their respective offices. About an hour later Bob came bounding into John's office.

John: "Well, how did it go with Earl?"

Bob: "I got a sweet deal thanks, but you could have used a 10-pound bowing ball instead of a 16-pounder rolling over Earl. He seems to be an ok guy, but I appreciate the help."

John laughing: "Well, let's take a look at the paper work. Bob handed the paperwork to John" John looked at the numbers: "I think you did get a good deal, very fair, I will have to stop by and see Earl and thank him." Well, it looks like you have a great deal to do, I may not see you for a month."

Bob smiling: "Nice try, I don't think that's going to happen." Bob grabbed the paperwork and left the office.

CHAPTER ELEVEN

"The BIXX"

07:30 John's office:

John was playing hard on the "PINBALL" game, he came in a little early to go for an all-time high score, he was almost there, and he was on his last ball. Jenny suddenly opened the office door. John looked at Jenny and when he looked back his last ball went buy the flippers—GAME OVER.

John: "Ahhhhhh."

Jenny smiling: "Oh, did I make you lose that game, sorry, you have a visitor."

John: "Send them in please." Jenny left the office and Kaylon walked in.

John looked around for a comm disk, found one and put it on his sleeve: "Kaylon, to what do I owe to this visit?"

Kaylon: "I had remembered on a couple of occasions the area of the Council planets was mentioned in various talks in your presence. I realized you had no information on that subject, so I brought you some material to look at."

John walked around the desk and shook hands with Kaylon and motioned to sit at the table. They both sat down. Kaylon took a folder he had brought with him and passed it to John.

John opened the folder and looked at the paperwork, it had a space map of the region that all the Council planets occupied. It also had a mini-synopsis of each civilization and various comments and descriptions about them and why they had access to the Council (Space craft, "VOID" or both).

John: "This is great, I have wondered if this information existed. Thank you, Kaylon." John pulled out the synopsis on Earth. He glanced through the pages. It was quite a lot of valuable information. He put the synopsis of Earth back and removed the space map of the Council planet locations. He looked at the area in space occupied by the Council planets. It was large.

John used the speaker phone to call Jenny. Jenny appeared at the door. Kaylon, would you like a glass of orange juice? Kaylon nodded. Jenny, make that two please. Jenny went to get the OJ.

John: "Kaylon, how much of our galaxy has the Council planets explored?"

Kaylon: "Only about 8 or 9 percent outside that map. What is out there is still unknown."

John: "Earth people are very curious, especially me. I would be much more comfortable if I knew what was out there, the old saying, "What you don't know can hurt you." is very appropriate when I look at this map."

Kaylon: "The only way to really explore the unknown area is using the "VOID", using spacecraft takes too long, and you are the only one so far that has that wonderful craft you built, that is because your vehicle does not have wheels, those are a huge disadvantage."

John: "I guess that explains why no one else has built a craft to use on long range missions, and we have built three. Wait a minute we have built three but you only gave us two fusion reactors. John picked up the phone on the table and called Izzy using the speakerphone. Izzy answered, Izzy, how can we build three "Bullets" if we only got two fusion reactors from the *OMER*?"

Izzy was laughing and said: "I wondered when you would notice that. You knew we were going to take apart the one reactor, we had an "*OMER*" expert with us when we took it apart. We were close to making fusion work. We had made a couple of stupid assumptions. The "*OMER*" pointed them out. After that we were able to make a fusion reactor half the size as the two, we got from the "*OMER*" and it produced 50 percent more power, all because of our advanced electronics. We shared all the knowledge with the "*OMER*" and helped them with their electronics."

John looked at Kaylon who nodded: "Izzy, how long would it take to build more "Bullets"?"

Izzy: "John this is classified information, we have 4 "Bullets" being built right now, two of them will go to the "OMER", Oh, that reminds me, can I send someone to pick up your "Bullet" we would like to do some upgrades to it. It should take 3 or 4 days and after it is done, I will send Sgt. Carter to update you and your crew on the upgrades."

John: "Yes, that's ok, thank you Izzy for the info." John hung up the phone."

Kaylon: "I am sorry, I thought you had been included in the loop with that information. I believe our two cultures are forever bound together. I made the decision to send the scientist to oversee the fusion reactor when it was taken apart. The information we both gathered about the fusion reactor is confidential and will not be shared with other planets."

John: "Thank you for sharing that. It helps relieve my anxiety about what might be out there. This is a normal consequence for me. Did Izzy give you a finish time on the "Bullets"?"

Kaylon: "Yes, they have been under way for many months and will be finished in one month, then another two weeks for testing with an "*OMER*" crew. What was your anxiety about?"

John: "I believe some current events that happen can drastically affect the future, the fusion reactor cooperation has caused a closer relationship between our people, however, that same event will lead to shared missions inside the "VOID" that were not planned before that cooperation. The fact we will now have extra "Bullets" relieves my anxiety about protection against what may be out there. Technology is not always a good thing, like everything else invention brings good and bad, hopefully the good will be stronger."

Kaylon: "I think I understand."

John: "What's really interesting is I have recently been thinking of getting my crew together and checking out some of those regions we just talked about, then Izzy wants to update my "Faraday 1" "Bullet" systems. Is that coincidence or a possible future event slapping us in the face?"

Kaylon: "I'm beginning to understand your theory a little better. Well, it's time to head back to "CEBO"."

John: "How is Kayla and Topa doing. I can tell she is very happy?"

Kaylon: "They are doing fine; I saw her yesterday and you are right she is very happy." Kaylon got up to go."

John stood up also.

Kaylon: "By the way I would like to go on that mission with you if you wouldn't mind?"

John shook Kaylon's hand: "Not at all, I would love to have you along." Kaylon turned and left the office. John went back to playing the "PINBALL" machine. The day passed and John walked home. He noticed the "Faraday 1" was gone. He went through the "doorway" into the workshop, turned off the "doorway", and went to the house.

One week later:

08:00 Friday

John was waiting for Bob, Donna, and Jack. They were going to get a briefing on the updates to "Faraday 1" from Sgt. Carter. Bob came into the office and sat down at the table.

John: "Well how's everything at the new store?"

Bob: "Couldn't be better, the inside is finished, the prototype of the new flashlight has been approved, the first delivery date for the flashlights is in two weeks. A large quantity of empty orange bars arrived today, the several pieces of floor material has been gathered like you showed me and stored in glass containers. The big roll of stainless foil is sitting in the storage waiting to be cut up. I hired 4 local students to work part time plus 3 full time seniors who applied for work. They all show up tomorrow and we will start making orange bars. I also hired a salesperson to handle the front of the store, she starts in three weeks."

John: "Wow, Bob that all sounds great. Good luck with all that." About that time Donna and Jack walked in.

Jack: "So what are we being briefed on?"

John: "They added some new stuff to "Faraday 1" and Sgt. Carter is bringing it here to brief us on the updates.

Bob: "Ooooo, more firepower I bet."

John: "Now that we are all here, let's go downstairs and see if Sgt. Carter is here yet, we can use my office "doorway" it is already set for the "VOID" parking lot. John opened his office "doorway" and they all went through to the "VOID" parking lot. Bullet "Faraday 1" was there and Sgt. Carter was standing in the door. He saw them coming and walked down the ramp to meet them. Donna gave Sgt. Carter a hug.

Upgrade #1

Sgt. Carter: "Let's start on the outside, John we tested your idea about the stainless fine mesh embedded in the windshield or just laid on the windshield with a clear coat of plastic. Embedded in the windshield kept penetration only to the mesh layer. Laid on the windshield and coated with a clear coat of plastic was the winner. The windshield like the hull could not be penetrated, we couldn't even make a scratch on it.

Izzy said thanks for the idea.

Upgrade #2

The next upgrade is on the top left corner of the vehicle. Sgt. Carter walked around to the other side of the "Bullet. As you can see, we have added a stainless-steel cylinder like what is in a revolver pistol. This cylinder holds 8 3/4 size AIM-92 fire and forget stinger missiles, and can be reloaded from inside the vehicle.

Upgrade #3

The next upgrade is the laser, the power was doubled and can now be focused into the "VOID" also and through the under floor "doorway", target settings were not changed. Dwell time on your target now is automatic at 3 seconds.

Upgrade #4

The next upgrade is the fanjets on top of the "Bullet" all four were updated to the latest electric motors with a 30 percent increase in fanjet power.

Upgrade #5

The last upgrade is the storage batteries aboard will now last for 4 days without fusion power charging. All systems now operate from the batteries. The on-board laser will draw direct power from the fusion generator if needed.

All 7 "Bullet" vehicles now have identical weapons, communication and navigation systems. A new comm system transceiver has been erected atop the "Earth" and the "CEBO" "doorways" linking "Bullet" communications available through cell, comm disk, "doorway" and all radio hardware. The plan is to erect "Transceivers" on all Council "doorway" stations, this will be part of the training mission for the "CEBO" "Bullets", the problem is only about a third of the Council

planets have "VOID" access. It is forbidden to give "VOID" access to those that have not discovered it, so the range of the communication is limited. The problem is being worked on. Are there any questions?"
John: "Can all of the "Bullets" communicate with each other?"

Sgt. Carter: "Yes, and the new comm badges also."
Donna: "Wait, did you say there were now 7 "Bullets"?"
Sgt. Carter: "Yes, four more were built, numbers 4 and 5 for us, the "OMER" vehicles were designated as "CEBO" 1 and 2." Are there any more questions?"

John: "Is the voltage to the hull always on or is there a control switch?"
Sgt. Carter: "There used to be a switch, it was tied to the stealth system, not anymore, voltage is always applied, why take a chance, are there any more questions?"
No questions. Sgt. Cater took a box from the floor and opened it. Inside are the new comm badges, they are the same size as before but the range has been increased by 1000 percent. A comm badge can communicate with the "Bullet" for 10 miles inside the "VOID".
Donna: "How do you use the comm badges to communicate?"

Sgt. Carter: "You put on the comm badge, it doesn't matter where and you touch it and speak. He handed Donna a comm badge and he put one on himself, he touched his and said: "Donna where are you. The sound came out of Donna's comm badge and she jumped. She said: "I am standing in the "VOID"." And the sound came out of Sgt. Carters comm badge.
Donna: "How does it do that?"

Sgt. Carter: "The comm system learns who is who by voice pattern, that information is stored in the system "Transceivers." When you all are together for the first time do what I just did with Donna and the system will learn your voice pattern. It also learns from "Bullet" transmissions.

If you all would take 3 or 4 comm badges I will return the "Faraday 1" home, to John's workshop. John you and Bob can ride with me if you wish."

John: "Bob, Jack, and Donna, I would like to see to you Monday morning in my office." They all nodded. Bob and John, and Sgt. Carter got into the "Bullet", John shut the door and Sgt. Carter took them to his workshop. Before Sgt. Carter left, John asked Sgt. Carter, if possible, to attend the Monday morning meeting.
08:00 next Monday

John in his office waiting for the others to arrive. Bob comes in and sits at the table.
John: "Well, you could have brought donuts."
Bob: "That's a good idea." He got up as Jenny brought in a box of donuts and a pitcher of orange juice and sat them down in front of Bob. Bob nodded at John who was smiling and sat down. Donna and Jack arrived with Sgt. Carter closely behind. They all sat down at the table. As they started on the donuts Kaylon appeared and sat down at the table. Everyone took a comm badge from the bowl on the table except Kaylon, Sgt. Carter and John who were already wearing them.

Kaylon: "I heard you were having a meeting from Kayla; I didn't think you would mind."
John: "Oh, I haven't talked to Kayla, but I have been thinking about the meeting so that explains it. Welcome Kaylon, actually this could not have worked out better. Have some orange juice while we all talk". They all talked for a while as if they were all family.

John: "Alright, I have been thinking that we need to do a reconnaissance mission out into the regions outside of the Council of planets space. John got up and moved to the wall next to the table. This map shows all of the Council of planets locations. The ones marked in green have "VOID" access, the ones marked in red have space craft, and the ones marked in white have both. As you can see the green and white ones are about a third of the Council planets. The ideal situation is that all the green and white ones with "VOID" access should be able to communicate through the "VOID", but the distance between them is too great. That problem I'm sure will be solved. Anyway, I want to take us on a look-see mission outside the area of the Council of planets. We are talking a mission of at least a week and possibly two weeks. Bob, I know you are in a critical time in your company start-up so it would not be a good time for you to go. We can talk later, and I have another job for you, I want you to certify Jack and Donna on hand guns. Take them to the range here and have them shoot and get them certified and accustomed to a handgun caliber larger than 22 cal. up to 9mm. Kaylon do you own a hand weapon?"

Kaylon said: "No, but I would love to learn. Bob, you have Jack, Donna, and Kaylon to train. I may even come over to do some target practice with you."
Bob: "We have a range on the moon?"

John: "Yes Bob, it is in the dome next to us. It is an indoor range, So, get them all qualified with weapons and ammo, put the weapons and ammo in a lock box for each of them and bring the boxes here, we will put them into "Faraday 1" for storage.

John: "Ok, let's move on, we will all wear the new uniforms, Bob make sure the weapons we take have a waist belt and a shoulder holster setup that can be worn over the new uniform. I would like to leave this Saturday morning at 08:00 and we will be leaving our sector here. (John pointed to the "VOID" planet closest to the edge of the Council planet area). Kaylon does that time work for you? Kaylon nodded.

Sgt. Carter you will bring 4 squad members, (I'm thinking of two stewards to take care of the cooking and kitchen but sleeping space is limited)."

Sgt. Carter: "One of my squad is a chef, let me call him (Sgt. Carter took out his cell phone and made his call. "Johnny, this is Tim, listen we may be going on a mission starting this Saturday with Mr. Faraday for two weeks, how would you like to cook for the trip for us and four others a total of 9 people. Ok, great—who? Oh, really, alright I will get back to you, thanks.")

Sgt. Carter: "Johnny said he would love to do that for us and Larry one of the other squad members is in Marine cooking school and will graduate this Thursday."
John: "Perfect now we don't need to waste the space for stewards and we can also help in the kitchen if needed. Ok, lets list what we need to do before we leave.
One---
Bob, you need to get Jack, Donna, and Kaylon certified on hand guns to bring with us.
Two---
Sgt. Carter you will get you and your squad ready to go, Johnny and Larry will take care of the food for the trip to be loaded onboard and get whatever they need to provide meals, etc. Oh, Sgt. make sure there are enough of the new uniforms aboard, I'm thinking 50 is enough. We have a combo washer and dryer on board if needed. I would think 4 uniforms each would work. Load all weapons and store extra ammo into the lockers.
Does anyone else have a suggestion?" John waited.
No other suggestions. We will see you Saturday morning about 08:00 at my workshop.

I need Kaylon and Sgt. Carter to stay a minute please. Donna and Jack thanks for coming. Jack and Donna got up and left. Sgt. How many rockets are loaded onboard the "Faraday 1"?"

Sgt. Carter: "The ammo lockers directly behind the cabin wall were made larger in the last upgrade. They were 18 inches deep; they are now 40 inches deep to accommodate 48 rockets. In the first locker, you probably didn't notice but the "Bullets" are 42 inches shorter. They made the 4 bedrooms 1 foot smaller and remodeled the storage space in the rear of the vehicle. The other large locker has mini-gun ammo canisters stored. Each canister holds 1000 rounds and there are 12 canisters. The third locker stores small arms ammo, handgun 9mm, rifle 5.56mm for our M4 carbines, 6 extra M4 carbines, and 5 extra 9mm hand guns."

John: "And all 7 "Bullets" are equipped the same, So, if we decide to start a small war, we can finish it also?" Sgt. Carter laughed: "Yes Sir, we can."
John pulled out his drawing he made and pushed it to Sgt. Carter. I would like you to give this to Izzy, it might solve the "VOID" transceiver problem. Sgt. Carter looked at the drawing, he studied it for a few minutes and started to laugh: "John, Izzy has had 4 scientists and 2 electronics experts working on that problem for weeks. It looks to me that your solution totally solves all the initial problems and then it exceeds the specifications for the system, Amazing."

John: "Well, if they can quickly build and test a couple of them, we can take a few with us to put in the "VOID" to close some of those communication range gaps. Izzy can call Bob for the lights and the orange bars."
Kaylon was now looking at the drawing: "John when did you think of this?"

John: "I started to think about it after the "Bullet" briefing Sgt. Carter gave us. It just seemed to work, after all I have been involved in the "VOID" since I discovered it."

Kaylon smiled: "Another proof of your theory maybe?" He gave the drawing to Sgt. Carter."

John smiled: "Maybe not, but then again. Kaylon, do you need a ride home?"

Kaylon: "No, I drove the golf cart again, thank you." anyway."

John: "Sgt. How did you get here?"

Sgt. Carter: "I was dropped off."

Kaylon: "How about giving us a ride to my workshop, and Sgt. Carter you can take "Faraday 1" with you?" Sgt. Carter nodded ok.

They went to the parking spot and Kaylon took them to John's workshop. John and Sgt. Carter got out of the golf cart.

John: "Kaylon, I will see you Saturday at the "CEBO" "doorway" station around 08:30 my time." They both waved to Kaylon as he started home.

John: "Tim, how is Carla?"

Sgt. Carter: "She is fine. She is still looking for an apartment to live in."

John: "I understand, women stuff." Tim did I ever mention the apartments here, they are very nice?"

Sgt. Carter: "I know they are but we couldn't afford the rent."

John: "Tim: I swore I mentioned this to Bob, at least I thought I did. Tim you are authorized to live here because you provide a service to Faraday Corp. You have the same benefits as any one employed by the Corporation. And so, does your squad. Those benefits include your residence and low-cost food. You tell Carla she can stop looking for a place to live. You let me know, I will inform Grace downstairs (you met her when the" Greys" brought the returnees back.) and she will help you with the apartment."

Tim: "John I don't know what to say."

John: "Tim you don't have to say anything, you are entitled to this, and so is the squad, it is me that should apologize for not following up. Anyway, take the

"Faraday 1" and go home and tell Carla the news. I will
see you Saturday morning", Tim thanked John and took
the "Bullet" home.

CHAPTER TWELVE

"Be Prepared"

08:00 Saturday morning:

Bob and John were standing outside the workshop. They could see Donna and Jack walking towards them in the distance, St. Carter was due any minute. Donna and Jack arrived just as the "Faraday 1" showed up. The "Bullet" stopped and Sgt. Carter opened the door.

Bob: "John I just realized that the door has no button to open the door from the outside, why not?"

John: "Actually there is an open button, it is hidden on the opposite side of the "Bullet", all of you need to know where it is, follow me. John led them to the other side of the "Bullet", Bob, put your fingers just under the bottom right bumper where the curve to the front starts and feel around."

Bob did: "I feel the button it is slightly indented." John let the others feel for the button.

John: "Now we can all get aboard." They all followed John up the ramp and took their places inside the cabin. John closed the door and sat down with his folder on his lap: "He looked around the cabin, Sgt. Carter how many people do we have on board?"

Sgt. Carter: "We have 5 Marines, you all and Kaylon coming. Johnny and Larry are in the kitchen."

John nodding: "Ok, Sgt. first stop is "CEBO" to pick up Kaylon please." Donna input the course and nodded to Sgt. Carter." They started to "CEBO".

John: "By the way Sgt. What did Izzy think of the transceiver drawing I gave you."
Sgt. Carter laughing: "He looked at it and went nuts, he called in the team who had been working on the problem and showed it to them. They of course could see immediately that it might work. He told them to get at least 3 ready and tested for our trip or they all would be fired. There are 4 tested "Transceivers" in the rear storage. "
John: "That's great, we will be installing them in the void on our trip."

In a few minutes they were at "CEBO", Kaylon was standing in the "VOID" waiting for them.
John opened the door: "Welcome Kaylon, Kaylon came up the ramp, said hello to everyone and sat down."

Donna: "John, where to next?" John opened his folder and pulled out a map of the Council planets, got up and moved over to Donna and gave it to Donna:" This is a map of the territory of the Council of planets. As you can see the planets names are here and they have a color. The colors are explained at the bottom of the map. Anyway, we are going to explore the area outside the Council area, and we will start from here. John pointed to a planet at the edge of the area, I am starting here at (he looked at the planet name) Tooder, the reason is that most of the planets that have "VOID" access are well inside the Council area. Tooder does not have "VOID" access, only space flight. Also, all of the "VOID" planets have had "Transceivers" added to their "doorway" stations as of last Friday, last week. So, Donna if you would put up the map between "CEBO" and Tooder we can make a decision where to put the first transceiver to test." Donna put up the map on the big screen. The map showed a line from "CEBO" to Tooder.

John: "Now if you would look at the map and put the planets that have "VOID" access on the map that are on the Council area side near Tooder." Donna did that, four more planets showed on the map."

John: "These four planets have all had the "Transceivers" installed but these two (John pointed to the outmost two planets) are still outside the grid. So, a second part of our mission will be to put the test "Transceivers" in the "VOID" and see if they work. So, Donna, input coordinates for 75 grid "VOID" miles from (John pointed to the nearest planet that was working in the grid) and the nearest to the one that was not working and that is where the first test transceiver will be placed. And that is where we are headed Donna, standard speed Sgt. please. "

Donna was way ahead of John. She nodded to Sgt, Carter, and he moved the throttle forward.

John looked at Kaylon and he nodded. About then Bob spoke: "What is that wonderful smell?"
John: "That smells like cinnamon rolls." About that time Johnny and Larry entered the main cabin with a plate of cinnamon rolls, plates, glasses and two large pitchers of orange juice, pulled up and locked a rear counter on the wall and sat the food and stuff down on the rear counter.

Larry: "There also is fresh coffee made in the kitchen."
Kaylon was already pouring himself a glass of orange juice, and checking out the cinnamon rolls. John: "Got up and went to the cinnamon rolls, put one on a plate and tasted it. Oh, my he exclaimed these are wonderful." Johnny and Larry smiled nodded and disappeared back into the kitchen."

John: "Donna, how far to the first test transceiver site?"

Donna: "About 90 minutes at standard speed."
John: "Sgt. Carter we are going 80 mph, correct?"
Sgt. Carter: "Yes sir."

John: "Let's try bumping that up to 160 and see how she does?" Sgt. Carter: "Yes sir and pushed the throttle forward." Forty-five minutes later Donna said: "John, we are at the first test location."

John: "Ok, stop the vehicle and we will set up the first transceiver." Sgt. Carter stopped the vehicle, John got up and opened the door. Everyone got out and walked back to the rear of the vehicle. Sgt. Carter opened a large panel and 4 transceiver units were visible.
John: "Take one out and set it on the "VOID" floor please." Bob and Sgt. Carter lifted out one unit by the handles and set it on the "VOID" floor. John looked the unit over. It was a good replica of the drawing. The bottom was a poured concrete shell. The top of the shell had a square glass indented top that was darkened to keep as much light inside the base as possible, they had put a tab on the glass to make it easy to remove, and a stainless-steel antenna was pushed down to its minimum height. The antenna had a round plastic attachment at the top of the antenna. (he would ask Sgt. Carter what that was) John removed the glass top, and looked inside. Inside the concrete base was the light wrapped in tinfoil and he could see the electronic box up against the side of the concrete base at the top. John pulled up the antenna to its full height of 30 feet, removed the tin foil from the light. The light lit up the entire area it was so bright. John put the light into the base using its holder plate with the light pointing down onto the solar cells. A green light on top of the unit turned on and so did a green light on the electrotonic box.

John: "That's it, let's go see if it works." They all went back into the main cabin and sat down.

John: "Ok, Donna, display unit 000204 on your transceiver screen please, everyone looked at the transceiver display on the big screen, the one marked 000204 was blinking like the rest."

Kaylon: "John it seems to be working."
John: "Not just yet, we see it working because we are sitting next to it, remember we have a transceiver on the "Bullet, Donna display the transceiver number closest to us, it will show what it sees. Donna selected the closest transceiver. They looked at its display, 000204 was blinking.

John: "Now we know that 000204 is working. Now we are going to move 000204 another 25 miles out and see if it still works." They pushed the antenna down to minimum and put it back into the storage area. Sgt. Carter pushed the throttle forward. In a few minutes they stopped again after going another 25 miles, unloaded the transceiver and put it on the "VOID" floor.

John: "Donna, before we raise the antenna, go back inside and see if we see the transceiver, then yell out and we will raise the antenna so you can do the same test with the other transceiver." Donna went back to the cabin. In a minute she yelled out she could see the transceiver. John raised the antenna to 30 feet and waited for Donna. Donna came back from the cabin and told them she could no longer see 000204 from the other transceiver behind them.

John: "Ok, we guessed that the best range was between 75 and 100 miles, so we back up 25 miles and put 204 back where we had it before." They did so, and made sure 204 was working again. They all were in the main cabin again.

John: "Donna, pull the transceiver display up again please." Donna did so. John looked at the screen. Donna asked: "John how many "VOID" planets are there?"

John: "There are 11 Council planets now, 4 have "VOID" access.

Donna: "We have 5 "Transceivers" showing." John thought about what Donna said: "Oh, that's right 3 planets one new one, and the "Bullet" you forgot we have a "Transceiver" on the "Bullet". Click on the furthest "Transceiver", Donna did, the display came up and the name was "Faraday 1"."

John: "Ok, let's go plant the next "Transceiver", and that will go here, this one will connect all the "Transceivers" together. (John pointed to the next location on the map he had given Donna.) About 50 minutes later they were at the next location. They unloaded the next" Transceiver", set it up and tested the unit. Everything tested ok.

John: "Sgt. Carter I forgot to ask; did Izzy tell you what the round plastic attachment on top of the antenna is?"
Sgt. Carter: "I forgot also, he said it was a wireless motion detector and a 4-direction video camera, it is hooked into the "Transceiver.""
John: "That Izzy is crazy, but I like the idea. Ok, Donna we go here next. (John pointed at the map)"
The next "Transceiver" will be on the edge of the Council of planets territory.

Donna we can go a couple of directions because we are less than 75 "Void" miles from the edge, so pick a spot towards Tooder using the 75 miles as a guide."
Donna: "Got it. She entered the coordinates and nodded at Sgt. Carter."

John: "Jack, you haven't said much today, what's up?"
Jack: "Oh, nothing, I am just watching Donna to learn as much as I can about her job, it is fascinating, he looked at Donna and said: "Like you Mrs. Foster", Donna smiled.
About an hour later they were at the location to install the "Transceiver #3". Bob and Sgt. Carter unloaded the

"Transceiver" and put it on the "VOID" floor. Jack bent down to watch John set it up.

Jack: "You hope the floor of the "VOID" grows up on the concrete holding the "Transceiver" permanently to the floor and stops at the glass, is that right?"
John: "Hopefully so, I just assume the glass will stop it. We will check the first one we installed and see if that is correct on the way back." They tested the #3 "Transceiver" and everything tested ok."

John: "I know a perfect way to test the "Transceivers", I will give Izzy a call." John got out his cell phone and called Izzy, Izzy answered his phone."

Izzy: "Hi John, I see the installs are going great. I have been watching your progress as the new "Transceivers" are installed. In fact, I am looking at the top of "Faraday 1" through the camera of the one you just installed."
John: "Well considering we are more than 150 miles into the "VOID" that is pretty good. Listen I have another idea I would love to talk about when I get back. Well, we have more work to do, talk to you later. John disconnected from Izzy and put the phone back in his pocket."
Kaylon: "So, the "Transceivers" can be used to connect communications devices through the network?"
John: "Yes, yours also, it was part of the plan from the beginning." Kaylon nodded.
Donna: "John, where are we going to plant the last "Transceiver"?"
John: "That will be 75 miles outside the Council planets territory."

John looked at his watch, "it's about lunch time, let's eat and cross into the other side after lunch." They all went into the kitchen. Johnny and Larry were ready for them, the food was laid out on the counter like a buffet. John looked at the food, it was high quality food that you would get in a fancy restaurant. He was expecting a ham

sandwich and a diet drink. He picked up a plate and got in line. They all sat down and had a wonderful lunch. John insisted that Johnny and Larry sit and eat with them.
Bob: "John I don't think I have ever had a lunch like that."

John: "I know, I ate so much; I want to take a nap." They both laughed. There was more than enough food left over for dinner later. They went back to the main cabin. John opened the cabin door.

John: "I need to take a walk; he grabbed a light from the locker and went down the ramp. He carefully removed the tin foil to reuse; the light came on and he walked around in the "VOID" for thirty minutes. John came back to the cabin and put the tin foil around the light again, the light went out and he put it back into the storage locker. Everyone was back in the cabin including Johnny and Larry.

John: "Anyone feel like exploring?" (All hands went up) Donna I want to go forward from where we are, and I want you to loop back and forth like a snake. Let's see what we run into." Donna when we get out 75 miles, we will stop and install the last transceiver. Sgt. Carter make 20-mile loops wide and 10-mile loops out. Sgt. Carter nodded. Sgt. Carter started the loops back and forth. After 3 hours went by, as they looped back and forth, they ran into nothing. As the fourth hour started Donna said: "I have a solar system coming up. "

John: "How far out are we?" Donna: "We are out 50 miles."
John: "Let's take a look. Let's see if there is a Goldilocks planet?"

Kaylon: "What is a Goldilocks planet?"
John: "That is a planet fit for human life, it is not too hot or too cold, it is just right, the term is from an old human fairytale."
Kaylon: "What is a fairytale?"

John: "I will do my best; it is a parable. Do you know what a parable is?"

Kaylon: "Maybe."

John: "Take my hand I will show you the parable of Goldilocks, Kaylon laid his hand on John's hand, a few minutes passed, Kaylon started to laugh.

Kaylon: "I get it, now I understand, we have the same thing. Sometimes things don't translate well. Thank you, John."

Donna: "We have scanned the system and there are no Goldilocks planets."

John: "Thank you, please start the loop again." Sgt. Carter started to loop again. Another hour went by.

Donna: "I have another solar system coming up."

John: "Same procedure please." John looked over at Bob, he was napping. (lucky guy) he thought.

Donna: "This system is a lot like Earths. I have two, planets 3 and 4 that would equate to Mars and Earth. Planet number 4 has some plant life but no oceans, planet 3 has, whoa, what do we have here, I see ships in orbit and bright lights on the surface."

John: "Bring up the cameras and let's take a much closer look." As they got closer you could see as many as fifty ships in orbit, some going down and some coming up from the surface. The bright lights on the surface were explosions."

Donna: "Get close-ups of those ships and let's see what is happening on the surface." Donna started to take pictures of the ships in orbit. Everyone watched on the big screen as Donna came much closer to the surface. Some kind of War was going on, the inhabitants were humanoid, and fighting some kind of Robots. They were using explosives to try and stop the Robots and were losing badly. They all watched as a row of 10 Robots 10 feet apart just walked in a line and used some kind of energy weapons to mow down the humanoids. There were dead humanoid bodies everywhere and Robot parts scattered all over.

John: "Did you see the small wheeled vehicle about 30 yards behind that line of Robots. Donna get some pictures of those. There were also some damaged small wheeled vehicles. "

Jack: "Two of the ships are going down to the surface." They watched as two ships broke orbit and proceeded to land behind a large number of Robots on the ground. As soon as the ships landed the Robots turned and headed towards the ship and the small wheeled vehicles followed. They started to enter the ships and when all of them were onboard the ships left and went back into orbit. Several of the ships left orbit and headed into space.

Donna: "Get a direction on those ships please." The rest of the ships left orbit and went the same direction. They watched as the humanoids started to pick up their dead and attend to the wounded.
John: "I would like to help them but I don't know where to start."

Sgt. Carter: "Let's watch and see what kind of medical help they give their wounded, maybe we can help with medical supplies. We have a large cache aboard. They watched as the wounded were cared for. The medical supplies they were using were normal medical supplies but they were running out."

John: "I see it, let's get ready to give them more supplies. I am going to open a "doorway" on the surface. We can toss out supplies until they get curious." John opened a "doorway" and the Marines started to stack up supplies near the "doorway", as the humanoids supplies dwindled John got ready to toss some supplies through the "doorway", he picked up supplies and tossed them through the "doorway". The humanoids watched as the supplies fell to the ground appearing from nowhere. They

turned and called out to someone behind them. A
humanoid dressed in some kind of uniform came up to the
supplies laying on the ground. He walked up to the
supplies, he bent down and looked at the supplies, then
picked one up and tossed it to one of the other humanoids.
He motioned for more to come forward and pick up the
supplies. As they did John tossed out more supplies as
they picked them up. The humanoid in the uniform looked
at where the supplies were coming from. He came closer
to the "doorway and motioned for someone to come
forward then held his hands up.
John: "Kaylon what do you think?"

Kaylon: "I think he wants to know where the supplies
are coming from."
John: "Anybody got a couple of comm badges?" Sgt.
Carter handed John a few comm badges.

John: "Kaylon shall we." John stepped through the
"doorway" with his hands up, Kaylon followed with his
hands up. The man in the uniform didn't seem surprised.
John held out his hand with the comm badges, and
pointed to the one on his arm and the one on Kaylon. He
pointed to the badges in his hand and then the humanoid
in the uniform and motioned for him to put one on. The
humanoid in the uniform looked at John and Kaylon who
were both smiling and back to John's hand with the comm
badges, he stepped forward and took a badge and put it on
his sleeve.

John: "Can you understand me yet?" The humanoid in
the uniform: "I understand you very well. Thank you for
the supplies."
John: "We have more if you need them. What is your
name? "
The man in the uniform: "My name is Gorton; I and a few
others are what's left of the group of people sent here to
fight the Robots."
John: "Who were they?"

Gorton: "We don't know, we have never seen them before and we had no weapons except the explosives to fight them with. They arrived here two days ago and started killing us, we have lost a third of our population. We have no idea why they came or what they wanted."

John: "My name is John Faraday, and the man next to me is Kaylon. We have more medical supplies we can spare to give you. We would like to pick up some of the Robot pieces to study if that is alright with you."

Gorton: "Take what you like, we have no need for them."

John: "Thank you, I will arrange to put out the rest of the medical supplies." John went back through the "doorway".

John: "Sgt. We need to put the rest of the supplies in a pile for them, Bob get some large boxes to pick up Robot parts and I want one of the small things on wheels also."

Sgt. Carter grabbed supplies and stepped through the "doorway and started to pile them on the ground. Bob brought several large boxes to John. John brought the boxes through the "doorway" and started to collect Robot parts with Kaylon. He tossed them into the boxes. They picked up one of the wheeled things and carried it through the "doorway" into the cabin, then went back through the "doorway". Sgt. Carter finished piling up the supplies and dragged the boxes full of Robot parts back through the "doorway". The squad put the boxes and the wheeled thing into the infirmary for study.

Suddenly Donna spoke over John's comm badge: "John there are two of those same ships coming into the solar system."

John touched the comm badge: Thank you Donna we are on the way."

John: "Gorton we have to go, do you have a safe place for your people to go. We must go but I promise we will return later, by the way what is the name of your planet?"

Gorton: "Its name is "Prema" and yes, there are caves in the mountains where we can go."

John: "Good luck Gorton, keep the comm badge for later." Gorton nodded, John and Kaylon went back through the "doorway", closed it up and went back to the "Bullet". John closed the cabin door. Donna had the two ships on the big screen. In a few minutes they both arrived and went into orbit.

John: "If they attempt to go down to the planet fire the laser across the bow of the ship. If that doesn't stop them fire through the ship. One of the ships started to go down to the planet. Sgt. Carter fired the laser across the bow of the ship. It kept going, he fired the laser through the ship, it exploded in a fireball. Then the pieces started to burn up as they fell into the atmosphere.

John: "I'll bet they saw that on the planet." The other ship did nothing. Suddenly the other ship left orbit and headed into space."

John: "Donna: "Is that the same coordinates as the two before?"
Donna: "Yes sir they are."
John: "Bob what do you think we should do next?"
Bob: "We should follow them to see where they live?"

John: "Donna, how close are we to the 75-mile marker where we wanted to install the #4 transceiver?"
Donna looked at her console, winked at Jack and said: "15 miles."
John: "Ok, take us out 15 miles, we will install the transceiver and then do a little following of the "bad guys"."
Donna nodded to Sgt. Carter and they were off to install the last transceiver. In a few minutes they arrived at the spot. Bob and Sgt. Carter removed the #4 transceiver and put it on the "VOID" floor.

John: "Jack, would you like to install the last transceiver?"

Jack: "I would actually. Jack pulled up the antenna, opened the glass, took out the light. He took off the tin foil and the light lit. He placed the light inside the transceiver, watched for the two green lights, and replaced the glass.
John: "Very nice Jack." John Jack Bob and Sgt. Carter went back to the main cabin.

John: "Donna as soon as the transceiver is checked out, please set a course for the "bad guys."

Donna: "Transceiver all checked out sir, coordinates set, Sgt. Carter at your leisure." Sgt. Carter pushed the throttle forward. John smiled.

John: "When we catch them just follow them at a good distance, we don't want them to know we are here. Bob, Kaylon and Jack follow me to the infirmary, we are going to do a little surgery, and any of you Marines that want to watch are welcome." They all went to the infirmary. John pulled a Robot arm, a head, and a chest out of one of the boxes and put them on one of the patient tables. I want to know what is inside these. John looked at one of the Marines, do you know where a tool kit might be. One nodded and left the room, he came back with an actual tool kit. John thanked him.
John laid some tools out on the table that might be needed.

John: "Jack would you like to open the arm first?"
Jack: "I would love to, he looked at the arm and had it open in about a minute. The arm was a Robot arm, no organics."
John: "Good job Jack, open the head next please."
Jack studied the head and smiled and pulled off the top of the head with his fingers. Everyone looked inside. It was again a Robot with electronics inside no organics." Jack smiled.

John: "Well, how about three for three Jack, open the chest please?" Jack studied the chest: "Hummm, no screws, just the two buttons at the bottom, Jack pressed the two buttons simultaneously, the chest plate popped open. Jack removed the chest plate." Inside was more Robot stuff, John looked closely at the inside of the chest cavity. He pointed to a box attached to the spine running through the chest: "Does anyone notice something about that box?"

Jack: "It has a red light on the side of it."
John: "I'll bet the large 1 in. thick 4 x 6 box next to it is a battery. I bet it has a wireless connection to the wheeled thing. We need to disconnect the wire from the battery to the box with the light. That light is red because it can't communicate with the wheeled thing. And I don't want it to do so. Jack, disconnect the wire please." Jack looked closely at the wire, it was a round connection, he twisted the round connection and pulled, it disconnected and the red light went out."

John: "Excellent Jack, thank you. John tossed the parts back into the box. Is there another "chest" in the boxes, Bob looked and nodded no."
John: "Ok, let's put the wheeled thing on the table please, Bob and one of the Marines picked up the wheeled thing and placed it on the table."

John: "Jack, take a crack at it please." Jack looked over the wheeled thing, again no screws, but it had two buttons like the chest did. Jack pressed the buttons simultaneously and the whole top popped up and was easily removed. They all looked inside, it again was a Robot with a jumble of wires and connections. John looked closer at the insides, he pointed out the same box as the robot with the same battery next to it.

John: "Jack please disconnect the battery. Jack reached down turned the round connection and pulled, it disconnected for the box, did anyone pick up one of the weapons the Robots were using?" Bob looked in the box and started to rummage around: "Here's one, he pulled it out of the box and gave it to John. John looked at it and said: "We will not mess with this, too dangerous, Izzy and his geeks will get this. Bob put this energy weapon in a bag for Izzy please, Kaylon I will send the report from Izzy to you and Toma. Kaylon nodded. Well let's go back to the main cabin. They all went back to the cabin and sat down."

John: "Donna, how are we doing on the "bad guys"?"

Donna: "We are still following them, no solar system in sight yet."

John: "Well, we just wait then." Another hour went by.

Donna: "A solar system coming up, and they are heading straight for it."

John: "How far are we from the last transceiver?" Donna put the transceiver screen on the big screen: "We are too far past the last transceiver to use it."

John: "Keep the coordinates handy, we may need to make a fast break to get within its range." Donna nodded.

Donna: "The ship has gone into orbit of the number 4 planet, there are at least 75 other ships in orbit."

John: "Ok, let's take a close look, Donna shut down radar also." Donna nodded and the camera moved closer to the planet. Everybody watched the big screen. There was a huge industrial complex, they were producing ships and Robots at an amazing pace.

Donna: "I have located another 100 ships on the surface. "

John: "Donna, let's take a look at the other side of the planet please."

Sgt. Carter maneuvered the "Bullet" around to the other side of the planet. Donna moved the camera closer to the surface. The big screen started to show destroyed city after city with no population. They had been destroyed long ago; the plant life had taken back the cities.

John: "Look at that destruction, it has been a long time since that destruction happened. Perhaps hundreds of years ago. "

Donna: "I have a humanoid on the screen near one of the buildings. He just disappeared into the building. "
John: "Kaylon its time to find out what is going on here. Sgt. is the" doorway" still in the back wall operating?"

Sgt. Carter: "Yes sir, there is a small rocker switch, about half-way up the wall, John pressed the switch and the "doorway" opened showing the area many miles above the old city."

John: "Donna, show me the inside of the building and anyone inside on infrared please. "Donna brought up the building and as much of the first floor as she could see. The humanoid and about 25 others were in the building. John:" Sgt. take us down and put the "Bullet" parallel to the building wall and the "Doorway "facing across the entrance to the building." They all watched as Sgt. Carter maneuvered the "Bullet" into position."

Kaylon chuckled:" I am amazed every time I see this vehicle do these crazy things."
John: "Ok Kaylon are you ready, it's you and me again?"
Sgt. Carter handed John a few comm badges.
Kaylon: "I believe a human saying, "Once more into the breach" is correct."
John smiling: "Very appropriate."

John and Kaylon stepped onto the planet and into the wide doorway that went into the room, they raised their hands. They stood in the doorway. Inside the room the humanoid they first saw turned and looked at them. The others just stood still. The humanoid took a few steps toward them. The humanoid was clear now, they were very human looking, the only difference John could see was his eyebrows, they were not hair like what was on his head, but a couple of raised skin like scars the same size as eyebrows.

John put his hand in his pocket and pulled out the three comm badges and held his hand out to the humanoid, the humanoid looked at his hand, John pointed to the comm badge on his sleeve. The humanoid smiled and took a comm badge and placed it on his sleeve.
John: "Can you understand me now?"
The humanoid looked at Kaylon and John: "Yes, are you from the "dark place" and pointed up to the sky?"
John understood: "Yes, we call it the "VOID, tell us what happened here, and may I have your name please, my name is John Faraday and my friends name is Kaylon."

The humanoid: "The "VOID", yes that is a good description, my name is Hebber, this is the planet "Karon", we have waited for this day for a long time, we knew eventually someone would come from your "VOID". Hundreds of years ago, we used the "VOID" to travel our solar system. We had no curiosity to go further. Our society was spectacular at one point. Then one day we developed a Super Smart machine,
then we made a fatal mistake, we allowed the machine to communicate with our planetary communications network. Everything was fine in the beginning but what we didn't realize until it was too late, was that the machine was planning our demise.
It built secret factories to build the Robots and the small controllers. It wasn't mobile but its army was. When we discovered the intention of the Super Smart machine, it had built an army so large we could not destroy it. We know we only had a year or so before it would take over the planet. We concentrated on destroying the network of "VOID" access so the machine would not be able to use it. The machine never discovered the "VOID" network and we successfully destroyed all access to and all knowledge of the network. We knew if the machine ever discovered the "VOID" network the universe would be in chaos. Plans and blueprints of the network were saved and

hidden long ago, only a handful of us know where they are. We were satisfied the Smart machine would never know about the network. The machine destroyed our planet, we have only a few thousand people hiding in the old cities and the machine leaves us alone now that we can't hurt it. It sends a few Robots in every once and a while but we discovered early that if you destroy the small controller, you stop the Robots."

John: "Hebber is the Smart machine located in one place?"

Hebber: "Yes, there is a light blue building in the middle of the industrial complex. That is where the Smart machine is located. It is fully guarded by the Robots. The machine stopped learning when we disconnected ourselves from it. The Robots it builds are not very strong, they are easy to break with clubs. The problem is they have those energy weapons. Even the controller is not built very well, it has no weapons to protect itself. I assume with the number of ships the machine has built it has moved to attack other planets?"

John: "We were exploring this sector and that is how we encountered the Robots. A solar system near you was under attack and we stopped to see what was going on. We helped the residents with medical supplies after all of the Robot ships in orbit left. Later two of the Robot ships came back, When the acted like they were going to attack again we had to destroy one of them, the other left orbit and we followed it here. We have seen the massive build-up of ships and Robots on the planet."

Hebber: "You must destroy them if you have the ability, you must. They are a danger to the whole galaxy and the universe."

John: "We have to leave now, but I promise we will return, is there anything we can do for you?"

Hebber: "No, we have enough to sustain us, we grow our food outside the city, and live in the old buildings, but thank you." John nodded, he and Kaylon turned and left then entered the "doorway".

John closed the "doorway" and sat down. Bob and Kaylon watched John. John noticed them watching him and chuckled: "Are you waiting for me to form a plan, is that why you are watching me?" Bob nodded; Kaylon smiled

John: "Kaylon already knows what must be done." Kaylon nodded.

Bob: "John you had a purpose in opening the Robot parts and the controller, didn't you?"

John: "Yes, life is important, all life, I needed to know there was no active life, no organics in them.

Donna: "Lay in a course to within 75 miles of the last transceiver. And Sgt. Carter-step on it. It is time to call the cavalry."

Donna set the course and nodded to Sgt. Carter who punched it.

John looked at Johnny and Larry: "Now would be a good time to get a bite to eat."

Johnny and Larry nodded and headed to the kitchen. Everyone but John and Kaylon went to the kitchen.

John: "I assume you want to relay everything that happened to the Council, and inform them of what is going to happen next."

Kaylon smiling: "Yes, as soon as I know what that is."

John: "I intend to activate all 7 "Bullets" to wipe out the evil machine and everything it created., in a single attack."

John: "I had a plan as soon as Hebber explained about the Smart machine."

Kaylon: "I agree with your plan as long as you coordinate it."

John: "I had planned to do just that; we have all the information we need." John got up and Kaylon followed him to the kitchen."

About the time they all finished snacking, a computer message came on the screen in the kitchen that they had reached their destination. Everyone went back to the main cabin.

John: "Sgt. Carter is there a place in the back where Kaylon can speak to the Council on "CEBO"?"
Sgt. Carter: "Yes sir, there is a secondary communications office right next to the last bedroom. One of the squad can show him and assist if necessary." One of the squad got up to go with Kaylon.

John: "Thank you Sgt." John got his cell phone out and called Izzy. Izzy answered the phone:" John, how is the exploring going? I see you installed the fourth transceiver."

John: "Yes, but now we have a real problem, John explained what had happened and why he wanted all the "Bullets" to be sent to his location. Izzy said he was on "Bullet 5" and would command them all to John's location at full speed immediately, their training was over and they were supplied for two weeks."
John thanked Izzy and ended his call. Kaylon came back into the cabin with the squad member.

Kaylon: "John, I informed the Council on our experiences so far and they agreed the Robots are a definite danger to our sector. They agreed with the action that needed to be taken."
John: "Good, Izzy is on the way with the other 6 "Bullets", we will wait for Izzy."
Bob was listening to John and Kaylon: Ya know John, this whole thing is your fault. You discovered the "VOID" and the next thing that happens is interstellar war. You are just a trouble maker."

John: "Well thank you Bob, and I take full responsibility of course." Bob just chuckled.
John: "Donna how long will it take Izzy to get here?"
Donna: "Izzy at full speed is almost two hours away."

John: "In that case I will have a nap." John leaned back in his chair and drifted off to sleep."

Bob leaned over to Kaylon: "I couldn't sleep with what's about to happen, could you?"
Kaylon: "No, but that is what makes John the individual he is, he lets nothing bother him that would cloud his judgment."
Two hours later Izzy and the other 6 "Bullets" arrived, they made a circle around "Faraday 1" and all their doors opened to the inside of the circle. Izzy and the other Captains gathered in the middle of the circle.

John: "Thank you all for coming. Your training will be tested today. If you will follow me to our conference table, I will lay out each of your rolls. John turned and went up his ramp to the kitchen, the others followed. At the table John got up and started to talk to the Captains:

First: "Who is the Captain of "Faraday 4" and "CEBO 2?", Two Captains raised their hands. You will go to the planet where all this started, the planet is called "Prema" my navigator will send you the coordinates, you will be out of contact with the rest of us until the operation is over, your assignment is to stay in orbit and destroy any Robot ships that come into orbit. My navigator will also send pictures of the Robot ships so you can identify them. My navigator will notify you when the operation is complete as we pass within communication range of you.

Next is "Faraday 5" and "CEBO 1", or (Group 1): Your assignment is to destroy all ships in orbit at the Robot planet. If any try to escape "CEBO 1" will give chase and destroy them. If our coordination goes off as I expect, all of the ships will be destroyed before they even know we are there.

Next is "Faraday 2" and "Faraday 3", or (Group 2) your assignment is to destroy the Robot ships on the ground. There are as many on the ground as there are in orbit. When you finish you can help "Faraday 5" and "CEBO 1" if they need help, or vice-versa.

Next is "Faraday 1" my assignment is to destroy the Robot complex building where the alleged Smart machine resides.

The point here is this—No Robot ship survives, nor does the Smart machine. At the end of the mission General Lesson will be in command to return you home, are there any questions."

"Faraday 2" Captain: "Do you expect any problems sir?"

John: "No, I don't, we will all attack at the same time when I give the order to "Fire". Once we destroy their ships it is essentially over, they have nowhere to go. If you find large groups of Robots on the surface you can destroy them also."

Any more questions? If not return to your "Bullets" and my navigator will send you the coordinates you need. We will be leaving in 10 minutes. The Captains got up and went back to their "Bullets" Izzy stopped and said a few words to John then went to his "Bullet' John got back aboard "Faraday 1", closed the door, and sat down.

John: "Donna, send these coordinates he gave Jack a copy of the coordinates, to help Donna."

To "Faraday 4" and "CEBO 2" the coordinates to "Prema", and pictures of the Robot ships.

To "Faraday 2", "Faraday 3", "Faraday 5", and "CEBO 1" the coordinates for the Robot planet. Let me know when all have been notified, please. Also input the coordinates for us to go back to the Robot planet.

Donna 5 minutes later: "John, all coordinates have been sent and acknowledged."

John: "Donna, tell "Faraday 4" and "CEBO 2" they can go on to "Prema". John watched them head out to "Prema".

Donna, tell "Faraday 2", Faraday 3", Faraday 5", and "CEBO 1" to keep 1 mile distant from each other and follow us to the Robot planet." Donna sent the request,
Donna: "All acknowledged the message."
John: "If we are ready to go Sgt. Full power ahead."

Sgt. Carter pushed the throttle forward.
Twenty minutes later all "Bullets" were in orbit of the Robot planet.

John: "Sgt. Carter, your target is the light blue building in the middle of the industrial complex."
Donna: "Put all the "Bullets" on speaker please." Donna nodded.
John: "Bullets please acknowledge radio check,
"Faraday 2", "Faraday 2 acknowledge"
"Faraday 3", "Faraday 3 acknowledge"
"Faraday 5", "Faraday 5 acknowledge"
"CEBO 1", "CEBO 1" acknowledge"
Faraday 1, 2, 3, 5 and "CEBO 1" Lock on to your targets.

Just a reminder for each group shooting at the ships, cross connect your firing systems so the systems will not pick the same targets to shoot at.
Group 1 locked on targets.
Group 2 locked on targets.
Good luck Gentlemen.
Starting a 3 count, 3, 2, 1, "FIRE."
The 5 "Bullets "Opened fire on their targets.

John: "Sgt. Carter, keep firing until your target is glowing red and burning fiercely.

John watched the screen as the ships in space exploded one after another until they were gone, the debris from the explosions started to drift into the atmosphere and burn up, the ships on the ground started to explode taking out other ships with the debris. The last ships were finished off. The light blue building was no longer 4 stories tall; it was now a red-hot fiercely burning basement."

John: "Well done Captains."
John took has cell phone out of his pocket and called Izzy,
Izzy answered: "Great plan John."
John: "It is over now, go ahead and take your people
home. We will be leaving here after I talk to the survivors
on the ground, after that I will head to Prema to talk to
their survivors and see if the "Bullets" there had any
problems, then send them home also, thanks for the help,
make sure you tell everyone they did a great job."
Izzy: "Ok John, have a safe trip." And Izzy disconnected.
John: "Sgt. Carter take us back to the surface where
we were before, please." John got up and opened the back
wall "doorway" again. Sgt. Carter took them back to the
same spot as before. Kaylon and John went through the
"doorway" and into the building. There were a few people
still there, one of them was Hebber, he walked over to
John: "We saw the space debris thank you, John did you
find the light blue building?"
John: "We destroyed all the ships in space and on the
planet, the light blue building is a smoldering fire pit, we
left the industrial complex alone, I thought there might be
something there that would help you rebuild."
Hebber: "Oh, that is wonderful news."
John: "We belong to a Council of planets, when you
get back on your feet, with spacecraft or the "VOID" we
will get together and talk, in the mean time we will look
in on you occasionally as we pass your planet in the
"VOID". We wish you a peaceful recovery."
Kaylon and John waved goodbye and went back into the
"Bullet" John turned the wall "doorway" off.
John: "Donna set a course for "Prema" please."
Donna did so and nodded to Sgt. Carter, they were on the
way to "Prema". Less than an hour later they were at
"Prema" the two "Bullets" were still there watching."
John: "Donna let's get the two ships on the speaker
please." The two "Bullets" came over the cabin speaker."

John: "This is "Faraday 1" did you have any trouble here?"

'Faraday 4": "The Captain spoke up: ", We had 4 Robot ships show up and we destroyed them without any problems."

John: "That's great news, the rest of the "Bullets" were sent home and you both can follow, we will be right behind you after I talk to someone on the surface. Great job guys."

"CEBO 2": "Thanks John, great plan, we will see you later."

The two "Bullets" started to move away.

John: "Sgt. Carter take us down to the surface to the area we were if you can find it." John got up and turned on the wall "doorway" again. They watched as Sgt. Carter brought them to the same location. There were people still taking care of the wounded. John stepped through the "doorway" Gorton saw him come through the "doorway" and walked over to John."

John: "I just stopped to tell you the Robots won't bother you any more, all of their ships have been destroyed."

Gorton: "We watched the debris burn up in our atmosphere. We thank you."

John: "Someday we will meet again, until then good luck. John turned and went back through the "doorway", he watched as Gorton went back to helping the wounded. It is a shame we could not do more for them, they are a strong people." John turned off the wall "doorway" and sat down. John looked at his watch: "Hey why don't we end this mission, set a course for "CEBO" and heat up and finish off that wonderful food that Johnny and Larry made for us, all in favor raise your hand?" Johnny and Larry headed to the kitchen.

John: "Donna, set a course for "CEBO" to drop off Kaylon please." Donna did so and nodded to Sgt. Carter. Then they all went into the kitchen. After eating they went back to the main cabin. A few minutes later they arrived at "CEBO" John opened the door for Kaylon and Kayla walked up the ramp into the cabin. John gave her a hug and she gave Kaylon a hug: "Welcome home Father." Kayla stayed around for a few minutes and talked to her old friends. Then she and Kaylon left the "Bullet". John closed the door and they went on to his workshop. At his workshop John opened the door and told Jack and Donna, he would drop them off at the moon entrance, they said ok and waited in the golf cart. Sgt. Carter came over to John: "Carla wants to move to an apartment on "Faraday's" moon. She loved the idea, Thank you John."

John: "Well that's great, listen you take the boys home and we will swap the "Bullet" tomorrow. Come by the workshop in the morning. John walked down the ramp and waved at the Marines. He took Jack and Donna to "Faraday's" moon and went home to Lora who was very glad to see him.

Next morning workshop 08:00:

John was working on an experiment he had planned to check out before. He was using an old flashlight casing. He started by drilling a small hole in the back top of the casing, he inserted a small piece of lite green plastic into the hole with a little glue on it. He had put a reflector at the rear of the casing facing forward, he then slid a round 2 in. cylinder of the new light generating material into the casing, it fit up against the reflector in the rear. He had another reflector he had drilled a 3/8 in hole in the center. This reflector would face the other reflector. He then glued a slice of synthetic ruby just slightly larger than 3/8 of an inch around and 1/16 of an inch thick over the hole on the back of the second reflector.

John had made a trigger system that covered the ruby with a cap that had a layer of tin foil inside. He checked the trigger and made sure the cap fit snuggly on the piece of ruby. He tested the trigger several times until he was satisfied it worked properly.

John out loud: "I have to be careful, if this thing works, it could be very dangerous."

"What could be dangerous? ": asked Bob as he came into the workshop from the house. John jumped. He had not expected Bob.

Bob: "Sorry, I didn't mean to scare you." John laughed.

John: "I am about to test an idea I had before we went on our last journey." John set up a 1/2 in. steel plate in front of the "doorway", the plate was tilted down to the floor of the "VOID", and had a 1 in. piece of wood attached with a 1 in. separation between the wood and the steel plate. Bob handed John a box with plastic orange bar holders and a box of the new orange bars that his company had made for John after John had asked for them.

John: "Oh great, just in time. He set the box on the worktable and took out one bar holder. He picked up a tube of super glue, applied some to the bar holder and pressed the bar holder onto the top of the flashlight cylinder facing to the rear. Bob was fascinated, he had no idea what John was up to. John held the bar holder to the flashlight for a full 30 seconds. He let up the pressure on the bar holder and checked if it was solidly glued, it was glued fast to the flashlight cylinder. John repeated the same steps two more times to each side of the flashlight. When he finished, he looked at the flashlight cylinder. It had 3 orange bar holders, one on top and one on each side. Then he looked at Bob: "How's everything going at Johnson Lite Corp?"

Bob: "Things couldn't be better, we have almost more orders than we can fill, the flashlights have been a big seller on "Faraday's" moon, but the big buyer is the government of course. So exactly what are you making to test?"

John: "We are about to test it." John took one of the orange bars and shoved it into the bar holder on top of the flashlight casing, the small green light on the rear of the casing lit up.

Bob watched with intrigue: "No light came out the front."

John: "That's right, so far so good." Now Bob was really curious. John walked over to the open "doorway" and pointed the flashlight at the center of the steel plate and pulled the trigger. A white spot appeared in the steel plate. John let it shine for a few seconds. He let go of the trigger and moved his hand closer to where the white spot was, he felt a lot of heat. "Perfect": John said.

Bob: "You have made some kind of gun?" John took two more of the orange bars and shoved them into the empty bar holders on his now "GUN". The small green light was now a very bright green. He walked back to the open "doorway", pointed the "GUN" at the steel plate and pulled the trigger, the once white light was now a deep blue color and quickly burned a perfect 3/8 in. hole through the steel plate and the wood and caught the wood on fire. John quickly put out the fire.

Bob: "Whoa, you have made yourself a ray gun."
John: "One more test to do." John moved the steel plate stand into the "VOID", and removed the three orange bars and put them in his shirt pocket. He noticed the small green light was still lit, but not as bright. Again, he stepped in front of the steel plate, targeted the upper right side of the steel plate and pulled the trigger. A white light appeared on the steel plate and slowly turned the plate red hot. John stopped and inserted one of the orange bars he had brought with him. Again, he stepped in front of the steel plate, pointed at the steel plate that was now just turning lite red and pulled the trigger. A beam of blue light came out and immediately turned the steel white hot. John let up on the trigger, pulled the other two orange bars out of his pocket and shoved them into place on the

"GUN", again he pulled the trigger, this time a very dark blue beam of light immediately burned a hole through the steel and wood, set the wood on fire again and started to melt the "VOID" floor. He let up on the trigger.
Bob, "That was incredible."

Sgt. Carter spoke up: "That sure was, John what have you invented this time?" John saw Sgt. Carter standing off a small distance, he could see the "Faraday 1" and the "Faraday 2" parked in the "VOID".
John: "Oh, it was just a thought I had, I was surprised it actually worked. Just then Izzy appeared from the "Faraday2" "Bullet".

John: "Well, I have one more test to do."
Izzy: "I can hardly wait to see this one."
John removed the steel plate with the wood attached and took it back into the workshop. He came back with two steel plates and another stand; he replaced the original steel plate and attached the second steel plate to the second stand, and asked Bob to take the second stand and put it 30 feet further out. Bob did so and came back.
John lined up the first steel plate with the second one, he took careful aim at the center of the steel plate and pulled the trigger and counted 1,2 and let up on the trigger. They all walked to the second plate and saw the perfect 3/8 hole in the center of the plate.

Izzy: "John we tested the Robot energy weapon you sent me. It was not anywhere near as powerful as what I just saw."
John: "It seems to work well outside the "VOID" by adding three orange bars, to the case, that was my original intent, I was just curious about whether it would work as well inside the void. The nice thing is just adding the three orange bars is enough to make it a formidable laser weapon outside the "VOID" with again, no batteries.

Izzy: "Well, I know someone that will like the laser pistol, that would be "Uncle Sam"."

John: "Izzy, Let's do this, you are still testing and installing the Transceiver, correct? "

Izzy: "Testing yes, we have not installed any more than the ones you did."

John: "Bob, you start the paperwork to file a co-patent for the Transceiver for Faraday Corp and whoever came up with the electronics for it, Izzy can get that information for you. Izzy nodded at Bob. Do the paperwork and I will sign for Faraday Corp, Bob, you also file a patent through Johnson Lite Corp for the flashlights and the laser system pistol."

Bob: "I like it, what are you going to call the laser gun?"

John thinking: "How about The BR laser system pistol, and when the patents come through you will manufacture the "Transceivers", the flashlights, and the laser system pistols."

Bob: "That sounds great, what does the BR stand for?"

John smiling: "The **B**uck **R**odgers laser system pistol, Sgt. Carter, what is your opinion of the pistol name?"

Sgt. Carter laughing: "I love it."

John: "Bob, I believe you are going to need a special division to serve our military." I will get the company attorney to set that up for you.

Bob: "That sounds great."

John: "Izzy can I speak to you outside of the workshop a minute please. John and Izzy left the workshop and stood in the back yard.

John: "Izzy, when do you retire?"

Izzy: "I can retire in 60 days if I want to turn in my papers, but I wasn't going to put in my papers, why?"

John smiling: "Bob is going to start a new division to serve our military, he will need an experienced ex-military Officer with connections as his CEO, would you know where he could find such an ex-military Officer?"

Izzy looked at John: "John, I don't know what to say?"

John: "Well, you think about it. Bob will be manufacturing the flashlights, laser pistols, and the "Transceivers", he needs someone like you to get it done correctly. Besides, it might be fun. Can you imagine building and testing a laser rifle for a tank, or naval vessel."

Izzy eyes glazed over thinking about a laser rifle: "I don't have to think about it, the answer is YES."

John smiled: "Put in your paperwork and let me know, then I will tell Bob who his next division CEO is going to be."

They both walked back into the workshop. Izzy and Sgt. Carter got into the "Faraday 2" and left."

John picked up the laser gun, he removed the three orange bars and handed the gun to Bob, show this to your flashlight guy, here's what it needs.

First: "A new trigger operation, maybe one that pulls the cap over the ruby downward, the cap works with the tin foil inside, stay with that theme, the trigger can be located further back on the cylinder, see if he can come up with a better trigger, the trigger cannot interfere with the seal of the front reflector, no light must pass around the front reflector. Look inside the front, the trigger must cover the ruby so it will not leak light through the hole, the cylinder size is ok.

Second: The small green led size lens at the rear is necessary to see if the inside of the gun is lit.

Third: The case can be plastic, the reflectors just need to be very shiny, metal reflectors will probably work best.

Fourth: Put a screw on front plastic lens with a 1/2-inch hole in the center. Bring me the first draft I will test it and see if it is ok."

Bob finished his notes: "Ok, I got it, I will get this to my flashlight guy, thanks John, you know the perfect guy to be the CEO of the new division would be Izzy, I don't know if he would be interested though."

John smiling: "Don't worry about that now, I'm sure we can find the right person for your new CEO."

Bob: "Alright, I will see you Monday at work." John and Bob left for the house.

CHAPTER THIRTEEN

"The Searchers"

Monday 08:00

John was working on a serious new best high game on the "PINBALL" machine. His last ball just went through the flippers, he looked at the score, it was his best score to date. John went to his desk and got a pen, and marked the new score on the piece of paper he had taped to the glass back section. Bob walked into the office.

Bob: "Oh, you finally got a best score, that old one had the best of you for a while."

John: "Is there something you want or are you here to just spoil my Monday?"

Bob chuckling: "NASA sent me over, they have spotted a large object apparently heading straight towards you."

John: "Did they say what it is?"

Bob: "No, it was too far away yet, but they did say it was about a week away."

John: "Well, tell NASA to wait until Thursday and if they can tell then what it looks like send me over a picture."

Bob said ok and left.

John went back to another game of "PINBALL"

Thursday 10:00

Bob came bounding into John's office waving a picture in his hand: "NASA gave me a picture, you need to look at this, he handed it to John."

John looked at the picture, then at the stars around it.

Bob: "It is just like the "Greys" big black ship."
John thinking turning his head sideways: "Actually it isn't."
Bob: "What do you mean?"
John: "This ship is at least a third bigger than the "GREYs" ship and according to where the stars behind it are, it is coming from the wrong direction; did NASA say when it will be here?"
Bob: "Yes, Tomorrow afternoon about noon, do I call everyone to board the "Bullet"?" What are we going to do?"
John: "We are going to do nothing, but wait for it to get here."
Bob: "I don't understand."
John smiling: "You will, and I will be expecting a guest in the morning."
Bob: "John, who is coming, who?"
John: "You will just have to wait and see. John closed his eyes and sent a message to Kayla. Bob, have you heard anything on the new laser pistol yet? Bob said the first one will be ready late Friday afternoon or Saturday morning. As soon as I get it, I will bring it by your house. Ok, great how about some lunch?"
Bob: "Sounds great." and they went to lunch.
    Friday Morning 08:30
John is standing at the window looking down at the dock. He watched as Jack and Donna got off the boat and went into the building. Jenny came to the office door and said: "You have a visitor" John continued to watch Jack and Donna disappear through the entrance, without turning around John said to Jenny: "Send "Toby" in please."
Toby: "Toby is already in John." John turned around to see Toby standing in the doorway: Come on in, and sit down."

Toby:" You were expecting me, how?" John smiling
pushed the spacecraft picture over to Toby. Toby laughed
and said: "Yes, they are coming here today."
John: "That's not all, you are about to get a big bear hug."
Toby looked puzzled then Kayla came into the office,
waited for Toby to stand up, and gave him a big bear hug.

John handed Kayla a comm badge: "Ok, how has
everybody been, Kayla you start?" Kayla started to talk
about the last month for her and Topa. She went on for
almost an hour. John and Toby enjoyed every minute of
it. Then Toby started to talk about his last month for more
than half an hour." Jenny brought them all a glass of
orange juice. they sipped the juice and talked some more.
John called Jenny and asked her to call Jack and Donna
to come up to the office. A few minutes later they arrived.
Donna supplied the hugs and Jack smiled and watched
with John.

John: "About noon a Searcher ship will land here
somewhere, Toby interjected, he said the ship will land on
the large lake about a mile from the dome. Well, Jack I
guess we could use your houseboat to go to the ship."
Jack: "That could be fun." They all sat and talked till
11:30.

John: "Ok, let's all go down to the dock and wait for
the ship to land." They all left the office and walked to the
dock. A few minutes later a large spacecraft appeared in
the sky and started to descend towards the large lake. As
it got lower and lower, they all got on the houseboat. John
and Toby took care of the lines and Jack headed down the
inlet toward the large lake. As they rounded the corner of
the inlet the large ship came into view, it was floating
about a foot above the water. As the houseboat got closer
a ramp like the one on Toby's spacecraft, but larger
opened up and went down and stopped about a foot into
the water. The houseboat pulled up to the ramp and two
tie-up posts rose up from the ramp door. John and Toby

tied up the houseboat. As they finished a tall humanoid of almost 7 feet appeared at the top of the ramp. Toby yelled: "Ander Father, Toby jumped from the houseboat onto the ramp and ran to the humanoid who had now gone to his knees with his arms open. Toby disappeared into the humanoid's chest and arms. The others carefully left the houseboat and walked up the ramp to Toby who was still hugging the humanoid. Big tears were streaming down Toby's face as was Donna and Kayla. Finally, Toby stopped hugging and turned to the group.
Toby: "This is my Father Ander, he introduced all of them to Ander."

Ander in English: "Thank you for coming to our ship, I would like to give you a tour of the ship and for you to have lunch with us." They all followed Ander into the ship. The tour took almost an hour, it would be talked about for years. After the tour Ander took them to a room with a table large enough for them all to sit and have lunch. After lunch Ander stood up: "We came here to "Faraday's" moon to thank John Faraday for the kindness he showed the people of the planet "Skimm" and also of course for fixing the problem and eliminating the cause.

We were on the way to the planet you call the "Robot" planet to take care of that problem, and then we discovered you had already taken care of the problem. We also thank you for that. I was happy we were back here in this galaxy, I got to see my son again, so it was all worth it. We left this galaxy many years ago after we accomplished our goal here. Do you have any questions?" John asked: "What goal was that my I ask?"

Ander: "We spend our lives seeding planets with life. The planets are the ones you call Goldilocks planets. When we left "Skimm" years ago, the planet was already habitable for what you call Humanoid life, we just had to collect it from Earth. We gave the "Greys" as you call them a place of their own, to live and grow with our help in their beginning. When that was finished our goal in this Galaxy was finished and we moved on to the next Galaxy, the one we are in now." We would check on civilizations occasionally after they were seeded to see if nature had taken its course."

John: "How many planets were seeded in this Galaxy?"
Ander: "Many thousands, they only required helping what life was already there or seeding the planet with Humanoid life. "
John: "That does explain the large number of Humanoid species in our sector of space."
Ander: "I know what question you want to ask next, but do you really want to know?"

John: "Humans have insatiable curiosity; I am one of those and I would like to hear the story of Earth."
Ander: "Alright, your Earth was seeded three times. The planet lost its life forms several times through different calamities. The last one was the large asteroid that collided with the planet 65 million of your years ago. It wiped out the reptilian life form that was evolving. We reseeded the planet again. We waited and waited and finally after about 6 million years passed Humans emerged on your planet. Ander looked at Kayla, and a few million years before that we seeded the planet "CEBO". We watched "Earth" and "CEBO" develop for thousands of century's as we continued to seed other planets in this sector. We knew that someday you would meet and form a strong bond. We are extremely proud of your actions in this sector and we see a long-lasting bond between the two of your peoples. I hope that the answer is the one you were hoping for. We have enjoyed your company, but we have to leave. You are now on your own. To use one of your sayings "We have other fish to fry", Ander smiled.

John: "Ander thank you for everything, who knows, someday we might meet again in the other Galaxy."

Ander: "John, of that I have no doubt." Ander led them back to the ramp and the houseboat. Ander and "TOBY" spent a couple of minutes talking, then they all got on the houseboat and went back into the lake, they all waved as the spacecraft lifted up and disappeared into the sky. Jack took them back to the dock at the office building.

Monday Morning Johns workshop 07:30:

John was cleaning up the workbench from the experimenting he and Bob were doing last week. Bob popped in from the house, he was carrying a small box, he sat it down on the workbench.

John: "What's in the box?"

Bob: "It is the first copy of the laser gun I sent to my guy that makes my lights. Open it up." John picked up the box, grabbed a box cutter and opened the box. He pulled out the new gun. It was plastic, had a very nice trigger, it had three orange bar holders just where he wanted them, he screwed off the end and looked inside. John stuck in his fingers and removed the reflectors; they were shiny metal and the one up front had the ruby re-glued just where the other one was. He pulled the trigger several times, the mechanism was built into the trigger housing that could be removed if necessary.

John: "This is exactly the idea I had in mind; all the improvements are here. John picked up a small ruler and measured the new size for the cylinder of cone material and cut a piece off the roll he had. He inserted the new roll, placed the front reflector into the gun barrel and it locked into place. John screwed the front of the gun back on, he then looked at the hole in the plastic in the front cover. John walked over and turned on the "doorway", Bob put that steel plate back into the "VOID" and we will test it out. Bob retrieved the steel plate that was sitting over by the wood pile and carried it into the "VOID". John picked up an orange bar from the box on the workbench and shoved it into the top holder on the gun.

He watched as the green light on the end started to glow. He put the other two orange bars into the holders on both sides of the gun. John stepped up to the steel plate and pointed the gun at one corner of the steel plate. Before he pulled the trigger, he turned and looked at Bob: "Bob would you like to test the gun?"

Bob: "Absolutely I would." John gave the gun to Bob." Bob looked the gun over and stepped up to the steel plate, he picked out the same corner that John was going to shoot.

John: "'Just a short burst to be safe." Bob pulled the trigger; a dark blue beam shot out of the gun and drilled a perfect hole in the steel plate.

Bob: "That was so cool." He handed the gun back to John: "John removed the three orange bars and put them back into the box on the workbench, then he re-inspected the gun. Everything looked fine, no burning or singe marks inside the front of the gun.

John: "Bob, I think we have a winner. Order a couple of boxes of the guns, I will start making a dozen or so ruby slices. You can give this one to Izzy, when he tests it ask him to test it on a solid block of metal maybe a foot thick, we need to know if the beam will sustain a continuous trigger pull. They might need to put the block of metal in water. It also needs to be tested on thick concrete."

Bob: "He will get the gun tomorrow."

John: "Let's get in the golf cart and go to work." John and Bob did just that.

Saturday 5 days later:

John was in his workshop again cleaning up the mess he made on the workbench cutting the synthetic ruby rod for the new plastic guns. Lora came into the workshop:

"John, Bob and another man are in the Florida room eating breakfast."
John: "Who is the other man?"

Lora: "I don't know, I have never seen him before."
John: "Ok, I will be right in." John finished his clean up and went to the Florida room. He opened the door to find Bob and Izzy eating breakfast that Lora had made them. Lora was also sitting at the table.

John: "Well, I didn't know this food shop was open for breakfast after (John looked at his watch) 9:30 am."
Bob smiling: "Lora asked if we wanted breakfast and it would have been rude to say no." John sat down next to Lora across from Bob and Izzy.

John: "And you Izzy, you just went along with it, huh."
Izzy: "No, actually I did not have breakfast yet, and thank you very much Lora." Lora trying to keep from laughing: "You are welcome Mr. Izzy." They all laughed.

John: "So, for what do we owe this visit?"
Bob: "Well, I brought a case of sixteen laser pistols, and a box of 50 orange bars. They are sitting on the floor over by the door, and my light guy noticed the synthetic ruby on the original gun and because we have given him so much business, he had a ruby rod cut to the same specs as yours. He said it was necessary to make sure the trigger cap fit perfectly he made the trigger and the front reflector a single removable assembly. "

John: "Well since he doesn't know what they are for, that will work for me, now I don't have to cut any more, *like I did,* this morning."
Bob: "Oh, sorry about that."
Lora: "What is a laser pistol?" John: "Do you really want to know?"

Lora: "Yes, you never tell me or show me anything."
John got up and went over to the big box, opened the top, and took out one box from inside and sat in on the table,

he then opened the small box and took out 3 orange bars. John opened the laser pistol box and looked over the pistol. He noticed the button lock on the trigger assembly. He pressed the button and the trigger assembly opened and dropped down slightly and was able to be pulled out of the pistol, the front reflector attached to the assembly came out a slot in the barrel. John looked over the trigger assembly and nodded.

John looked inside the barrel: "Oh yes, this was a good idea. John inserted the trigger assembly back into the pistol and pulled the trigger a few times: Bob go to the workshop and get one of the steel plates, the roll of the white new cone material, and a pair of scissors laying on the workbench please." Bob went to the workshop and returned with the three items. John again removed the trigger assembly and unscrewed the front cover and laid them on the table, he then cut a piece of the new cone material, rolled it up and shoved it down the barrel of the gun until it stopped up against the rear reflector. He marked the end sticking out and withdrew the cone material., he then cut off the cone material with the scissors and put the cut piece back into the barrel, he checked to be sure it was seated properly. He reinserted the trigger assembly and screwed the front cover back on, and handed the laser pistol to Lora: "Now take a good look at it, look it over it is completely safe. Lora looked at the pistol: "Is this some kind of gun?"

John: "Very good, (he picked up the 3 orange bars), now bring the gun and come with me. John walked into the back yard. Bob holding the steel plate and Izzy followed; they weren't going to miss this. John pointed to Bob and Izzy: "Izzy stay on the sidewalk; Bob, take the steel plate and put it on the ground in front of me." Bob did so, then stepped back onto the sidewalk with Izzy. John: "Lora come over next to me on the grass." Lora did.

John handed Lora the gun: "Put the gun in your hand
and move it around, pull the trigger and get the feel of it,
go ahead it is still safe right now. Lora did so and
wondered now if she should have kept quiet. John took
the laser pistol from Lora and inserted the 3 orange bars.
He noticed the green light was bright green. I am going to
give the gun back to you, do not point it at anyone, point
it at the steel plate on the ground and pull the trigger just
for a second."

Lora carefully pointed the pistol towards the ground
and then at the steel plate laying in front of her. Then she
pulled the trigger, a dark blue beam of light drilled into
the steel plate and started the grass underneath the plate
on fire. She jumped, John raised her arm up with the gun
pointed into the sky, and he stepped on the fire and put it
out. He released Lora's arm: "That was fun and pointed
the pistol at the steel plate and shot three more holes into
the steel plate." Bob and Izzy started laughing, John a
little stunned took back the laser pistol and removed the 3
orange bars.

Lora was laughing: "Thank you for the lesson and
later I want to know how that laser pistol works please."
John just nodded, Lora went back into the house and
disappeared. John, Bob and Izzy went back into the
Florida room and sat down.

Izzy: "John we tested the laser pistol you made; we
couldn't find any material it wouldn't burn through. We
tried the foot-thick steel, 10 feet of concrete, we even
fired it through water at a steel plate 50 feet away. No
matter what we did it bored through all the material. That
pistol is more powerful than our own laser on the 'Bullets
and requires no power. One of your concerns was the
length of time you could hold the trigger down. Our laser
on the "Bullets" can only operate for 5 seconds, until auto
shutdown. We took the laser pistol to a mountain that was
solid granite and held the trigger for a full minute, it

drilled a hole in the granite that was more than a mile deep and the pistol never even got warm. Right now, we still do not know how far the laser will go inside the "VOID" and still burn through the material, that is our next test. I'm thinking that normally only two orange bars are needed to operate the gun with more safety. But this weapon is extremely dangerous. We will be putting 3 of these pistols and 9 orange bars into all the "Bullets" when testing is done."

John: "Izzy thank you for that report, I'm kinda sorry now I had the idea to build it. By the way, why are you with Bob today?"

Izzy: "We met at a meeting very early this morning and Bob said he was going to visit you, so I hung out with Bob to give you the report on the laser pistol." Bob and Izzy got up to leave, John walked them to the front door and said goodbye.

Lora came out of the back bedroom and stood next to John in the hallway 10 feet from the front door: "Was that the General Leeson you call Izzy." John nodded yes.

John: "Well what is for lunch?"

Lora: "It is whatever you want to make, Donna and I are going shopping, she will be here any minute. The doorbell rang and Lora tilted her head and pointed to the front door, she walked to the door and opened it, Donna and Jack were standing on the front porch. Lora went out the door and Donna followed her to the car. They got in and disappeared down the street.

Jack was still standing on the front porch: "I thought I would come and hang out with you." John and Jack went to the Florida room. Jack watched John cut two more pieces of the new core material and load it into two more guns. Then he took Jack into the back yard and let him test both of the new laser pistols. Jack was very excited to do so. John put the three new laser pistols, and the big box and the small box of orange bars into the workshop. He

decided he would put the three pistols into "Faraday 1" later. Jack and John sat and watched TV until the women came home. Donna and Jack stayed for dinner and left about 10:00 pm. John and Lora went to bed.
Sunday morning 09:00

John and Lora were in the Florida room eating breakfast and talking. John was explaining to Lora how and why the laser pistol worked and that it was his idea to build it, and he felt a little bad about building it.
Lora: "I don't think it was a bad idea, after all you had no idea, it would be so good."
The doorbell rang, Lora got up to see who I was. She came back with Bob.
John: "I thought we got rid of you and Izzy."

Bob:" Izzy sent me back, he said two of the "Bullets", "Faraday 5" and "CEBO 1" may be in trouble. They lost contact with them an hour ago. They were on a routine mission on the western edge of our sector installing "Transceivers". The last message they got was garbled, but they said they were under fire. There has been no contact since. Izzy is sending the squad here. Your vehicle is the only one that is operational all the others are down for minor repairs or updates. The squad in being delivered by Izzy in "Faraday 4" that can be driven but is still not operational. Jack and Donna will be here shortly.

John: "Alright, go open the workshop "doorway" for Jack and Donna. Bob headed to the workshop and returned.
Lora: "What is west of our "doorway" station?"

John: "Nothing, that area has not been explored, there is one Council planet out there but they do not have "VOID" access. Probably that is the reason the two "Bullets" were installing "Transceivers" out there. Well, we will get the latest information from the squad when they arrive. Five minutes later Donna and Jack arrived through the workshop. John informed them what was happening. They all went through the workshop to wait for Izzy, including Lora. Izzy arrived 10 minutes later with the squad in "Bullet". They got off "Faraday 4". Sgt. Carter opened "Faraday 1" and the squad boarded the vehicle and started to bring up the systems. Donna and Jack also boarded "Faraday 1". John, Bob and Lora were still standing in the "VOID".

Bob: "Are we waiting for something?"
John: "Yes, Kayla is 5 minutes out, we are waiting for her to get here." John walked up the ramp of" Faraday 4" to talk to Izzy. A few minutes later John came out of "Faraday 4" and Izzy closed the door and left. Kayla pulled up in her golf cart and parked it next to John's golf cart. She gave Bob, and John, and Lora a hug.
Kayla smiling, "Thank you for waiting for me, I came because my Father is on "CEBO 1"."
John: "What is Kaylon doing on "CEBO 1"?"
Kayla: "He said he was bored and got a ride on their mission."
John: "Wonderful, I'm sure it will all work out."
Lora: "All you guys be careful, Kayla you keep these two boys straight."
Kayla holding Lora's and Bob's hand: "Don't worry, John is with us, everything will be alright. "

John, Bob, and Kayla boarded "Faraday 1". John waved to Lora and closed the cabin door. John was about to sit down: "Oh, I forgot something, he opened the cabin door, walked down the ramp past Lora and went into the workshop, he picked up the three boxes of laser pistols and the 9 orange bars and returned to the "VOID". He gave Lora a kiss and went back to the cabin. He waved to Lora and again closed the cabin door and sat down. He placed the big box and the small box on the floor next to his seat.

John: "First everyone put on a comm badge please, John watched as the comm badges were displayed. For those of you that need to updated on the situation, "Faraday 5" and "CEBO 1" may be in some trouble. They were out on the western edge of our sector installing "Transceivers". We believe they installed three and were on the way to install number 4 when all contact was lost. The last contact was garbled but may have said "we are under fire",
Donna, please verify "Transceivers" with serial numbers of the 300 series. Put the map on the screen please."
Donna input instructions and the serial numbers 000300,301,302 showed active and blinking.

John: "It looks like the information we have is correct, they were on the way to install 000303 when they ran into some kind of problem. Donna input a course to Transceiver 000302 please, Sgt. Set speed at 200 mph."
Donna nodded at Sgt. Carter. And he pushed the throttles forward.
John: "Since we are going into an unknown situation, I want everyone to wear a sidearm. Sgt. Carter if one or two of your Marines would kindly help those of us that don't have one, get one."
Sgt. Carter: "Johnny and Larry, take the ladies and Jack to the gun locker and outfit them with their weapons please."

John got up and walked over to the cabin storage opened it and took out his sidearm that he had stored there weeks ago. It was in a large belt and with the gun backwards on his left side, he put it on and adjusted the belt. He said hello to Johnny and Larry as they passed by him to Jack, Kayla, and Donna. A few minutes later Kayla and Donna came back to the cabin with a weapon on like Johns. John was watching the look on Bob's face as the two women came back into the cabin, he leaned over to Bob and whispered: "Nothing like a weapon to make a woman look even better is there." Bob just nodded. John chuckled. Jack and the Marines came back next.

John watched the big screen as the "Faraday 1" and the blinking 000302 got closer: "Donna how long to 000302?"

Donna: "35 minutes.", Donna smiling put a descending clock up on the big screen. John nodded and smiled at her.

John: "10 minutes left, anyone that needs the restroom, now is the time." Jack, Donna, Bob and Kayla got up and went to the back. John looked over at the Marines, they smiled and Larry said: "We are good." Sgt. Carter looked at John and smiled. Bob, Jack, Kayla, and Donna came back and took their seats.

Donna: "5 minutes to the Transceiver."

John: "Donna, how far are we looking out on radar"

Donna checked her console: "20 miles John."

John: "Thank you that is good."

Donna: "Transceiver 302, fifty feet in front of us."

John looked at the big screen: "No sign of any of the "Bullets", Sgt. Normal speed forward until we see the vehicles on radar, please. "Sgt. Carter pushed the throttle forward. Ten minutes later. Donna: "John, I have two vehicles on my screen, they are ten miles from us."

John: "Bring us within two miles to stay unseen, all lights out please, let's go dark, all weapons ready."

Sgt. Carter acknowledged all weapons ready, going dark."

Donna: "We are two miles out."

John: "Sgt. All stop, Donna let's see what we can see."

Donna brought up the camera on the screen. Both vehicles were visible and something else was familiar, a "doorway" structure.

John: "Donna, let's see the planet please." The camera looked at the pale blue planet. Water and rock, another Earth like planet. Can the cameras get closer to the planet, Donna got closer, an ocean, lakes and cities appeared?

Donna, do we see the "Transceivers" of the two vehicles?" Donna put all the "Transceivers" within 50 miles on screen. John: "Well, I see the two vehicle "Transceivers". Donna go back and put the camera on the two vehicles again." Donna did.

John: "They don't seem to be damaged, can we see who the residents are please, Donna brought up an image of one of the people hiding behind the concrete pillars, they looked human but were tall and thin, like a 5ft. 10 in. human had been stretched to 6ft. 8 inches. Donna contact the two vehicles and put it on speaker please." Donna: "Comm open"

John: "This is "Faraday 1" are you two vehicles just out for a Sunday stroll, come back?" Suddenly a voice cracked over the speaker: "John is that you, this is Kaylon?"

John smiling at Kayla: "Kaylon, yes, we are two miles from you, what is going on?"

Kaylon: "We were out installing "Transceivers" and stumbled on the "doorway" station, we went in for a closer look and got out of range of the last "Transceiver" we installed. When we got to close to the "Doorway" station they started to attack us with small arms fire and small explosive devices. When they realized they couldn't hurt us they stopped firing?"

John: "Have you tried talking to them through the language translator?"

Kaylon: "No, both our translators are inoperative for updates, we left to install the "Transceivers" never thinking we would run into anyone that would require the translator we didn't want to hurt them so we assumed someone would come and see why we haven't communicated."

John looked at Bob: Bob, what rule of mine did they break?"

Bob frowning: "Always be prepared." John nodded, everyone laughed.

John: "Kaylon, we are coming in and we will park next to you. Sgt. Carter please lay us up alongside of the other two vehicles"

Sgt. Carter with a smile: "Yes, sir." The "Faraday 1" pulled up next to the other vehicles. The unknown owners of the "doorway opened fire on the "Faraday 1" with the same result, no damage."

John: "Donna, please point the language translator at our almost new friends and let's see if we can understand each other, on speaker please and connect to the other two "Bullets" please." They listened to the garbled talk until it turned to English."

Donna: "John, you are on."

John: "My friends, we have had the ability to harm you since we met, we chose not to, we are from the Council of planets, your neighbors, and we would love to talk to you. Are any of your planet leaders available to talk, just talk to us we can understand you?"

Unknown people: "We have sent for someone to talk to you."

John: "Thank you, would you mind if we came out and walked around a little, next to our vehicle?"

Unknown people: "Alright, but just next to your vehicle."

John: "Thank you. Kayla and Donna, how about a small walk just outside the vehicle with me."

Kayla: "You mean where they could see us?"

John smiling: "Especially where they can see you and Donna."

Donna: "Oh, I get it, ok"

John opened the cabin door, and slowly walked down the ramp, then Kayla and then Donna. John could hear the commotion near the concrete pillars.

John: "Ok, ladies, wave at our new friends. Kayla and Donna did. The noise at the pillars got much louder. Ok ladies, I think we have made some friends you can go back now, thank you." Kayla and Donna waved again then went back into the vehicle, John closed the door. John pressed his comm badge: "Kaylon are you there?"

Kaylon: "Yes, John what have you got planned?" John thinking to himself that Kaylon has gotten to know him too well.

John: "I think we will need a diplomat today; do you know where we can find one?"

Kaylon laughing: "When they are ready to talk, I will join you, where do you want to hold the talks?"

John: "I believe your kitchen table will do just fine, that way we would not have to stay."

Kaylon: "I see, I don't mind, that's a good idea."

A few minutes later three of the unknown people arrived to talk, John, Kaylon, and the "Faraday 5" Captain met them halfway to the vehicles. The three unknown people were given comm badges, Kaylon invited them to his vehicle to talk, they agreed, he led them to the vehicle and they walked up the ramp into the "Bullet", then into the kitchen. They all sat down at the table, the three-unknown people on one side and the three Council of planets representatives on the other.

Kaylon: "My name is Kaylon I am from the planet "CEBO", the man on my left is Captain Trane he is from Earth, and on my right is John Faraday also from Earth. My I ask your names please."

The unknown in the middle: "My name is Trabor, I am the head of the Council of three on our planet. To my left is Turbok and to my right is Larno. The name of our planet is Grinder."

Kaylon: "How long have you had access to what we call the "VOID"?"

Trabor: "About 1 year. We just started to understand how to use it. We had no idea there were other beings in the universe. You said you represent the Council of planets; how many planets is that?"

Kaylon: "At the moment it is 11. To become a Council member, you have to have "VOID" access as you do or Faster than Light spacecraft. All members support each other and if one is attacked for any reason the others respond. We would like you to join the Council but it is not required. If you want to go your own way that is fine, we only wanted you to know we are here. We are exploring this sector that is why we found you. Every once and a while we will check on you to see if you are doing alright. We can show you how to use your "doorways" also. We don't believe anyone owns the "VOID" everyone is free to go as they please. We were installing communication devices in this sector; we have one more to install and we will be gone."

Trabor: "We understand, I see a possible future for your people and ours but right now we have to accept that we are not alone, that will take some time, I'm sure you understand."

Kaylon: "We do understand, we all had the same reaction to discovering we were not alone in the universe. There are many more beings out there that we have not met yet. But it gets easier after a while. Trabor it was nice to meet you and your Council and I hope to speak to you again."

With that the meeting broke up and the Grinders went back to their planet. John suggested that they finish installing their Transceiver about 5 miles away from the Grinders "Doorway". They took that suggestion. After stopping to install the new Transceiver Kaylon and Kayla got to talk a little before John and the crew headed home. Two weeks passed.

Monday
08:30

John was sitting in his office waiting for Bob. Five minutes later Bob came into this office and at down.
Bob: "So, what is going on, anything?"

John: "No, things are kind of boring. I hear all the "Bullets "are finally up and running?"

Bob: "Yes, I talked to Izzy about an hour ago, he said they had made a terrible mistake letting all the "Bullets" be down at the same time. It wasn't planned that way it just happened, he said from now on only 2 "Bullets" can be down at the same time. He also mentioned the "Faraday 1" needed an upgrade of minor stuff and he will send a mechanic to do the upgrades at the workshop, and they will be complete by 10:00."

John looked at his watch, it was 09:30: "Come on Bob, I want to talk to the mechanic before he leaves." Bob and John went down to the parking lot and jumped into the golf cart and headed to the workshop. They got there just as the mechanic finished, the cabin door was still open. The mechanic was a little surprised when they pulled up and stopped.
John got out and walked over to the mechanic, He stuck out his hand and shook the mechanic's hand: I have a question to ask if I may?"
The mechanic: "Yes Mr. Faraday ask me anything."

John: "I was just curious about what upgrades you did?"
The mechanic: "Oh, no upgrades just some regular maintenance, like check for leaking fluids, wipe the windshield, check the windshield micro stainless mesh. stuff like that."

John: "Did everything check out ok?"
The mechanic: "Yes sir Mr. Faraday it did, "Faraday 1" is in top shape
 Bob knew John was leading up to something but it hadn't happened yet.

John: "Let me ask another question, Is the voltage applied to the stainless-steel skin changeable. I know it is a constant 12 volts now?" Bob—thinking here it comes. The mechanic: "Actually yes, at first, we had to change out an electronic board, we got tired of that and instead installed a potentiometer. It allows from 0 volts to 24 volts and you are correct the current voltage is 12 volts. It works like a light dimmer."

John: "Yes, I know what it is and how it works, can you tell me where it is located, I want to test some different setting, and run some experiments?"
The mechanic thought about John's question: "Sure I guess that is alright, the switch is located under the weapons console, let me show you." The mechanic went up the ramp into the cabin and stopped at the front of the weapons console, he moved the chair back out of the way and got on a knee on the floor. John got down with him. The mechanic put two fingers in a small oval hole on the top of the panel and pulled downward, the whole panel opened and swung to the floor: "If you look inside the potentiometer is hanging on the right side just inside the panel he pointed to the small wheel. John looked inside where he was pointing and saw what he wanted to see. John: "Well, thank you for showing me where it was." The mechanic nodded and closed up the panel". He got up and walked down the ramp. John followed him down.

John: "Listen can I give you a lift somewhere?" The mechanic: "No sir, I have a ride coming any minute." As he said that another person in a small cart stopped to pick him up. The mechanic got into the cart and they started to leave. Bob and John heard the mechanic say to the man who picked him up: "That was John Faraday and he asked *me* questions."

Bob: "I assume you got what you wanted to know." John: "But of course I did, it was where I suspected, it turned out to be easier to change than I thought and that's

great. Bob come here in the morning first before we go to
work say 08:00, oh, did you notice the push button they
installed on the outside of the door, John pointed to the
button?"
Bob: "No, what is that for?"
John walked over to the button and pushed it. The ramp
went up and the door closed.
     Bob: "Well isn't that just swell?"
John: "Actually yes, it is, beats the hell out of having to
go to the other side under the bumper to close the door."
     Bob: "Well, does it open the door also?"
John: "Of course not, it just closes it."
Bob: "Ok, see you in the morning." They both walked
through the workshop and into the house, John walked
Bob to the front door and Bob left.
Tuesday 08:00-John's workshop
     John was getting ready to try his experiment, he was
waiting for Bob to show up. Bob came into the workshop.
Bob: "What are we going to try today?"
John: "I want to experiment with the voltage on the skin
of the "Bullet", when they discovered that a small voltage
of 2-3 volts made the vehicle invisible to radar, they then
put twelve volts to the skin and discovered the hull could
not be penetrated. They stopped testing after that. I think
had they continued even better protection might occur.
John handed Bob a small hand sledge hammer. So, follow
me and we will see." John opened the "doorway" and he
and Bob entered the "VOID".
     John: "First I want to see if something works like it
should, I have never tested this. Go press the door open
switch please, John stood in front of the door. Bob handed
the hand sledge hammer back to John and went to the
other side of the "Bullet", reached under the front bumper
and pressed the button he found there. John watched as
the door opened and the ramp started to extend, however
this time the ramp stopped because he was in the way.

Bob came around the end of the "Bullet" to see what John was testing. He saw John standing in front of the door and the ramp partially extended."

Bob: "Were you testing the ramp?"

John: "Yes, I wanted to know if they had installed a sensor to stop the ramp from hitting anyone standing in the way, I guess they did." John moved out of the way of the ramp and the ramp continued to deploy normally, he handed the hand sledge hammer back to Bob and went up the ramp and into the cabin, he went over to the weapons console bent down, inserted two fingers into the slot at the top of the panel and pulled it open and let it lay on the floor. He stood up and powered up the "Bullet" and went to the door, down the ramp and stood next to Bob.

John: "Let's go up front of the "Bullet", John walked to the front of the "Bullet" and Bob followed. Bob, I want you to hit the "Bullet" with the hammer."

Bob took a swing at the center of the "Bullet" below the windshield. Nothing happened, the hammer bounced off.

John: "Now press the hammer against the "Bullet" and tell me what you feel, move it around a little. Bob did so, it feels like it is slippery, not hard at all."

John: "Good, now stay here, I will be right back." John went up the ramp and back to the weapons console. He got down on the floor and reached in and gently pulled out the voltage potentiometer. It was a dial switch made to be inserted into a hole drilled into a panel, there was a rotating wheel and numbers on the wheel from 0 to 24 and the word "Volts" stamped on the middle of the plastic wheel. John could see the holding nut under the wheel that held it tight after inserting it into a hole through a panel. The dial was set on 12 volts, he moved it to 14 volts. John got up and went back to Bob standing in front of the vehicle.

John: "Ok Bob, do the same thing again, just press the hammer into the metal." Bob again pressed the hammer into the "Bullet": It feels about the same, slippery."

John: "Keep pressing.", John looked at the top of the hammer, he could see a small space between the hammer and the hull of the "Bullet". He showed it to Bob. John went back into the cabin and turned the dial to 18 volts., then went back to Bob.

John: "Ok, do it again, John looked at the top of the hammer again, now there was at least an inch from the top of the hammer to the hull, Bob saw it also."
Bob: "Is that some kind of force field forming on the hull?"

John: "Yes, just what I was hoping would happen, one more change to go." John went back into the cabin and bent down and turned the dial to 24 volts. He started to go out the door when he ran into a soft wall, John stepped back and put his hands forward, they stopped at the edge of the door, He pushed into the invisible wall and it just pushed his hands back.

John: "Bob come here and walk up the ramp, Bob come over to the ramp and he got stopped by the invisible wall. Bob, try and force the handle through the force field. Bob tried to push the wood handle through the force field and couldn't do it. John went back to the switch and turned the voltage back to 18 volts. Now try it Bob, Bob was able to come into the cabin."
Bob: "Well, it seems you have once more stumbled onto something important." John went to the console and turned the dial back to 24 volts: Bob, stand back and throw the hammer at the open area of the door, try for the center top. Bob threw the hammer at the force field, the hammer hit the field and dropped straight down to the floor.

John: "Ok, I am lowering the voltage, take the hammer out and look and see how much distance there is between the hammer and the hull. John changed the dial back to 18 volts, and Bob went out, as he did John changed the dial back to 24 volts. In a minute Bob came back to the end of the ramp: "There is now a good 4 inches of space between the hammer and the hull."

John: "One more test, test the hammer on the windscreen." Bob nodded, and went to the front of the "Bullet", he came back and said: "Still 4 inches."

John turned the dial back to 12 volts. John walked down the ramp, took the hammer from Bob and went back into the workshop. He put the hammer back into the tool box under the worktable and sat down. Bob came into the workshop. John was thinking.

John: "I need my hand drill, bits, foil and a rag, my tape writer, black marker and needle-nose pliers, he started with getting the drill out of the tool box, then the drill bits, and the needle-nose pliers. He got the box of tin foil, took out a large sheet and covered the drill with tinfoil keeping the air vents open. He picked up a clean rag and the tape writer from the shelf behind him, all the tools he had gathered, got the black marker from the big plastic cup on the workbench and went back into the "VOID" and entered the "Bullet" cabin. He laid the tools on the floor, picked up the drill and pulled the trigger to see if it worked, it did. John pulled out the volt switch carefully to see how much slack was in it. It had plenty of slack, he removed the plastic dial and laid it on the console top.

John: "Bob where would be a good place to drill a hole in the console top to put the volt switch?" Bob looked at the volt switch and pointed to an empty place on the console top, a small plate 4X4 inches. John looked at the space Bob had pointed out, and then checked under the console to look at the space underneath." I agree Bob."

John opened the drill bits to find the correct size drill to use. He pulled out a drill bit, unscrewed the lock nut on the switch and laid it next to the plastic dial on the console top, he put the drill bit next to the dial post to check the size. It was a good guess on John's part. He put a dot with the marker on the space Bob pointed out, put the needle-nose pliers on the console, put the drill bit in the drill. Bob, take the rag and put it on the floor under the console to pick up any drill mess when I drill the hole. Bob picked up the rag, got down on the floor and placed the rag under the console.

John picked up the drill and proceeded to drill a hole in the console, then put the drill on the floor.
John: "Bob put the switch dial post end up through the hole please and I will start the locknut onto it. "Bob reached inside for the switch and put the dial post up through the hole. John started the lock nut on: "Ok, Bob that is good." Bob stood up out of the way, John reached under the console and held the switch and tightened the lock nut with the needle-nose pliers. After it was tightened good, he put the dial on and adjusted the switch level. He picked up the tape writer and made a label called "Hull Volts" tore off the sticky protection and placed the label on the console above the switch.

John: "What do you think Bob?" Bob: "Looks great, give it a quick test." John turned the dial to 24 volts and told Bob to go to the door and check it. "Bob walked up to the door and pushed out his hands. Bob smiled; the wall was there: "Another victory for TEAM FARADAY." John laughed: "Ok, all I need is to get a picture of the switch for Izzy." He turned the switch back to 12 volts."

John: "Bob, I need to go into the house for may digital camera, I will be right back." John went down the ramp, through the workshop and into the house. Bob sat down in one of the chairs and waited for John. John returned with his camera and took several pictures of the installed switch.

John: "Bob, I will print these and bring them back in a minute, why don't you just sit in that chair." Bob smiled at John and nodded. John returned some minutes later and gave Bob the pictures to give to Izzy.

John: "Give Izzy the pictures and fill him in on what we found."

Bob: "Ok, I will see you tomorrow at work." Bob left the "Bullet", went through the workshop, into the house and home.

Wednesday 08:00

John was on another high game run on the "PINBALL" machine. He was carefully playing his fourth ball with one ball left. Jenny wandered into his office and watched John play. She also loved to play the "PINBALL" machine when John wasn't around, but she had never gotten a really high score like John was about to do. She looked at the piece of paper John had put on the rear of the machine with the high score written on it. John now was very close to another high score, just another few thousand points. As John approached the new high score the "PINBALL" machine went dark, it had powered off.

John: "No, no, no—I was about to make another high score, I had another ball left." He pushed the new game start red button, nothing happened. John turned off the power rocker switch he had installed and then back on, nothing happened. He turned around to see Jenny standing behind him.

John: "Jenny, call the repair number on the side label of the "PINBALL" machine and ask Vinnie to send a repairman please."

Jenny: "I'm sorry John, I will call it in for repair." Jenny left the office. John sat down at his desk. Bob came into his office and sat down in front of John's desk, he looked at John: "What are you bummed out about."

John: "My "PINBALL" machine just broke, just as I was about to break my high score."

Bob feigning concern: "Oh, no, do we need to call the president or something?"
John looked at Bob: "Thanks for your concern, did you give the pictures to Izzy yet?"

Bob: "I did so yesterday, after reviewing your notes and the pictures he decided to change out the current potentiometer and the round dial to a larger selector switch with, OFF, 12, 18, and 24 volts that locks into each selection. Izzy said the place we selected to put the switch was perfect because of the small plate, and he is sending a repairman to change out the new switch on the "Faraday 1" this morning as the first "Bullet" to get the new switch, He said it would only take a couple of hours."
John: "Has Izzy ordered any of the new "Transceivers" from you yet?"

Bob: "Yes, he ordered 50, we delivered 25 last Friday."
John: "Call Izzy and asked him if he could deliver 5 or 6 "Transceivers" for us to install south of "Faraday's" moon, next Monday, we will need the squad and will be gone two or three days, I'm kind of bored." Bob: "I will call right now. How about a donut?"

John: "Ya, I could eat a donut, ask Jenny if she wants one too?" Bob got up and left the office. Thirty minutes later Bob returned, and gave John his donut. Jenny brought in an orange juice for John and a coffee for Bob and returned to her desk.

Bob: "I talked to Izzy, he said along with the technician to change out the voltage controller he will put 6 "Transceivers" in the rear storage area, they are of the 000400 series, these are the first of the new ones we made to be installed. He also will have the squad outfit the "Faraday 1" with supplies for 1 week."

John: "Call Jack, and Donna, and I will ask Kayla and Topa if they want to come long, yes, that sounds like a fun few days." Bob nodded.

John: "I just thought of something else, this is important, if a missile is fired with the skin voltage set to 24-volts, the missile will blow up coming out of the cylinder when it hits the force field. This only effects the rocket launcher. Call Izzy back and have him tie the skin voltage circuit into the missile firing system to turn off the voltage for 4 seconds before firing the missile." Bob: "Right now John." Bob took out his cell phone and called Izzy: "Izzy John wants to pass on that you need to tie in the skin voltage circuit to the rocket launcher to turn off the voltage for 4 seconds before launching the rocket so the rocket won't explode trying to go through the force field the 24-volt setting makes, alright thanks Izzy, I will."

Bob: "Izzy says thanks for the info, it would not have been fun to find out the hard way what might have happened, he will have the technician do the work when they come and pick up the "Faraday 1" on Saturday and return it Monday morning at 08:00."
John: "Ok, I'm glad we got that out of the way."

Thursday 08:00
John was sitting at his desk thinking about his broken PINBALL" machine, and directing a thought to Kayla about the trip Monday. Bob rolled into his office and sat down at the table.
John picked up the drawing he had been working on and went to the table and sat down. Bob, look at this and tell me what you think, John shoved the drawing over to Bob. Bob started to look over the drawing plans.

Bob: "This is in the same cement case we use now for the "Transceivers"?" John nodded.
Bob: "I assume that is a new type power supply on the left of your drawing?"
John: "Yes, the small 1 in. thick, 6X6 wide orange plastic box has a flat piece of cone material fastened to the inside rear of the box with plastic rivets, the front of the box

facing the solar cells in clear plastic, on the back of the
orange plastic box is two slots for orange bars. That turns
the box into a light for the solar cells that power the mini-
"doorway" and the extending probe."
Bob: "What does the probe do?"

John: "It goes through the open "doorway" into space
and provides video of that section of space using the three
cameras on the end of the probe, and sends the image
wirelessly to the Transceiver."

Bob: "Well, we would have to build the new solar
power source, and it could be used on all the new
"Transceivers" built and replace the flashlights in all the
present "Transceivers"."

John smiling: "We just need to add the electronics for the
video and wireless system, none of which is a big
problem, most of the space inside the present "doorways"
is battery space, this also changes the power supply on the
"doorways", we no longer need an electrical connection.
We need to get your flashlight guy to make us a handful
of the new plastic light case ASAP so we can test it."

Bob: "I will call him right now; this is a revelation
John, on your part, this will change a lot of stuff. Do you
realize that the power pack you just invented can be used
in almost every electronic device on the planet, most of
those use 120vac to 6-12vdc transformers?"
John: "I actually had not thought about it that much, but
you are right."

Bob: "I am going to see my flashlight guy right now,
take me to your workshop, I will get what's left of the roll
of white cone material and give it to my flashlight guy for
the new lights. Make me a quick drawing of the new light
box, I will take it with me also." John made a quick
drawing of the plastic light case and gave it to Bob. John
and Bob went to the "VOID" and John took Bob to the
workshop, John gave Bob the last of the white cone
material and they went back to "Faraday's" moon. John

said goodbye to Bob and went back to the office. A few minutes later a repairman for his "PINBALL" machine showed up. John watched as he opened up the top and looked inside.

The repairman: "Here is the problem, he pulled out a fuse and showed it to John, this is a 10-amp fuse, I'm surprised the machine worked this long, it should be a 20-amp fuse, he unplugged the machine from the wall, got a new 20-amp fuse from his toolbox, put it in the "PINBALL" machine. He plugged in the "PINBALL" machine and pushed the red button, the lights all came on. "Wonderful John said." The repairman gave John an extra fuse and taped it to the inside bottom of the machine and closed the top.

John: "Please thank Vinnie for me?" The repairman nodded and left the office. John played "PINBALL" the rest of the afternoon.

Friday 08:00

John got to the office about 09:00. He sat down at his desk and remembered he needed to tell Kayla about the trip on Monday. He closed his eyes and told Kayla about the trip and she could bring TOPA if he wanted to come. A few minutes later Kayla answered, she would love to come but TOPA had a few meetings he could not skip and she would come to the workshop on Monday morning by 08:00. About lunch time Bob excitedly came into the office carrying a box, he put the box on the table.

John: "So, what's all the excitement about?"

Bob opened the box and pulled out an orange new light box. and a solar cell used in the "Transceivers". John came over to the table and sat down. He picked up the light box. It was an inch thick, and 6X6 wide and long, one side had a plastic cover with screws, John could see the white cone material inside with plastic rivets holding it in, the other side had three orange bar slots.

John: "Oh Bob, this is perfect, even better than the drawing. Give me some orange bars?" Bob pulled out three orange bars and handed them to John. John held the light in one hand and pushed in an orange bar, light came out the front, he pushed in another orange bar, more light came out the front, John pushed in the third orange bar, the light coming out the front lit up the whole office. John removed the three orange bars and the light ceased.

Bob: "My guy also gave me these, he handed John some clips that were for the solar panel and the new light, it allowed the light to clip onto the solar panel. Anyway, I have twelve new lights and twelve solar panels in the box."

John: "Where did you get the solar panels?"

Bob: "Izzy gave them to me for testing when I told him about the new light."

John: "Ok, I will take the box home with me today and tomorrow you can come over and we will test stuff until our brains turn to mush." Bob nodded and went to his office. John was thinking that tomorrow was going to be a fun day.

John finished his day with a new "PINBALL" record recorded on the paper taped to the machine.

Saturday 08:00

John was sitting at his workshop table. He had a solar panel and a light clipped together. He had a voltage/amp test box to hook the solar panel power plug to. Bob came into the workshop and sat down at the table.

John: "Ok, the first thing is we cut the plug off of the power supply so I can hook it to my test box. I want to know voltage and amperage." John picked up a pair of wire cutters and cut the plug off the solar power supply. He cut a split in the two-wire cord so he could pull apart the two wires. He cut off the cord on both ends to get to the bare copper wire underneath, he attached the minus wire to the minus post and the plus wire to the plus post on the testing machine.

Bob: "What does the test machine do?"

John: "It measures the voltage coming from the solar cells and puts a load on the panel to measure the amps. I will put one orange bar in the light, John got 1 orange bar from the table and shoved it into one slot on the back of the light. The light turned on. John and Bob looked at the test machine display results. The voltage read 12 volts at 4 amps. John put another orange bar into a slot, On the test machine the voltage was still 12 volts at 8 amps.

John: "The 8 amps is more than enough to run any electronic device. John put 1 more orange bar into the last slot, the voltage held steady at 12 volts at 12 amps. You were right Bob, this small plastic case could power almost every electronic device on the planet, no batteries or input electricity. This is crazy stuff."

Bob: "Ya-crazy like a fox stuff."

John smiled: "The next thing we do is I will get with my "doorway" builder and see what needs to be done to get all this to work together after we get back next week."

Bob: "Sounds like a plan." Bob left the workshop and went back through the house.

John looked at the test box and the display readings and muttered to himself: "This is going to be crazy, then another thought came in to his mind, this could be even bigger than we thought."

.

CHAPTER FOURTEEN

"The Repubs and the Demos"

Monday 08:00

John and Bob were in John's workshop. John was puttering around with the new flat light and the solar panel. They were waiting for the rest of the crew to install some more "Transceivers" south of "Faraday's" moon. Donna and Jack came into the workshop. Donna: "Hi guys, John the "Faraday 1" just pulled up with Sgt. Carter and the squad. John put down the light assembly and they all walked out to the "VOID". As they did Kayla rolled up on her golf cart. She parked the golf cart and gave everyone a hug, then they all went into the cabin, John shut the door and sat down. John went over to the weapons console and looked at the new voltage switch.

John: "Very nice job on the switch. Bob come and see the new switch." Bob came over and looked: "Yes, they did a great job."

Sgt. Carter: "Maybe you would explain about the new switch, we were rushed out this morning to get here and Izzy said you would explain the new switch."

John: "The old one was a dial inside and under the weapons console, normally you could not access it without opening the front panel. It supplied 12 volts to the skin of the "Bullet". That voltage made the skin impenetrable. I had some curiosity about the voltage, so Bob and I tested the voltage Saturday. We discovered that

24 volts applied to the skin of the "Bullet" produced a 4-inch force field around the "Bullet", Sgt. put the selector switch to 24-volts please. Sgt. Carter moved the switch to 24-volts John opened the cabin door. Kayla, go to the door and slowly push your hand out the open door. Kayla slowly started to push her hand out the door and discovered the force field in place. I would like all of you to do the same test please, the squad, Jack, and Donna tested the force field. As crazy as it might seem, nothing can penetrate that force field. It has one problem, if we were to fire a missile, the missile would explode as it left the cylinder, because of the force field, so when on the 24-volt setting a 4 second delay turns off the skin voltage long enough to fire the missile. Sgt. return the voltage setting to a normal 12-volts please, Now knowing how Izzy thinks, Sgt. activate the missile system please. Sgt. Carter did so and the voltage switch automatically went to 24-volts, Yup, I know that Izzy, ok Sgt. put the voltage back to 12-volts. Sgt. Carter did so."

John: "Today we are installing more "Transceivers" south of "Faraday's" moon. Donna, put the map of our sector with the council planets on the big screen please. John stood up and pointed to the last planet on the edge of the sector. Donna set a course for 75 miles from Earth towards the planet "TETO" please. Donna set the course and nodded at Sgt. Carter.

John: "By the way, nice to see you again Johnny and Larry, thank you for coming they both smiled and nodded. Sgt. forward please, normal speed. Sgt. Carter pushed the throttle forward. About an hour later Donna said: "We are at the first install point. Everybody got out except Sgt. Carter and went to the back of the "Bullet" John opened the storage panel and 6 "Transceivers" came into view. Let's find 000400 and put it on the "VOID" floor please. Bob checked out the serial numbers and discovered they were in order from left to right. Bob and one of the Marines lifted out the Transceiver and set it on the "VOID" floor.

John" Kayla, you have never set up one of these, correct?"

Kayla: "No, I haven't."

John" Well today is your lucky day, let me show you how to do it. The rest watched as John showed Kayla how to set up the new Transceiver. Kayla would ask questions as they proceeded and John would explain as they went forward and finished, then they all went back aboard. John closed the door an sat down: "Donna please test the new Transceiver. Donna verified the Transceiver was on and working then put up the Transceiver map on the big screen. Everyone could see that the Transceiver at the Earth "doorway" station saw 000400 blinking.

John: "Good job crew, Donna set course for 75 more miles please, again towards the planet "TETO."

Donna set the course and nodded to Sgt. Carter and they were off again. About an hour later Donna said they were at the next point.

John: "Who would like to learn how to install a Transceiver this time, Donna raised her hand."

Jack: "Come on Mrs. Foster I will go with you." Donna smiled at Jack and Bob, Kayla, Donna, Jack and one of the Marines left the cabin and went to the back of the "Bullet", John again opened the back panel and Bob and the Marine unloaded the Transceiver and placed it on the "VOID" floor. John and Donna gathered near the Transceiver and John explained what she needed to do. Donna asked no questions; she had watched two other installs and did the install perfectly. They all went back into the Bullet" cabin. John closed the door and sat down. Donna did the testing and this time choose 000400 to see if it saw 000401: "Number 000401 is ok John."

John: "Thank you Donna, set course for here, John pointed to the map, the next location was on the edge of

our sector and 25 miles beyond planet "TETO". Donna
set course and nodded at Sgt. Carter."
John: "Sgt. let's slow down to 40mph, and Donna put
space on the big screen please." John watched as the
video of space appeared on the big screen.
 John: "Space is so beautiful, isn't it?" The others
agreed, they had never seen it from this angle."
Kayla: "Oh look, a large asteroid field came into view."
John: "Sgt. stop and we will watch the asteroids for a
while. They watched as the asteroids crawled by at a slow
pace.
 Donna: "Look some of them even sparkle."
John: "Donna, take a closer look at the sparkle please."
Donna panned the camera closer to the asteroid field, one
asteroid gave off a gold sparkle, Donna moved the camera
in on that asteroid. John stood up: "That asteroid is a solid
gold rock the size of a city bus, these must have come
from a planet breakup. Check out some of the other large
ones Donna. Donna panned over more of the large
asteroids.
 Kayla: "Look at that one, it has a lot of sparkles in
it." Donna panned to the one Kayla had noticed, on
closeup John said: "That one is full of diamonds" Bob
watched John as he started to scheme.
 John: "I think the large nugget would make a nice
donation to the "Vets" fund, all we have to do is get it
back and smelted. Any ideas how to do that?" John
directly looked at Kayla and smiled: "I'm waiting for Jack
to speak up." Kayla smiled and nodded.
 Jack: "I may have an idea, John."
John still smiling at Kayla: Yes Jack, what would that
be?"
Jack: "We could do like we did before with that "Greys"
asteroid piece."
 John: "I don't think we could use a cable on it, we
want it to be stable and not move around when we tow it."

Sgt. Carter: "We have a six-foot 2X2 inch tow bar with a hook on one end, the other end has a foot with two holes that can be bolted to the "Bullet"."

Jack: "That would be perfect, but how would we hook the towbar to the asteroid?" Sgt. Carter: "Let's go look at what is stored in the rear for towing stuff." Bob, Jack, and Sgt. Carter went to the rear of the vehicle. John opened the panel and they looked inside. They found the tow bar and pulled it out."

Jack: "Well look what we have here, Jack pulled out a foot with two holes in it and a hook welded to it. This is what we need."

John: "Jack is right, we open a "doorway" and bring the front of the asteroid inside like before, we attach the hook with the foot and two holes to the asteroid with screws, then attach the other hook and then attach the tow bar to the "Bullet".

Jack: "That will work but we need to keep the hooks from swinging around as the asteroid is towed. How about some metal blades or something and masking tape?" Sgt. Carter looked in the toolbox in the storage area, he pulled out two 1-foot metal rulers and a large roll of masking tape."

John: "I will get the "doorway" John went back into the cabin and got the portable "doorway" and came back behind the "Bullet", ok Jack do your stuff." Jack set up the "doorway" on the "VOID" floor. We have to put the hook on the asteroid first. Jack and John set up, and opened the doorway, he and John located the asteroid and adjusted the "doorway" to bring the asteroid four feet into the void. Since the foot had bolt holes, they decided to drill holes into the asteroid and use screws. Bob found a drill and bits inside the tool box, they found 1/2 in. bolts and bit. First, they attached the tow bar to the "Bullet", then decided where to align the foot with the hook. Bob marked the holes with a black marker. They drilled the holes deep and attached the foot with the hook, then Sgt. Carter backed up the "Bullet" and slowly put the two hooks together. John held the two rulers while Bob used the masking tape to make the two hooks solid. They checked their work.

John: "Alright the final step is to disconnect the towbar from the "Bullet" and gently shove it through the "doorway".

Jack: "Why are you putting the tow bar into space."

John: "Think back to the "Greys" asteroid, we only used the doorway to start moving the asteroid and then we cut the cable away. We need to tow the asteroid to where we need it to go, to do that we need to mount the "doorway" on the towbar so the doorway is towed with the asteroid." Jack thought about it for a few seconds: So, you want to disconnect the towbar, push it into space, and move the "doorway" from the "VOID" floor to the towbar. John nodded."

John: "Now we need something to somehow mount the "doorway" onto the towbar with masking tape.

Bob was looking again in the storage space: "John there are some pieces of 2X4 wood that you may be able to use for the towbar. "Bob picked up three-foot section of 2X4 and a couple of 1-foot pieces and tossed them to the "VOID" floor.

John: "Bob those are perfect, Jack tape two of the small pieces to together, Jack did so. Now tape the three-foot section to the two other pieces making a cross, the three-foot section will stick out from the sides of the towbar and we will tape the "doorway" antennas and the box to the towbar.

First: Disconnect the towbar from the "Bullet" and gently push it into space. Sgt. Carter and Bob did so, the asteroid with the towbar on the front moved very slowly through the "doorway"."

Second: John took the antennas and made a curve in both of them.

Third: "Now I will turn on the "doorway" again and we will pick up the plastic feet of the now curved "doorway" and gently put the tow bar back through and then mount them on the cross under the tow bar just before the masking tape." John turned the "doorway" back on and a now round "doorway" opened. John moved the "doorway" to the asteroid and then he and Bob each held an antenna as they brought the towbar back into the "VOID". Jack and Sgt. Carter carefully using the masking tape mounted the wood cross about a foot from the tow bar masking tape, and then they carefully mounted the two antennas on each side of the 3-foot piece of wood. And last they mounted the "doorway" box on the towbar after folding the wires with masking tape so they would not drag on the "VOID" floor."
Jack, Bob, and Sgt. Carter now all saw what John was trying to explain earlier. Now they could drag the asteroid behind the "Bullet" anywhere they wanted. They all went back into the cabin, John sat down.

Jack: "Where are we going to take the asteroid."
John: "Bob, did we not build a joint Military-Civilian moon base last year on the Earth moon to get samples and mine things if they found stuff to mine?"
Bob: "Call Izzy and see if he has any info on the moon base." Bob called Izzy, they talked for a few minutes, Bob was laughing like hell when he disconnected with Izzy.

John: "What's so funny Bob?"
Bob trying to keep from laughing: "Izzy said you are right about the Moon base, the Officer in charge is a Major Towers. And he said that Congress has put you back into the Air Force again, the Air Force Reserve with a rank of Full Colonel."

John laughing and shaking his head: "Donna, see if you can contact the Moon base, and Major Towers and put him on speaker please." Donna started to try and contact the Earth moon base. Suddenly someone came on and said they were Moon Base 1, Donna looked at John and nodded, Moon Base 1, this is John Faraday in "Faraday1", I would like to talk to Major Towers please." Moon Base 1: "Yes sir I will get him, it will only take a minute." They waited.

Moon Base 1:" This is Major Towers, Colonel Faraday how can I help you? John rolled his eyes, Major Towers, we have a nugget of gold the size of a school bus we plucked out of an asteroid belt, we would like to leave it with someone to smelt, is that something you have the ability to do?"

Major Towers: "How are you getting it here sir?"

John: "We are towing it and intend to place it where ever you need it to be. We will be there in about (John looked at Donna) she held up two fingers, in about two hours."

Major Towers: "Yes sir we will expect you, Moon Base 1 out."

John: "Donna set a course for Moon Base 1, Sgt. Normal speed please." Donna nodded at Sgt. Carter.

Sgt. Carter pushed the throttle forward laughing: "Yes, sir, normal speed Colonel."

John looked at Kayla who was covering her mouth and chuckling: "Ok, everyone, get it all out so we can get back to business. How about some lunch?" John noticed Johnny and Larry were absent from the cabin. About that time Larry came to the cabin and said lunch was ready. They all went to lunch, they all kept watch on the kitchen screen of the cargo to Moon Base 1 as they ate. It was a great lunch. About two hours later they arrived at Moon Base 1.

John: "Donna open a channel please. Donna did and nodded to John: "Moon Base 1, this is "Faraday 1" with a small delivery-over."

Moon base 1: "This is Moon base 1 Colonel Faraday; we have marked the landing zone for your cargo."

Sgt. Carter: "We see it, John."

John: "Moon Base 1, can you handle this rock the way it is or would you like us to slice it up for you?"

Moon Base 1: "We can handle it Colonel thank you for asking."

John: "Moon Base 1, would the Civilian contractor be handy to talk to?"

Moon Base 1: "Yes Colonel, my name is Dan Henley, I will have the gold smelted and an account transfer ready for you whenever you say."

John: "Moon Base 1, Mr. Henley, thank you, your part of the bargain is10 percent of the gold value. I assume that is ok with you?"

Moon Base 1: "Yes, that is fine Colonel Faraday, thank you for the business."

John: "I will contact you next week for the transfer, thank you Mr. Henley, Sgt. Let's park this big rock where they want it." They all watched as Sgt. Carter brought the asteroid down in the middle of the landing zone.

John, Bob and Sgt. Carter left the cabin and went to the rear of the vehicle. They carefully removed the box from the towbar, then the antennas from the wood cross member, then moved the "doorway" so about two feet of the asteroid came into the "VOID", Bob removed the foot screws from the asteroid and John moved the "doorway back away from the asteroid and turned it off. Sgt. Carter pulled up the "Bullet" and they removed the intact towbar and put it away in the storage locker. They all went back to the cabin. John sat down.

John: "Donna set a course for "Transceiver" number 000402 please and Sgt. double speed to 000402."

Sgt. Carter smiling: "Yes, sir John."

John smiling: "That's better. "

Donna: "We are 90 minutes out from our next "Transceiver" install."

John: "Thank you Donna, I will take a short nap and John nodded off."

Donna: "John we are here for number 3 "Transceiver" install." John woke up, got up and opened the cabin door.

John: "Who would like to try your luck in this "Transceiver", Let's see, Donna, Jack Kayla, Bob, and Sgt.Carter has done one, how about one of you Marines, come on don't be shy, Danny raised his hand, we have a winner, give that man a Cupie doll. Danny, Bob, and John went down the ramp and to the rear of the "Bullet"?" John opened the rear panel, Bob and Danny unloaded number 000402 and placed it on the "VOID" floor. John and Danny hovered over the "Transceiver"; John relayed the steps to Danny. Danny followed the steps like a trooper. The first green light came on but not the second. John took out the light to use to look inside the concrete base. Danny pointed to the loose power cable.

John: "Danny, you found it; you fix it. Danny reached into the concrete base and pulled out the power cable then reinserted the cable and twisted it to lock. The second green light came on.

John: "Good job, Danny you are now an official certified electronics technician." Danny smiled and nodded. John closed up the rear panel and they all got back in the "Bullet". John closed the door.

John: "Donna, give it a test, please." Donna entered a few commands: "Good to go John."

John: "Ok, three down three to go, Let's look at the map, John looked up at the map, well we have a planet to our left that is a "VOID" planet, Donna can you see their "Transceiver" signal?" Donna put the "Transceiver" screen up next to the map, no signal John. We are a few miles out of range."

John: "Ok, let's go toward that "VOID" planet until we get a signal, then go five more miles, and we will install another "Transceiver." Donna input the coordinates and nodded at Sgt. Carter who pushed forward the throttle. John watched the "Transceiver" display on the big screen. As he watched the "Transceiver" of the left planet started to blink green. A minute later Donna announced we were at the next install site.

John got up, and opened the door, he looked at Bob: "Come on Roberto, we will do this one. Bob got up and followed John to the rear of the" Bullet", John opened the panel and he and Bob unloaded number 000403 and sat it on the "VOID" floor. John bent over and set the "Transceiver" up, got two green lights, closed the rear panel and went back to the "Bullet" cabin. John closed the door and sat down: "Four "Transceivers" down, two to go."

Donna: "The "Transceiver" is good to go. "John looked at the map again: "Ok, we are sitting in between two "Transceivers", Donna go back 32 miles and make a hard left and go out 75 miles and we will install number 000404." Donna input the coordinates and nodded to Sgt. Carter. Who pushed the throttles forward, 32 miles later they made a hard left and headed out 75 miles further? In about 50 minutes Donna announced they were there at the install site. John got up to open the cabin door.

Donna: "John I have an incoming something. Sgt. Carter, the voltage setting just changed to 24 volts."
John: "Donna can you tell what it is, how far away it is?"
Donna: "It is 4 miles out and coming right at us."

John: "Sgt. Turn up the mini-gun and track whatever it is."
Donna: "It is now 3 miles out; it looks like a missile."
John: "Sgt. change course turn left for a hundred yards then back to this course."

Donna:" The missile has not changed course it is on its original course.

John: "The missile doesn't see us. Sgt. fire at it when it closes to 1 mile from us."

Donna: "Missile 2 miles out and still on original course."

Donna: "Missile 1.5 miles out, still on original course."

Sgt. Carter opened fire on the missile with the mini-gun, you could hear the "BURRRRP" of the gun. The missile exploded, half a mile from the "Bullet."

John: "Sgt. Let's go dark, slow ahead, Donna keep an eye out for anything we can blame for the missile. The "Bullet" moved slowly ahead."

Donna: "I have several contacts now, 7 to 10 moving objects."

John: "Keep moving closer, go to night vision on the screen. A bunch of vehicles appeared, there were 10 vehicles, John continued to watch."

Donna: "They are shooting at each other; the vehicles are wheeled mini-tanks. They watched and came closer."

John: "Donna how close are we?"

Donna: "We are at two miles."

John: "Sgt. stop here." The "Bullet" stopped. Donna go to normal cameras please." Donna changed to normal cameras.

Donna: "The tanks are two colors, Red and Blue, I don't think they see us."

John: "I agree and we are also out of range of their guns Donna, bring up the space cameras, let's see what is around us, they had to come from somewhere."

The display on the big screen showed a large planet close to them.

Donna: "Two of the Red tanks have seen us and are approaching."

John: "Sgt. warm up the stingers, you may shoot any tanks that fire on us. They watched the Red tanks get closer; they were still a mile away. The two Red tanks fired at the "Bullet"; the rounds fell way short.

John shaking his head: "Sgt. show them the mistake they made. "Sgt. Carter fired two stinger missiles at the two Red tanks, both exploded in a huge fireball. The other Red tanks turned and ran. The five Blue tanks turned their guns away from the "Bullet" and stood still. In a few minutes two of the Blue tanks opened their lids and two people got out from each tank.

John: "Donna get a close up please." Donna zoomed in on the four people standing in front of the tanks. They all watched as the camera showed four very short humans, none of them were over four feet tall.

John: "Wonderful, I just blew up four little people."

Kayla: "They gave you no choice, they fired on you."

John: "That doesn't help me much, Sgt. move slowly towards the Blue tanks; Donna point the Language Translator at them while we approach them." They were hearing English before they got closer, Sgt. Take us to 50 yards and point the door towards them please. Inside speaker please Donna. Donna nodded at John. "We would like to speak to you if you are inclined. The little people said they would talk. John opened the cabin door. Kayla, would you join me at the door ramp bottom. John and Kayla walked to the bottom of the ramp. Two of the little people started to walk to John and Kayla. As they go to within 10 feet Kayla took some comm badges from her pocket and held them out in her hand. The little people looked at Kayla and then the comm badges. Kayla motioned for them to put them on their sleeve like hers. They each took a badge and placed them on their sleeve.

John: "Can you understand us now?

The little people: "Yes, do the badges let us hear your language?"

John: "Yes, that is their purpose, my name is John and her name is Kayla, may we know yours?"

The little people: "My name is Emery and his name is Larno, we are curious about your vehicle. Ours have wheels yours does not."

John: "If you like, you and your other two friends can come into our vehicle and we can talk."

Larno: "Emery we must move the tanks or they will be stuck to the floor."

Emery:" I know, go back to the tanks, have all the tanks taken back to base and ask Will and Tatum if they want to come with us." Larno went back to the tanks the other two little people started to walk towards John and Kayla, two other little people came out of the tanks and all the tanks left. The four little people followed John and Kayla into the "Bullet". They stared at Donna for a minute, then followed John and Kayla to the table in the kitchen. Kayla gave the new two people comm badges.

John: "We call this dark place the "VOID", how long have you been using it?"

Emery: "We discovered it about 4 months ago. We know almost nothing about it. Are there other kinds of people in here also?"

John: "Do you have space travel in ships?"

Emery: "No, we are not developing that yet.

John: "There are many other kinds of people out there in space. You can see I look like you only bigger, yet Kayla is similar to you but different. Well, that is the way it is in the universe, many different kinds of people working together. We are part of a Council of planets that govern space and the "VOID" in our sector. Some planets have "VOID" access, some use space craft, some have both. We are free of war because our rule is if one is attacked all the others respond against the attacker. It makes war too terrible to do. Every planet is run by their own people without interference from the Council. We trade, we share ideas and all are better off. But we also have one more rule, no war in the "VOID". Tell me about your people."

Emery: "We have two clans, The Repubs and the Demos. Our leaders are a Council of 5, Two Repubs(elected), two Demos(elected), and 1 selected at random from a lottery from all the people. We have elections every 4 years for the Two clans among themselves.

John: "What is the name of your Planet, and why are you at war with the Repubs?"

Emery: "We call our planet PREZ; they didn't like the results of the last election; they say the 1 council member who is random was fraudulently picked because he sides to much with the Demos. They claim the Demos rigged the lottery. Of course, they have no proof, but they refused to follow the rulings made by the Council vote and occasionally start trouble. That is what you saw today. This was the first time anything happened inside the "VOID". I'm sure the two Repubs tanks that you destroyed will be blamed on us,"

John: "We are sorry for that but they fired on us first, we had no choice."

Emery: "Oh, I understand that, but it won't matter, they will just lie about the whole thing and stir up their clan against us."

John: "What if we go to your council and explain?"

Emery: "Right now that won't work because our people think we are the only people in the universe."

John: "Yes, that is a big surprise when planets find out they are not alone."

Emery: "We will have to digest what happened today."

John: "Well, because you have access to the "VOID" you can join the Council of planets, that is one of the requirements. But I must warn you and you need to take this message back to your Council, you must not bring your violence into the "VOID" or space, the other planets won't allow it. And they have terrible weapons to defend all the Council planets."

Emery: "I will take that message back to the Council, and hopefully in the near future things will change, they must change."

John: "We wish you good luck and I hope to hear from you." Do you need a lift home?"

Emery: "No, they will come back for us soon."

John: "We will stay and wait for them to come and get you, then leave. We will also put a "Transceiver" 1 mile from this location, if you need to talk to me, wear your comm badge and come into the" VOID", press your finger to the comm badge and ask for me. Someone will answer you and get a message to me, alright?"

Emery: "Thank you John, I will remember."

Emery and his friends left the "Bullet". The "Bullet waited for the Little People to get picked up.

John: "Ok, that is over for now, I have a bad feeling about it though, Donna take us back 1 mile and we will install another "Transceiver"." Donna input the coordinates and nodded at Sgt. Carter. They reached the install location. John opened the door: "Come on Bob we will do another one." John and Bob left the "Bullet" went to the rear of the "Bullet". John opened the panel and they removed 000404 and put it on the "VOID" floor. John set it up, closed the panel and he and Bob went back to the cabin.

John: "Ok, Donna check 000404 out please. Donna ran her checks:" John, the "Transceiver" is ok."

John looking at the map: "Let's put the last one "HERE". Donna looked at the map and set coordinates then nodded at Sgt. Carter. They were off to install the last "Transceiver". About an hour later they arrived at the install site.

John: "Any volunteers for the last "Transceiver"?"

Jack: "Donna and I will do the last one, Donna nodded."

John: "Ok, he opened the cabin door and the three of them went to the rear of the "Bullet". John opened the panel and he and Jack took out the last "Transceiver" and placed it on the "VOID" floor. Donna and Jack stood over the "Transceiver", then knelt down and finished the install, all lights were green. John closed the panel and they went back into the cabin.

John looking at his watch: Well, it's about 5pm. We finished everything way to soon, how about some food, I'm hungry. He noticed Johnny and Larry missing from the cabin, Let's see if we have anything to eat around here. They all got up and headed to the kitchen, Johnny and Larry were way ahead of them, the food was just put out on the counter and it smelled wonderful."
They spent the next hour having good food and good conversation.
John: "Who wants to go check out that other asteroid we found, the one full of diamonds?" Everybody raised their hands.

John: "Donna put in the course. How far away is the asteroid field?" Donna: "It is about three hours."
John: "Here's what we will do. We will go check out the asteroid. If it is towable, we will get a good night's sleep and try to set it up to tow to Moon Base 1. If it is not towable, we will just all go home." Everybody agreed.
John: "Ok, head us. to the asteroid belt." Sgt. Carter pushed the throttle forward.
Two Hours later:

Donna was attempting to locate the asteroid they were looking for. The field had moved since they were there the last time. The asteroids were still all flying at the same speed. Donna put the asteroid field up on the big screen so everyone could look for the one they wanted. The search went on for an hour.
Kayla spoke up: "I see one that is sparkling, she pointed to the one she was talking about."

John: "Donna get us closer. Donna adjusted the camera and the asteroid became closer. Kayla was right, the asteroid she had spotted was the one they were looking for. They moved right up to the asteroid.
Jack: "It doesn't seem to be solid rock, it's more like compressed gravel, almost like concrete, but it is three times the size of the gold one."

John: "Let's put it through a "doorway" and inspect it. Maybe that will give us some ideas on how to capture it."
Donna: "I like that idea, let's do it John." John: "Ok."

CHAPTER FIFTEEN

"Diamonds are a Girl's Best Friend"

John opened the cabin door, he took a "portable "doorway" out of the storage bin and went out to the "VOID", everyone followed him out. John set up the "Doorway", and Bob helped him expand it to accept the front of the asteroid. They slowly moved the "Doorway" until about 10 feet of the asteroid was inside the" VOID".

John: "Sgt. Carter please get some of the gloves and a small pick or something to pound on the asteroid if there is anything like that in the toolbox. "Sgt. Carter took Danny with him to the rear of the "Bullet" They came back with two hammers, several chisels. the drill and bits, some wrenches, two pair of safety glasses and the tow bar with the two taped up hooks on one end."

John put the gloves on and picked up one of the hammers, and a chisel. He and Bob stood next to the asteroid and checked out what Jack had said about the composition of the rock. The looked very close at the rock without touching it.

John: "I think Jack is correct, it does look like compressed rock, but look at it, it is full of diamonds of all sizes." John put on one of the safety glasses and stepped up to the rock, set the chisel up against the asteroid and hit the chisel with the hammer. A shower of a few handfuls of rock separated from the asteroid and fell onto the "VOID" floor. Bob scooped up the debris and looked at it.

Bob: "My hands are full of diamonds and rock. He showed the stuff to the girls, they started to pick out the diamonds. John attacked the asteroid again for a few more hits, everyone picked up the diamonds from the "VOID" floor.

John: "Let's pick up the tools and put them inside the cabin and go wash off the diamonds and we can see what we have." The Marines helped pick up all the tools and all the diamonds were taken into the kitchen and washed in the sink. Donna put all the diamonds on two pieces of paper towels and laid them on the kitchen table. There were 20 or thirty diamonds of different sizes, none were smaller than a peanut, there were some as large as a walnut.

John: "Does anyone know anything about diamonds?"
Donna: "I see these and they are remarkable, these were formed deep underground, look at the different colors, they would need to be cut into gem stones, but John some of the big ones are priceless."
John: "Would everyone agree that it doesn't look like towing the thing would not be an easy thing to do?"
They all nodded.
John: "What if we filled a box or two with diamonds, we mine ourselves, it might be fun. We each can keep two large diamonds and the rest go to the "Vets" fund."
They all thought that was a great idea.
"John: "Alright, since it is getting late, let's all go to bed and tomorrow morning we start mining?"
Bob: "I'm ready to go to bed, I'm tired now."

John: "Donna, why don't you and Kayla go check out the rooms, then we can assign rooms and all hit the sack." Donna and Kayla got up and went back to the rooms, 30 minutes later they returned and handed out room assignments. John went into the "VOID" moved the "doorway" so the asteroid went back into space and turned off the "doorway." He picked up the antennas and the doorway box and headed back to the cabin. He needed to charge the "doorway" batteries anyway to be sure they were fully charged. He went back to the cabin and plugged the "doorway" box into an outlet. Everyone went to their rooms and went to sleep.

Next Morning:

John awoke at 06:00 like every morning. He looked over at Bob sound asleep. John washed up in the sink and shook Bob awake.

John: "I am going to the kitchen; I will see you there." Bob nodded and sat up with his feet on the floor. John went to the kitchen. The Marines, Donna, Jack and Kayla were already there.

John: "It's nice to see everyone bright and early." Johnny and Larry had made food and it was on the counter. John filled a plate with food, filled a glass with orange juice and sat at the table next to Kayla. John looked at Kayla directly and said: "You look nice this morning Princess."

Kayla squinted her eyes at John: "Thank you John, where is Bob?"

John: "He is up and washing his face." About that time Bob showed up, grabbed a coffee and sat down at the table.

Bob: "I will eat in a minute, let me start my heart going first."

Kayla: "Bob, is there something wrong with your heart?" John chuckling" 'No Kayla, it just an expression that humans say when they haven't quite woken up yet?" Kayla smiled chuckled and nodded.

John: "As soon as Mr. Johnson has eaten, we will start mining, we have two hammers and several chisels. We can take turns hammering and picking up the debris, when one box is filled, we can start on another box, meanwhile

220

the first box can be cleaned. Then we can sort out the
large diamonds and put the rest away. Does everyone
agree to that? All nodded except Bob who was stuffing
his face as fast as he could." Bob finally finished eating
and everyone went out to the "Bullet" cabin, Johnny and
Larry stayed in the kitchen to clean up.
John: "Bob, get a couple of boxes out of storage please."
Bob got two boxes 1x1x1 ft.

John: "The two hammers and the chisels are on the
floor over in the corner. Who would like to be first to start
mining?" Jack and Donna raised their hands and the
Marine Danny and Bob.
John: "Please, the one hammering must wear safety
glasses, the other can put debris in the box. Take your
time we are not in a hurry. Look for large diamonds to
hack out. Ladies and gentlemen start your HAMMERS."
John opened the cabin door. John removed the "doorway"
box from the outlet and picked up the antennas, then he
and Sgt. Carter went down the ramp to the area there were
yesterday. John put the antennas on the "VOID" floor and
opened the "doorway". They guided the asteroid back into
the "VOID". The "Miners" started to hack at the asteroid.
Danny was using the hammer; Bob was picking up the
debris. Donna was carefully checking out the asteroid,
then would hammer out a few sections. The two teams
went at it for more than hour. The first box was half filled.
As the hackers got tired the other on the team would take
over hacking, Jack and Bob were hacking now, as Danny
and Donna were filling the box with debris. Kayla was
watching all the hacking. John walked over and stood
next to Kayla.
John smiling: "If you want to try hacking, I will pick up
debris for you."
Kayla: "I don't care about the diamonds but it might
be fun to hack them out of the asteroid."

The first box was full. Bob opened the second box and put it on the "VOID" floor. Jack and Donna put down their tools, picked up the box and headed to the kitchen to clean it up. John picked up the hammer and chisel, and a pair of safety glasses. John handed the safety glasses to Kayla, she put them on. He handed her the hammer and chisel: "Try not to hit your hand with the hammer, go slow." Kayla put the chisel up to the asteroid and gently hit the top of the chisel. She practiced for a few minutes, picking out areas to hack. John smiled as she got better at it. After a few minutes she was hacking like she had done it her whole life and was having a good time. John was putting the debris into the box. It seemed in no time the box was half full again.

John: "Kayla are you ready to quit yet?"
Kayla: "No, this is really fun and kept hacking away."
The second box was full now.

John chuckling: "Kayla you can stop now, the box is full, and you might want to wipe off the asteroid dirt from your front. She made a face and handed John the tools and started to pat off the dirt on her front. Bob handed John his tools and picked up the box and headed to the kitchen for cleanup. John handed the tools to Kayla and he moved the "doorway" back and the asteroid went back into the "VOID" a lot worse for wear. John closed the "doorway" and picked up the equipment and headed to the cabin with Kayla close behind. He put the "doorway" back in the bag and stored it in the storage locker. Sgt. Carter helped John pick up the tools and all the stuff they had removed from the rear of the "Bullet" and returned them to the rear of the "Bullet". John closed the rear panel and he and Sgt. Carter went back to the "Bullet" cabin. John went to the kitchen to see how things cleaned up. He entered the kitchen and looked at the cleanup piles. The two diamond piles were huge. Donna had put paper towels on the counter and Larry was washing the debris. As Larry finished washing, he handed the handful of diamonds to Donna who spread them out to dry. The first was almost done. The stack of diamonds was high, Donna had also laid out the large ones separately and there was plenty of them. John had no idea the diamonds were so abundant in the gravel-like makeup of the asteroid. They finished with the first box and Bob cleaned out the box with a damp paper towel to restore then to the first box. Donna laid down new paper towels and Larry started to wash the second box. John went to the fridge and got a diet soda and say down at the table to wait for the other box to finish. Bob was already sitting at the table sipping a beer.

John: "Where did you find the beer?"
Bob: "It was hidden in the very back of the fridge."
Donna: "Ok, the diamonds are cleaned, take a look."
John got up from the table and looked at the counter. They had put the diamonds in three piles. Box1, Box 2, and large diamonds. John checked out the large diamond pile. It was unbelievable, all of the large diamonds were as big as a walnut and different colors, there must have been fifty large ones, 3 or 4 of Red, Blue, Green and clear. In both the other piles none were smaller than a peanut also of different colors.

John: "I know that color, and clarity matter in diamonds. Cut diamonds are worth more than uncut diamonds. The only way we can find the best price is a gem expert. So, I will keep the diamonds in the boxes and get the best expert to look at them. Then I will find out who will cut them. Afterwards we will have a lottery for the large ones, remember I said everyone gets two, all the smaller ones go into the "VET" fund. Is that acceptable?" They all agreed. Now all we have to do is count the number of diamonds. They poured the first box back onto the paper towels and counted the diamonds. They separated out the big diamonds, then they counted the second box.

John: "Ok, Bob, when the count is done, wrap the big diamonds in something, maybe a large plastic freezer bag, box up the rest, mark the numbers, and put all of the diamonds away in the storage locker please." Bob started to box up the small diamonds, as he finished Larry handed him a large freezer bag, Bob wrapped the large diamonds in paper towels and stuffed them into two large freezer bags. Someone joked about putting the "ICE" on ice, Bob ignored them, then he put all the diamonds in the storage lockers. Everyone was now sitting in the main cabin.

John: "Bob, what was the final count on the boxes of diamonds?"
Bob: "There were 50 large diamonds and we made each box the same number of small diamonds there were 6006 small diamonds, in each box."

John: "WOW that is a lot of diamonds. We have an hour before lunch, does anyone want to do anything?"
Donna: "Why don't we look around in the asteroid field, who knows what we might find?" A bunch of hands went up.
John: "Alright Donna, turn up the cameras and let's look at stuff. Try looking for really large asteroids. If this was a planet breakup of some kind anything is possible."
Donna checked the radar screen, there was some very large asteroids, she put the cameras up on the big screen so everyone could watch.

Donna: "Let's get closer to that large asteroid, that thing is about a quarter size of the Earth's moon." Sgt. Carter maneuvered closer to the huge asteroid. The side they were looking at was jagged and torn like it was ripped from something else. It was miles long and miles wide.

Donna: "Sgt. maneuver around to the other side of the asteroid." Sgt. Carter took the "Bullet around to the other side of the now big rock. They were still many miles from the surface.

Donna: "Sgt. move closer maybe 2 or 3 miles from the surface and I will use the camera to do a closeup. Sgt. Carter moved closer to the big rock.

Suddenly Bob said: "Those look like buildings." Donna moved the camera closer to the surface. Now the buildings became clearer. There were streets and buildings for what could have been 12 or 14 city blocks. John was watching intently: "That was a big city not a town, I was right this was a planet breakup of some kind. Some of those buildings are 20 stories high. Let's get close and see if we can figure out what was in the buildings."

Donna started to pan each building as they got closer, they were no more than 30 feet from the front of the buildings. Store fronts with glass windows and displays in the windows were visible. Clothing was in one of the store fronts. The inhabitants were obviously humanoid. Some had posters in the windows, then they saw that the posters had pictures of the inhabitants. They were human. John: "I wonder if they were able to escape, if not some bodies would still be in the asteroid field floating somewhere."

Kayla: "John, that sign in the window, isn't that the language you call "English". Everyone looked closely at the poster, the writing was definitely "English"." It was an advertisement for the clothes in the window.

Donna: "John, how could that be?"

John: "Well, it looks like the inhabitants were human, it follows that a current human language like English could occur. They probably had a lot of things that would match us. "

Donna continued to move the camera down the street to a 4-way intersection. They looked at the buildings on each corner. One of the buildings looked like a department store, one was an open market of some kind, the tall one on the other corner said" GOVERNMENT DEPOSITORY".

Kayla: "Maybe that building is a records storage building. It would be interesting to find out about the people here."
John: "It might at that, it would be a good story to tell our kids, Donna, let's see if we can see inside the upper story windows." Donna moved the camera to the second story and looked through one of the windows. Inside you could see office cubicles that was strewn around. She moved the camera to the third floor; the same picture was seen there.

John: "Well, that makes sense, if it is record storage there would have to be offices to manage that storage and the damage occurred when the planet was torn apart." Sgt. go around to the back of the building and see if we can find anything else." Sgt. Carter moved around to the rear of the building which was on the next street intersection. Most of the street behind the building had sunk into the ground about 5 stories, the 5-story basement wall was visible all the way down to the bottom of the building, some of the walls had large cracks from the pressure of the top stories.

John: "I believe it is time to take a tour of what is in the basement, anyone curious? All hands went up." Sgt. Bring us down to the bottom of the hole and next to the building wall." Sgt. Carter did so.
John got the portable "doorway" from the storage locker, opened the cabin door and walked into the "VOID" with everyone behind him." He looked directly at Kayla:" I have a funny feeling about this, I have an idea what is stored on the ground floors." Kayla directly back: "Is it good or bad?" John directly back: "It is a crazy thing." John set up the "doorway" in front of the "Bullet" and turned it on. Sgt. Carter, do we have a cart of some kind on board?"

Sgt. Carter: "Yes there are 2 in the rear storage. They are 1/4 in stainless steel flat carts 3X5 ft. with a three-foot handle that fit into holes on the bottom of the cart. Would you retrieve one for us please?" Sgt. Carter went of the get the cart. He came back pulling the floating cart.
John looked at the cart: "Perfect, someone had a good idea, John put the cart to one side of the open "doorway"."
John: "Sgt. help me push the "doorway" towards the large crack in the wall in front of us, Sgt. Carter and John slowly moved the "doorway" closer to the large crack."
Bob: "There is something laying on the ground in front of the crack, it looks like they fell through the crack."
They all looked at the metal bricks laying on the ground.
John: "Sgt. do we still have those half suits we used on the asteroid to install the rocket stands?"

Sgt. Carter: "No sir, we have better, we had new suits made after that just for this kind circumstance, Danny go suit up." Danny left to go back into the main cabin, then disappeared. He came back 5 minutes later with a new suit of some kind. Sgt. Carter helped Danny get into the suit, it opened in the back with a zipper from lower back to the neck, it was a full pull over body suit with a full Helmut that attached to the ring at the neck. It also had two attachments at the waist for the two 1 in, 20 ft. hoses that were laying on the ground. The hoses were attached to a box with a fan to keep air from the "VOID" circulating in the suit, one hose was attached to the box with the fan, the other to the side of the box.

Sgt. Carter finished hooking Danny up: "Ok, Danny is ready to go. Larry was holding the box with the fan and controlling the 20 ft. of hose

John: "Danny, go through the "doorway" and pick up a couple of those bars and bring them back here and put them on the cart."

Danny stepped slowly through the "doorway" and stood a foot on the other side. He wiggled his arms testing the suit, then slowly walked over bent down and picked up two of the metal bars. He turned and came back through the "doorway" and put the bars on the cart, and took off the Helmut.

John: "Sgt. Where was the suit tested, in a chamber somewhere?"

Sgt. Carter: "Yes sir, no chamber we just tested it now."

John: "I wish you had told me that before we put Danny in the suit."

Danny: "The suit worked great Sgt., just like you expected."

John: "The suit was your idea Sgt?"

Sgt. Carter: "Yes sir, I saw the need for a suit of this design to be used for us in the "VOID", I took the idea to General Lesson and we went to NASA and worked with them to design the suit, we told them how the suits were going to be used. I know they tested the suit for space, but I don't know how they tested them but officially we just tested the suit, they made 4 suits for each "Bullet"."

John: "Well, I feel a lot better after that explanation, thank you Sgt." Sgt. Carter smiled and nodded. John bent down and touched one of the metal bars to see if it had warmed up enough, it had, he picked up the bar and looked at it: "We need to take these to the kitchen and take a closer look at them." John picked up the other one and headed to the kitchen. Danny stayed with the cart. They all sat down at the kitchen table to look at the bars. Now being in the better light the bars were a slightly greyish-silver color.

John: "Anyone know what this metal is?"

Donna: "It is a bar of platinum; I know Platinum and Gold when I see it." Jack smiled and laughed.

John: "You are right, it is a bar of platinum and there are more on the other side of the wall I'm sure, I suspected this was not a records depository, so do we continue or do we remember the location and come back later. Think about it and raise your hand if you want to see what is on the other side of the wall." All hands raised. John chuckled: Sgt. Carter, set the laser beam as small as it will go, cut a wedge out of the bottom of the wall, then cut a 10 ft. door in the wall, hopefully the wall will fall outward. Sgt. Carter set the laser to do what John asked, he cut a 10-foot-wide 4 in. wedge from the bottom of the wall, then he made a 10-foot-wide and 8 ft. high cut in the wall, when he finished the wall started to fall to the ground. Donna scanned inside the hole in the wall. Stacks and stacks of ingots to the celling were in iron cages all along the inside of the room, Gold, Silver and Platinum, and it was only a small room.

Bob: "Holy cow, there must be Billions in this building."

John: "Ok, if we are going to do this, we will do it right. Sgt. Carter, we need one more person in a suit." Sgt. Carter sent Larry for another suit.

John: "Sgt. Is there a way to raise the ramp without closing the door?" Sgt. Carter: "Yes, there is a button marked "Raise ramp" on the weapons console."

John: "Everyone out into the "VOID", Jack, raise the ramp before you exit the cabin." They all left the cabin; Jack raised the ramp and followed the group.

John: "Here's the plan, Sgt. Carter get the other cart out of storage and set it up. Danny and Larry will remove ingots from the building and put them on one cart, when that cart is full the cart will be taken to the cabin door and the ingots will be unloaded to the floor of the cabin, from there the ingots will be stacked anywhere in the "Bullet" until we run out of space. Sgt. You are in charge of the ingots in the "Bullet", Bob you and I will keep moving the" doorway" into the building so moving the ingots will only be a few feet to the cart. One cart will be empty

loading ingots, the other will be unloading ingots. We will take a break every hour or sooner if needed. Sgt. can one Marine take care of both suit fan boxes? Sgt. Carter nodded he could. Bob or I will take the full cart to the door to unload, when the other cart is empty someone will return the cart to the "doorway" for refilling. John went to the open "doorway" he and Bob and pushed it through the wall and the two Marines in the suits started loading Platinum bars onto the cart." They worked for an hour and John stopped to give everyone a break.
Sgt. Carter said the unloading and stacking inside the "Bullet" was going well, so far, no problems. They finished with the two large stacked piles of Platinum bars. John: "Sgt. Carter, you need to use the laser to chop off the bars of the three cages to get to the three stacks of Gold bars. John had the two Marines come out of the building and wait for Sgt. Carter to cut off the cage bars. After the bars were cut the loading began again. An hour later all the remaining stacks were loaded onto the "Bullet". John asked Danny to open the door to the next room and look and see what was inside, Danny opened the double doors and looked inside: "He said it was another room full of stacks of Gold and platinum bars but larger with five more cages of each. They stopped for another break.

John: "Sgt. Carter how much more room do we have to stack more stuff into the "Bullet", Danny said there is five more cages of Gold and Platinum bars in the next room?"

Sgt. Carter: "I think there is just enough room to get the next room." John nodded.
John backed out the "doorway" back into the "VOID" and moved it to go through the wall of the next room. The operation started again. One hour later John stopped again for a break.

John: "Sgt. Carter how much room is left in the "Bullet" now, there are two stacks left?"
Sgt. Carter: "I think that we can make room for the two last stacks, if we need to, we can put the last of them into the rear storage. They started again, one hour later they were finished. John backed out the "doorway" to the "VOID" and shut it down and put it away, The Marines put the carts away and the two suits, then they all sat down in the cabin.
John: "Well, are you ready to deliver all these ingots, then come back and do it again. Let's see hands for another run?" John waited. Bob raised his hand, no one else.
John: "Ok then, Bob has volunteered to come back and load up the "Bullet" all by himself. All in favor of that raise your hand, all the rest raised their hand."
Bob: "Very funny, you all are hilarious."

John looking at his watch: "Alright it is 6pm, let's have something to eat and head home I believe it is still two hours home, isn't it Donna? Donna nodded. I will talk to the Faraday Moon bank tomorrow morning and get the ingots into the vault's basement. Once there an expert will let me know what the value is, along with the diamonds and I will let everyone know, then after we eat, you all can pick out your diamonds to keep, along with one ingot, you decide which. All in favor of this plan raise a hand. All raised a hand, even Bob. Johnny and Larry headed to the kitchen, 40 minutes later dinner was ready and they all went to eat. They all talked and ate.

Bob: "So, what happens to all the other ingots inside the building?"
John: "Well, we don't know if there is any more, however before we leave, I want to do a walk through the building with my new goggles, that will answer your question, ok?" Bob nodded. After dinner they all went to the main cabin, John went to the storage locker and removed a very small bag, he opened the cabin door and walked down the

ramp to the "VOID". He walked over to the area he had the other "doorway" last opened before.

John put on the goggles and slung the box over his shoulder. It works like this, the goggles act as a small "doorway" for your eyes only. The box is a miniature version of the larger "doorway" box, and you can see on the cable from the box to the goggles is a small switch. The box is powered by the new power supply Bob and I just invented; it charges the batteries constantly. You never have to plug in power. So, let's take a look, John turned on the switch. He talked as he walked along.

John: "I am in the first room, there is nothing left here, except for silver, all the ingots are gone, I am going to the second room, you have to get used to going through walls, you have no way to open a door, I am now in the second room, this room is also empty no more ingots. I see another door at the far end, I guess that would be the third room from the end, oh Boy, this room is also full of ingots, they all seem to be Gold, there are 12 cages filled to the top like the other rooms. I see no other doors. I am walking back to the first room, there is a door at the back left I assume it is to a hallway, I am walking through the door, I was wrong it is another large room as long as the first three, it is filled with three rows of cages filled with Gold and, let me look closer, it looks like Silver ingots. There are 15 cages on each side of the room and 14 down the middle with walkways between the middle cages to move ingots into them. There is a small walled room at the back, I am going to look in inside it. I am passing through the door, oh my god the room is filled with human bodies all dead, I assume they came here to hide from whatever apocalypse occurred on the planet, there escape worked until the atmosphere was ripped away and they suffocated. I am going back to the other end of the large room; I saw stairs to the above floor next to a freight elevator. I am going up to the next floor, I see a door and I am passing through, this floor is exactly like the one below, 15 cages of ingots down one side 14 down the middle and 15 down the other side, the ingots are Silver in the middle, Gold and Platinum on both sides. I am going back to the end again; I saw another stairs. I am going up the stairs to the next floor, I believe this is the last basement floor, I am going through the door. I was right this floor is just like the one below, 15 cages on each side and 14 in the middle all filled with Gold bars, I have to see the next floor up it is the street access floor, I am walking to the stairs and going up, I am passing through the door, Yes, it is the first floor, an entrance from the street, a barrier for security and offices. I am turning and facing the rear of the building and coming out through the back wall. John turned off the goggles and took them off. He looked at the group that was listening to his walk. Well, I guess Bob was right, there is a lot more treasure here. What do you all suggest we do?"

Donna: "We know where the asteroid field is, it isn't going anywhere very fast. If we need to come back for some reason it would be easy to find again. I say we go home and worry about it later." They all agreed with Donna.

John: "Let's go back to the main cabin, they all went back. John closed the door, looked at Kayla and said, "Donna set a course for "CEBO" please. Sgt. FULL speed."
Donna nodded at Sgt. Carter and he pushed the throttle forward.
John: "I wonder if the extra weight will cause any problems, Let's go to the kitchen and you can pick out your diamonds and ingots?" They went to the kitchen and Bob brought the big diamonds. John wrote names down on a piece of paper and they drew lots for the drawing, Sgt. Carter was first, he picked out two diamonds, Donna was second, she picked out her choice, Danny was next,

he picked out two with Donnas help, Johnny was next, he picked out two, Kayla was next, she picked out two, Larry was next, he picked out two, David the last squad member picked out two, next was Bob who picked out two and last was Jack, who picked out two guided by Donna, now remember the diamonds are worth much more if they are cut, so I will let you all know who will cut them for you, now pick out one ingot and we will be done." They all picked one from the stacks in the kitchen.

Donna: "John what about you?" John picked out two diamonds and put them into this pocket. You know what, give me your diamonds in a plastic bag with your name in it, I will make as part of the diamond deal they cut all your diamonds first." They all were given plastic bags and they all put their names in the bag, so did John. They arrived at "CEBO" and dropped off Kayla. John walked her off the "Bullet:" What, are you going to do with your Gold bar?"

Kayla: "I will show it to Father and tell him all about the fun we had." John gave Kayla a hug and went back up the ramp. He waved to Kayla and shut the door. Sgt. Carter then took them to John's workshop. Sgt. Carter parked "Faraday 1". They left the "Bullet" and were standing in the "VOID", Sgt. Carter gave John the numbers on the ingots.

John looked at the numbers: "That's just incredible. Ok, Bob, I will see you tomorrow morning at work, Bob left going through the house. I can give Jack and Donna a ride to "Faraday's" moon and come back and give the squad a ride. The squad said ok. John took Jack and Donna to "Faraday's" Moon and dropped them off. He then went back to his workshop and all the squad got on his golf cart and he dropped them off after thanking them for all the help. Then he went home.

08:00 Next day

John had just dragged himself into the office, he was sitting at his desk. Bob came popping in and sat down.

John: "Bob we need to call Ed Long at the bank and arrange the transfer of all the ingots to the lower basement storage vaults. John walked over to the table and dialed Ed Long, Ed answered the phone, "This is Ed Long." Ed this is John Faraday how are you today?"

Ed Long: "I'm fine John, what can I do for you?"

John smiling: "Ed I have some ingots I need to store in your storage vaults until I can get an expert to look at them, is that something you can do?"

Ed Long: "Absolutely John, how many ingots are we talking about, John pulled the paper that Sgt. Carter had given him, that would be 3200 ingots of Platinum and 3800 ingots of Gold and a couple of boxes of uncut diamonds. There was total silence on the line, Bob was stifling a laugh, Ed are you there?"

Ed Long: "Sorry John, where do you have these ingots?"

John: "They are in my transportation vehicle at my home, I would bring it here and if you could furnish some people, we would unload them directly to the vault."

Ed Long: "How long before you could be here?"

John: "If you have enough people to unload, about an hour."

Ed Long: "How about 1pm after lunch?" Bob was splitting a gut.

John: "That would be fine Ed, thanks, we will see you in the vault at 1pm, oh Ed one more thing, Moon Base 1 smelter will be transferring an unknown amount to the "Vets" fund, I will tell them to call you to handle the transfer, is that ok with you?"

Ed Long: "Yes John, I can handle that also."

John: "Thank you Ed, see you at 1pm bye now." John hung up.

John: "Ok, next is Moon Base 1." John went out to Jenny's desk and asked her to get Moon Base 1 and Major Towers. He went back to the table and waited for Major Towers. A few minutes Jenny came into the office.

Jenny smiling: "Colonel Faraday, Major Towers is on line 1." Bob was splitting his side again.

John picked up line 1: "Major Towers how are you today?"

Major Towers: "Colonel Faraday I am just fine, what can I do for you?"

John: "Well, I am calling about the large Gold nugget we left to be smelted, can you give me an update on it?"

Major Towers: "Yes sir it is finished, all we need to know is how you want it, it was smelted into 400 oz. bars, you can take the bars or a check for the gold. There were 4200 bars."

John: "I would like to transfer the value of the Gold minus the 10 percent fee to the "Vets" account at Faraday bank on "Faraday's" moon. If that can be arranged just talk to Ed Long at the bank to handle the transaction, he is aware of the deal, and if you would mail me a copy of the transaction, please."

Major Towers: "That can be arranged, it was great working with you Colonel, thank you and goodbye." John hung up the phone.

Jenny smiling came back into the office: "Any more calls for you Colonel?" Bob was about to roll on the floor.

John: "No, Jenny, that will be all for now. Bob, I feel I need a donut and your buying, let's go." They asked Jenny if she wanted anything, she said no. John and Bob went downstairs to the donut shop.

12:30 pm

John and Bob had walked to the workshop to get the "Bullet" to take to "Faraday's" Moon bank. John opened the door and he and Bob got in. John sat at the weapons console and turned on the power.

Bob: "Can you drive this thing."

John: "I am fully trained and qualified to operate this vehicle. I ask Izzy not to put my name on the qualified list." John pushed the throttle forward and they headed to "Faraday's" moon, John stopped at the entrance and pulled off to the side.

John: "I will open the "doorway" and go to the vault; it probably will scare the hell out of Ed Long. John got the "doorway" and set it up in the "VOID", he took two orange cones, opened the "doorway", found the bank and went into the vault. They saw Ed and 5 or 6 people and several heavy carts to tote the bars. John tossed out the orange cones one for each side of the "doorway" and he and Bob went through the "doorway, scaring the hell out of Ed Long.

John: "Are you ready Ed?"

Ed recovered his wits: "Yes, I didn't realize that could be done. "

John: "Yes, anyone with a "doorway" could do what I just did, they could come in here and steal you blind, unless the motion sensors went off, you have motion sensors down here don't you Ed?"

Ed: "We will tomorrow."

John: "If you will put your carts up close to the orange cones we can start. Bob if you would be so kind as to show them." Bob walked over to a cart, grabbed the handle and went back through the "doorway" and disappeared. The people took another cart and followed Bob. Once the went through the "doorway" they caught on how to do it. John went through into the cabin and pulled up the ramp. Bob started to show them where the ingots were. John went to the rear of the "Bullet" and opened the panel and looked inside. There were ingots here also, he went to the cabin door and had one of the people bring a cart to the rear of the vehicle. He started to empty the storage area. In a few minutes John was done.

He took the cart back to the cabin door so they could fill it
up.

John found Bob in the "Bullet" he told Bob to finish the
unloading and add the boxes of diamonds to the last load,
and he would go supervise the vault loading. Bob nodded.
John went through the "doorway" into the bank vault. Ed
was showing his people where to put the ingots.

John went to Ed Long:" I would like separate vaults for
the ingots."

Ed Long: "Yes, I agree, I assumed that, may I ask
where these strange ingots came from?"

John smiling: "There were recovered on a remnant of a
destroyed planet in space, as were the two boxes of uncut
diamonds that will be put with the Gold bars."

Ed Long: "That is amazing, what are you going to do with
the treasure?"

John: "After its counted and weighed the Gold and
Platinum ingots will be sold, the profits will go into the
"Vets" fund along with the Gold sale from the smelter on
Moon Base 1. Who knows maybe it will be worth more
since it is "SPACE" treasure? If you were to make some
kind of deal with a buyer it would be a nice profit for the
bank, don't you think, imagine a certificate issued by the
"Faraday Moon Bank" certifying each ingot was found in
"SPACE", I would be inclined to authorize something
like that if it would help the "Vets" fund, I could even see
a small percentage say .5 percent of each ingot to the
person who would handle the transactions?" John could
see the wheels turning in Ed Longs mind. I would like
automatic vault lease payments taken from the "Vets"
fund and a bill, and a copy of monthly transactions on the
ingots sent to my office.

Ed Long: "Mr. Faraday I would love to handle those
transactions for Faraday Corp. "

John held out his hand: "Put all we talked about in writing
signed by you for you to handle the deal and bring it to

me for my signature." John walked over to the storage
vaults and watched the loading into the vaults. Two hours
later Bob came with the last cart and the diamonds to put
in vaults. They put the two boxes of diamonds into the
Gold vault. They waited 30 more minutes for the final
count. John compared the count to the piece of paper in
his pocket, the count was right. John picked up a Gold bar
and walked over to Ed Long: "Ed this is for all your
trouble and the help you gave us today, I appreciate it."
Ed Long: "I don't know what to say."
John: "You will earn it; I have no doubt." John and Bob
went back through the "doorway" to the "Bullet"
Bob: "What kind of deal did you make with Ed Long?"
John told Bob what he had done.

Bob: "I'm sorry I missed that fish being reeled in, and
then begging to get in the boat." They both had a good
laugh and went to the workshop.
08:00 two days later
John was going hard on the "PINBALL" machine, Bob
came into the office and sat at the table and waited for
John to finish. Jenny came in and sat next to Bob. John
finished the game and was about to start another when
Jenny spoke up: John you have a gentleman waiting to see
you, he said he was from the De Bears company. John
turned and noticed Bob: "Well send him in, and you guys
should make more noise."
John had the De Bears man sit at the table with him and
Bob.

Dr Bears man: "Mr. Faraday I just came from the
vault of the "Faraday's" Moon bank, I sampled the large
diamonds and several handfuls of the smaller diamonds, I
must ask, where on Earth did you find these diamonds. I
have never seen diamonds with such clarity, I didn't find
a single flaw in any of the diamonds I checked and the
colors were wonderful?"

John: "Well that's nice to know, but I already suspected that, we didn't find the diamonds on "Earth", they were discovered on an asteroid in space, the asteroid was about the size of three or four city busses, they were buried in a material I can describe as compressed sandy gravel, grey to black in color. I believe you call it Kimberlite. The diamonds 1/2 to 1in. apart and that spacing was standard throughout the asteroid, the number of diamonds you saw in the boxes was less than .5 percent of the asteroid, it took us 2 hours to hack them out of the rock."

De Bears man: "You got all those in two hours, that is amazing, what is it I can do for you?"

John: "I want to sell all the diamonds, but I don't want to dump them on the market, can you imagine what would happen if all those diamonds and the ones to come were suddenly dropped on the market. What I was thinking was this: These diamonds are special because they don't come from "Earth", presently they are uncut, imagine the price for cut and polished stones of all sizes of "SPACE" diamonds, especially if they were certified by De Bears, purchased from Faraday Corp., think about it for a minute or two." Bob watched as John reeled the De Bears man in, it was a masterpiece to watch.

De Bears man: "Mr. Faraday would you mind if I make a call from the hallway outside your office?"

John: "I can do better than that, Bob and I will go get some donuts downstairs, make your call from here and we will be back in about 10 minutes."

De Bears man: That will be fine, thank you." Bob and John got up and left the office, they asked Jenny if she wanted anything, she gave them her order and they went downstairs.

Bob: "I just watched the master at work, that guy was sweating bullets, he can't wait to make a deal."

John laughing: "Ya-but he doesn't know what the deal is yet." They got the donuts and hung around at the entrance of the building for another 10 minutes. John and Bob went back to the office and sat down at the table. John: "Well, what do you think, if you think it will work tell me, if we can reach a deal fine if not, I can move on."

De Bears man sweating profusely now: "Ok, we will buy all the diamonds for half of the price, as if the diamonds were already cut."

John: "Oh, only half, huh."

De Bears man: "Alright 70 percent of value."

John letting out his breath: "Ok, but with a couple of requests: John got a piece of paper to write the requests. **One:** All the diamonds are cut then appraised by my man and your man together, to get an accurate value. Or if you wish smaller amounts can be done to get the deal moving **Two:** I have about 20 large diamonds not in the collection that need to be cut, those will be cut and given back to me first, I would like you personally to pick those up in a couple of days, and when they are finished deliver them back to me.

Three: You will send a man to do the count of the diamonds, and the descriptions of the large ones. I will supply the counter with an apartment, full access to our facilities. and a safe to store the counted ones, again the large ones should be cut first. I will also supply an armed guard to be with the counter during the count.

Four: You can decide if you want to continue the deal later. If so, we will make another run and get two more boxes of diamonds for you.

If these terms are ok, then we have a deal."

De Bears man: "I have been authorized to make this deal."

John got up and held out his hand, the De Bears man shook on the deal.

John: "Let me make a quick copy of the deal so everybody remembers. John called Jenny in to make a copy of what they agreed to."

Jenny came back with a copy. John signed a copy and the De Bears man signed one, then they swapped copies. The De Bears man left after John told him to call with any changes.

Bob: "That was amazing, I thought the deal with the bank was slick, have you ever thought about selling time shares?"

John laughed:" Hey, if I could make deals like that selling timeshares I would do it. Nothing is too good for our Vets. I think we are out of great deals today, let's go home for the weekend. "

Bob: "I like that idea." They left the office and went down to the "VOID", and then to the workshop. John and Bob entered the workshop.

John: "I will see you here on Monday morning, I will have something new to show you." Bob nodded and they went to the house. Lora said hi to Bob and he left. It was just about supper time. John was thinking about tomorrow in the workshop, if he was correct, he would have another major project to show Bob on Monday.

Saturday morning 09:00

John was just completing his frame for the box he was building. He had cut out all the parts, now to nail in the end pieces of the box. The box was 3 feet long and two feet wide and two feet high. The bottom, the top, the back and the two end pieces were just cardboard. The frame inside was 3/8 square lengths of wood. He had 3/4 in wide pieces of wood between the frame for strength on the bottom and top, they also formed a base to slide in already made panels. John went to check on the slide in panels he had made last night. They were 2ft. by 2ft. slide panels with a sheet of stainless-steel foil between two thin clear plastic panels. He had added several thin pieces of

"VOID" floor to the stainless-steel foil front and back and let them sit overnight, he had made three of them.

John looked at the foil through the clear plastic panels. On the first panel, the "VOID" floor material had now completely covered the foil. He checked all the panels and they all were filled with "VOID" floor material. John took a slide in panel that had solar panels mounted on one side facing the right end of the box and slid it into the box. Next, he picked up a slide panel that had white cone material between two clear pieces of plastic. He slid that panel into the box.

The next slot was for the stainless foil panel but he did not slide it in, he skipped that hole and installed another white cone panel. They seemed to be sliding in ok.

John now was ready to test, he removed all the panels and started by reinstalling all the solar panels one at a time running the wire across the bottom of the box to the inverter at the far-right end of the box, after installing all the solar panels and wiring he reinstalled all the white cone panels. He picked up one foil panel and slowly pushed it into the slot. The white cone panel glowed brightly and the volt meter registered voltage and amps. He pulled the foil panel and installed it into another foil panel slot, again the cone panel glowed brightly and the volt meter registered voltage and amps, he tested the third foil panel in the last foil slot, and the white cone panel glowed brightly and registered voltage and amps on the volt meter. He pulled out the foil panel and laid it down with the other two. He was done testing until Monday morning when Bob would be here, John couldn't wait. Monday Morning 08:00

John was sitting in the Florida room with Lora eating breakfast, he pulled the plastic bag with the two diamonds in it out of his pocket and laid them on the table.
Lora: "Oh John, are those what I think they are?"

John: "They are two large uncut diamonds, if that is what you think they are." Lora took the two diamonds out of the plastic bag and carefully examined them.
Lora: "These are just beautiful, where did you get them?"
John: "In space, on our last mission we discovered a large nugget of Gold and an asteroid full of diamonds, where those came from."
Lora: "What do you mean a nugget of Gold?"
John laughed: "A nugget of Gold as big as a city bus. And an asteroid three times bigger full of diamonds."
Lora: "What are you going to do with the two diamonds?"
John: "I am going to get them cut and give them to you."
Lora: "Oh John, won't cutting them make them worth a lot of money?"
John: "Yes, but they will look nice on your neck, or on your finger."
Lora: "Well thank you, but I probably won't get to wear them to the grocery store. I will put them in my jewelry box. She put the diamonds back in the plastic bag and gave them back to John.
John: "That's ok too." The doorbell rang. John: "That's Bob, I will get the door." He went to the front door and let Bob in, they went to the Florida room and sat down.
Lora: "Bob, can I get you anything?"
Bob: "No, I'm fine thanks." John and Bob got up and went to the workshop.
Bob: "So, what are you going to show me?"
John: "It is on the workbench. I got this idea when we were working on the small power panels before, this is a large version, take a look at it before I see if it works."
Bob looked over the box: "I see what you are doing, what goes in the three slots that are empty?"
John: "Those slide in panels laying down behind you."
Bob turned around and picked up one of the foil panels and examined it. He again looked at the box and looked at

the panel he was holding. No way he said, is this like an orange bar?"

John: "Yes, would you like to slide it into its slot?"
Bob: "I sure would, he slid the panel into the first hole marked for it, the white cone material glowed brightly. Bob noticed the inverter on the end of the box and the two gauges lit up. One showed 12 volts and the other showed 80 amps. Oh John, this is crazy."

John: "Go ahead put the next foil panel into the box." Bob picked up the panel and slid it onto its slot, the next set of white cone material started to glow brightly and the amp gauge changed to 180 amps."
John: "Go ahead and slide in the last foil panel."
Bob picked up the third foil panel and slide it into the last open slot in the box, again white cone material glowed brightly and the amp gauge now said 300 amps: "John that is more than enough amps to run your whole house." John took the cardboard side for the open box front and covered up the panels to keep all the light inside the box. The amp gauge went to 320 amps.

Bob: "John this will drive the power companies absolutely bonkers, clean no fuel power, and my company makes all the inserts."
John: "Yes, just think of the deal we can make with them, remember the workers."
Bob: "Of course. What material are you thinking of enclosing the box in?"

John: "Well, a professional looking power plant in your garage would probably be sheet metal. The box would fit nicely above the current fuse panel in the garage or in the attic. It could be sold and installed by the local power company. I anticipate power rates would drop to maybe $50 a month or lower. With the unit going for $1500 including installation with easy payments and a lifetime guarantee. Bob why don't you call the CEOs of the local power companies have them bring a power expert with them and schedule a meeting tomorrow here in my driveway at 09:00".

Bob: "This is going to be great; I can't wait to make the calls."

John: "Well, I guess you have a day ahead of you. I am headed to work, see you tomorrow."

07:00 Tuesday

John and his electrician friend had just finished the installation of the power transfer switch to the fuse panel in his garage, it was one of those things that you use to switch power to a generator after a loss of local power. The electrician now hooked the new test box to the switch.

John thanked his friend and told him to send him a bill. The friend smiled, nodded and left. John had put a card table up against the wall where the fuse box was located in the garage then placed the new box on the card table to show how light the new box was.

08:00

Bob showed up grinning from ear to ear. John noticed.

John: "Well, I see you have a secret to tell me."

Bob smiling: "I called the 4 local power company CEO's, they called me back to acknowledge the meeting, and mentioned that other CEOs from a few more Florida power companies are coming also,"

John: "That's ok, the more the better, I do wish I had cleaned up the garage a little."

Bob: "That doesn't matter a bit. I wonder if the CEO's will be on time?" John: "I'm sure they will be early."

They waited. Lora brought out orange juice for John and Bob. The CEO's started arriving at 08:30.

Bob: "How did you know they would be early?"

John smiling: "Greed is always early."

The big cars were starting to pile up on the street, the CEO's and a good number of Johns neighbors were standing in his driveway. John asked Bob to get the large labels laying on the card table on the clipboard and ask each of the CEOs to put their last name on the label and the power company they represented at the bottom. Bob picked up the clipboard and started to get the names. John stood at the front of the garage and waited till 09:00.

John: "Thank you for giving us your time this morning for a demonstration, you must have thought it was important or you would not have come. If the power experts would come forward, please. Nine men stepped forward. I would like all the experts to come into the garage and inspect the hookup I have done and report back to their respective CEO's. John waved them to the card table. They all spent a minute looking at the box but did inspect closely the hookup, after they finished, they walked back and informed their CEOs of what they found."

John: "If the hookup is in question, please say something now, the hookup is no different than a generator for a local power outage, do any of the power experts deny that?" no denials. Ok, let's move on, John moved over to a lamp that was plugged in to the wall and turned it on. That lamp is plugged into the wall outlet and working on local power, Bob please slide in the foil panels, Bob slid in the foil panels then closed up the hole with the cardboard panel. Now would the experts look again at the box device and the power gauges. The experts came forward and looked at the gauges, then stepped back." John: "Any comments?"
One of the power experts:" It's a trick, that is impossible."

John: "John pointed at the power expert who said it was a trick, to go over to the transfer switch and throw the switch. He did, the lamp blinked but stayed on, now throw the main breaker in the fuse box to cut off any local power, he did so, the lamp was still on. He looked again at the inverter; the inverter says you are putting 36volts into the inverter with 230 volts out at 320 amps."

John: "That's right, 230volts, 320 amps with no fuel of any kind,"

One of the CEO's: "If that is the case, we all will be out of business in a year."

John: "And now you understand why you are here today. Putting you out of business is not my goal, my goal is an orderly transition to a new power source, one that provides cheap power to everyone using no coal, no oil, no nuclear and no dams. The current power companies still provide power, it is just going to be a lot cheaper." One of his neighbors: "John what to you is cheap power." John: "I believe a constant power bill of $50 or less a month is possible. And it's going to start right here in River City." His neighbors started to clap.

John: "If there no more questions I believe we can plan another meeting gentlemen to plan the future of US power starting in Florida. His neighbors went home, all the CEO's and their power experts left except one, he was one that John knew.

John: "Harry, how is your day going so far?" Harry Kent smiling: "Well, it started out good, but now after this I think it is better, John I never cease to be amazed by what you have accomplished." John: "I believe Bob here has the answer for us, go ahead Bob say it."

Bob: "With John, it just never stops, ever." Harry smiled, told John he would help any way he could, then left.

John walked over to the fuse panel and threw the main back on, then threw the transfer switch back to local power. John walked over to the new box opened the cardboard and pulled out the three foil panels, the box went dark.

John: "Well it already has been a day, Bob; I don't see how it could get more exciting." Bob nodded.

John: "Oh, now because of this box, the individual box we tested the other day will not be necessary for each small device. However, a version of somewhere between the two boxes will replace all the power supplies in the "Transceivers" and all the "doorways" operating in the world, *we* can now control the power to all the "doorways". We can now start making the boxes and all the foil inserts we need. You will need more white-cone material. Bob, there is one other place the power supplies will work also, that device in road vehicles. I don't even want to think of that now. Even though the "doorways" have reduced private vehicle transportation they all can be made electric. One of these and a backup would be great for Jack's houseboat."

From the comm badge on John's arm: "Hello is Mr. Faraday there?"

John touched the badge: "This is John Faraday, who is this?"

Comm badge: "This is Emery, the Repubs have moved all of their tanks into the "VOID"." They are daring your Council to come and stop them." We told them what you said, but as usual they only care about what they want."

John shaking his head looked at Bob: "Call Izzy, Jack Donna, and the squad, you are right Bob, it just never ends"

"THE END"
Watch for Book 4
Comments to: <u>JayTrees2@Bellsouth.net</u>

FE5-10-21-6B

Made in the USA
Columbia, SC
22 March 2023

14145508R00137